# IN TROUBLE WITH HIM

## STACY TRAVIS

FJP

FAST TURTLE
PRESS

IN TROUBLE WITH HIM

STACY TRAVIS

Copyright © 2020 by Stacy Kravetz

All rights received.

No part of this book may be reproduced in any form or by any electronic or mechanical means, including information storage and retrieval systems, without written permission from the author, except for the use of brief quotations in a book review.

This is a work of fiction. Names, characters, places and incidents either are products of the author's imagination or are used fictitiously. Any resemblance to actual events or locales or persons, living or dead, is entirely coincidental.

Cover Design: Alyssa Garcia, Uplifting Author Services

Copyediting: Blazing Butterfly edits, 2020

Publicity: Social Butterfly PR

# CHAPTER ONE

ANNIE

I CAUGHT a glimpse of myself in the mirror as I sat on a giant, round pouf of a chair. It was purple and squishy, and I almost fell off when I gave it a test bounce. I could see the headline in the gossip rags in the morning: "Guest at Celebrity Wedding Bashes Her Head While Avoiding Festivities."

I didn't need that. I just needed a moment, as one does when one is a bridesmaid. Again.

This was wedding number fourteen, and counting. Not that I was counting, because counting was liable to make me feel depressed about all the bad blind dates and internet match-ups that had not even led to a friend with benefits who'd throw on a tux and accompany me to my best friend Nikki's wedding.

I was batting a zero. Was that a thing? Whatever. This was not a time to feel sorry for myself. It was time to find the bar. Or, in the case of this particular wedding, the ice cave.

"Can you believe we have a vodka tasting room made of ice?" Nikki had asked, shaking her head in the bridal suite earlier. Apparently, the wedding planner was the boss of everything and she'd insisted on an igloo. "So keep your eyes peeled for the rack of PETA-friendly fur coats. Before you go into the tasting room, which is like twenty degrees below zero, you get to put on a coat and pose with a live seal," she said like that was normal.

Her now-husband Chris, who had gazillions of dollars thanks to the many, many superhero action films he'd starred in, had insisted on hiring the planner because he thought it would take some of the pressure off of Nikki. The result was a dove release at the end of the ceremony, a nineteen-piece orchestra playing at the reception, and a life-sized ice sculpture in the shape of Venus on the Half Shell, which held the largest display of seafood I'd ever seen.

I'd be right there. In a minute.

First, there was makeup to freshen and an attitude to adjust. In the mirror, I saw a thirty-one-year-old woman with a pile of peach silk and organza gathered from the floor and draped over one shoulder so as not to tempt fate and whatever unidentifiable germs lurked on the restroom floor. I also saw a tiara. Yup, a freaking tiara, courtesy of a best friend who'd apparently found a sale on princess gear and doled out sparkly headwear to her six bridesmaids without a whiff of irony.

Absent the other merry maids, I looked a little like a Disney princess on the walk of shame, so I took it off. The ceremony was over, photos had been taken, and I was free to pull my tumble of dark, bridesmaid-perfect waves into a haphazard knot that would keep the hair out of my face.

The dress, with its layer of organza over the silk and its spaghetti straps and square neckline—that was all my doing. I'd seen it and loved it on the hanger, convincing myself that it would look equally good on me. For the record, I don't have the body of a hanger, but the dress, as it turned out, looked even better with hips and other feminine curves filling it out.

On the day I'd bought the dress, I never imagined that three months later, I'd have moved from San Francisco, started a new job, and found myself sitting in a well-appointed restroom of a Bel

Air hotel. The room's design rivaled the nicest spaces I'd ever seen, rooms whose primary use was not primping or pooping. Metal flowers bloomed from the walls, and tall mirrors arched behind a series of pedestal sinks.

I'd timed my absence from wedding party activities precisely. The ceremony was over, we'd taken photos beforehand, and I knew I had at least an hour of cocktail mingling before we'd all be called into the ballroom for the bride and groom's first dance. I had such accurate knowledge of the timing because… fourteen wedding parties.

My time in the fancy restroom was designed to remind me that my horrible dating record was just a footnote. It didn't define me. I had a great career and that would fulfill all my earthy wants and needs. Defending white-collar criminals could do that, right?

So far, my job as a lawyer had provided everything a boyfriend couldn't: stability, activities that lasted late into the night, and the emotional high that came from compliments. "You write a beautiful brief, Annie." "Your torts make other lawyers jealous, Annie." "We could all learn a lot from watching Annie litigate."

Reminding myself of my priorities right after Beautiful Wedding Number Fourteen was the best way to get out of my head and into a party mood. Who cared that my most recent date had dared me to go to the restroom and come back without my skirt on in the middle of dinner?

I was done rehashing bad dates and bemoaning tiaras because now it was go time. From this point forward, I would live in LA and practice law with a single-minded focus. Work would be my great love.

And with that thought, I saw a person ready to celebrate her best friend's wedding with some tequila, some stupid fun on the dance floor, and an even more stupid hookup. Preferably in the form of one of the groom's hot fellow actors who had screen-perfect abs and would leave on the next plane to film a movie overseas.

There was at least one groomsman who I was pretty sure I'd seen without his shirt, playing an Air Force captain in a movie. I wasn't picky. Any actor/model/whatever would do. I just wanted to forget about being the new girl in a strange city for a while. That was tomorrow's problem.

Tonight's problem was easily solved at the ice cave and the singles table.

~

NIKKI HAD DESCRIBED the game of Tetris that had gone into fitting everyone into a seating chart, and she assured me that my table was the most fun. I assumed that meant she'd thrown me in with Chris's single actor friends, which boded well for my designs on a hot hookup.

But as it turned out, I never made it to Table Ten.

I found myself drawn to the vodka ice room because the promise of a kiss from a friendly seal was guaranteed action and I wasn't above stacking my odds. Plus, the mandate for a drink—any drink—topped all other needs.

Unfortunately, the line near the Swan Lake garden had morphed into a medusa of four or five sprawling lines that converged on a single immovable point in front of the fur coat display at the cave entrance. I wasn't a line cutter, but I also didn't have much patience. I looked around to see if any servers were walking around with trays of champagne. Or lithium.

"You know, there's another bar," said someone with a deep, quiet voice behind me. He spoke so quietly I felt fairly certain he had to be talking to someone else, but he'd spoken so near to my ear that it felt intimate. I turned around, expecting to see a man whispering to a woman close by.

I didn't care about the intrusion into my personal space. But I did want to follow his journey to this other mythical bar because the one where I stood was going nowhere fast.

When I turned, I met a pair of deep green eyes that immediately felt familiar. In a strange firing of synapses, my mind went straight to my favorite marble in the set I used to play with as a kid. It was the shooter, and as such, it was bigger than the others and weightier when I held it in my hand. However, it was the color that entranced me, a deep forest color with tiny yellow flecks.

I hadn't seen the marble set in two decades, but I was certain this man's eyes were the exact shade of green. I was struck by the idea that a memory could be so instantly triggered by a color.

I stared longer than I should have and immediately realized my mistake when his lips started moving and I didn't hear anything he said.

"I'm sorry, what?" I asked, finally pulling my focus away from his eyes and noticing that the rest of his face was equally arresting. It wasn't because he was trying to smolder in some model perfect way; he didn't need to try. He had a gorgeous, angular face, dark hair that was combed and gelled nicely, and crinkle lines around his eyes which indicated he either smiled a lot or had spent many hours squinting at the sun. He wasn't smiling at the moment, but it didn't dim the wattage of his bulb.

"I said there's another bar. A normal one. No one seems to have noticed." He pointed to the opposite corner of the lawn where we stood. Sure enough, there was a second bar with no more than four people standing around it. No fur coats required. It was a thing of beauty.

"Works for me." I tilted my head to indicate we should go. I weaved my way out of the crowd and walked through the verdant space toward the other bar. Carrying his suit jacket on a thumb over one shoulder like he'd walked out of a magazine spread, he turned to follow me.

Instead of striding next to me, however, he stayed a few paces behind, saying nothing. After a few moments, I turned to see if he was even still there and noticed he'd fallen farther back and was looking at his phone. He'd put on a pair of nerdy-looking reading glasses which made him look a little like Clark Kent.

When he saw me stop, he stowed the glasses and moved faster to catch up.

"Sorry. I'm on a short leash," he said, his voice still low. He seemed serious about whatever was going on in his world.

"Hopefully your leash is long enough for one drink," I said, wondering a little about what or who had him tied down. My initial thoughts ranged from girlfriend to serious corporate job. Or if he was an actor, a manager or agent might be a possibility. In my fantasy world of post-wedding hookups, it didn't matter. I was fine with him remaining mysterious.

"I think I can manage," he said.

I put his height at over six feet tall, which meant I had to stand back a bit so I wasn't awkwardly looking up at him. I was above average height for a female, but even in my tall stiletto heels, I was probably about five foot eight. I still had to tilt my chin upward to meet his gaze. And I wanted to meet his gaze. Those eyes.

"Your eyes are navy green," I said before I realized I was speaking.

"What does that mean? I thought the Navy wore blue," he said, a small smile telling me he was intrigued.

I shook my head to clear away the dreamy stare before the drooling came next. "When I was younger, I thought navy blue meant really dark blue. So when I wanted to describe dark green or dark purple, I assumed the word *navy* was correct."

"No one ever corrected you?"

"Oh, they did, but by that time I didn't care. I knew what I meant when I said navy green, so I went with it. Other people can catch up."

His smile broadened. "I like that. And by that definition, yes, I guess my eyes are navy green. Better than army green, I guess."

So much better.

We sidled up to the bar, where the bartender was looking across the lawn in sympathy. "People just follow people," my new companion said, indicating the other bar.

The bartender nodded. "Yeah, happens all the time. Most guests don't look around. They look for the crowd."

"Lucky us. What are you drinking?" he asked me.

"I'd love a tequila and soda with a lime."

"Sure thing," the bartender said. "How about you, sir?"

"Dry martini, please. One olive."

I raised an eyebrow. "Only one olive?"

He returned my skeptical gaze. "You think I'm making an olive faux pas?"

"I mean, it's your call, but I thought the whole point of drinking a martini was to provide a vehicle for eating olives."

"Make it two olives," he told the bartender, who nodded and went about making our drinks.

"Wow, careful. Two? Don't give in to peer pressure," I said, unable to keep my sarcasm at bay. An old boyfriend used to carp at me that "sarcasm is the lowest form of wit." Because I was insecure back then, I questioned my approach to humor until I learned he was quoting Oscar Wilde without realizing it. That was insult enough, but when I discovered that the actual Wilde quote was "Sarcasm is the lowest form of wit but the highest form of intelligence," I saw no need to temper my comebacks. Or date him anymore. For better or worse.

This man didn't seem perturbed. He extended his hand. "I'm Finn. And I'm quite interested in your olive theory."

I shook his hand and took the opportunity to look again at his eyes. Yup, exact color of my marble, and that gave me both comfort and a desire to gaze unabashedly. He was almost blindingly handsome. He had a strong jaw, high cheekbones, pretty lips, and the kind of furrow lines in his forehead that made him look brooding and hot. I laid odds he was probably an actor—his face practically required it—though I couldn't place him in anything I'd seen.

He was looking at me expectantly, and I realized I was still shaking his hand and had yet to introduce myself. "Annie. And

I'm not sure my thoughts on olives qualify as a theory. What would you like to know?"

"Well, by your logic, your drink should contain multiple limes, but you only asked for one."

I held up a finger. I liked that he was parsing condiments, but he was wrong. "The lime in my drink is for seasoning. The olive in yours is actually a snack."

"Ah, now I see. So really, to you, a martini is a marinating bowl for olives."

"Yes, but I don't drink martinis, so it's really just academic."

"Yet you have an opinion. I like that."

"I appreciate it."

His gaze worked its way over my face and settled on my eyes before making its way to my lips and back to my eyes. "Do you have opinions about other alcohol-soaked foods? I've always found it interesting that we tolerate olives and tiny onions in drinks, but not pickles or bananas," he said.

I considered this. "I'm not sure how many drinks would taste good with a banana, but I'm certainly not opposed to the concept. And I agree. Why does celery go in a bloody mary but not a string bean or an asparagus spear?"

"I think you and I could revolutionize the cocktail world if we gave it half an effort."

I couldn't help smiling at that. "It's been a while since I've revolutionized anything, so I'm up for the challenge. I'd even be willing to posit that a slice of bacon might go well in a martini," I said.

"With a wedge of cheese on the rim?"

"Ooh, now you're talking. I think all drinks should come with a snack attached, especially cheese."

He laughed and studied my face once more. It seemed like he was assessing something about me, but he didn't say anything. I knew that look. I'd cast the same glance at a jury when trying to size up the likelihood of them buying my argument. I wondered if he felt like he was trying to convince me of something.

I smiled at him again, a little wider this time, trying to communicate that he didn't need to work hard to convince me. He was exactly what I was looking for in a one-night stand: witty banter, handsome face, biceps which I could see straining at the fabric of his dress shirt, good hair that would look even better after I'd run my fingers through it. Check, check, and check.

He could distract me from thinking about any number of things—moving to LA or my new job or the fact that I'd need to glue myself to my desk in the morning and put in the time necessary to overachieve. He was doing it already.

When the bartender handed us our drinks, Finn made a point of stirring his with the toothpick that held the two olives before taking it out and offering one of the olives to me. It was sweet. "Is that why you agreed to two, because you thought I was after your olives?" I asked.

"Not going to lie, I kind of hoped you were after my olives," he said, a slight smirk forming on his lips. "But I'll just hang onto them for now. Maybe you'll find them more enticing after we get to know each other a little better." I felt certain we were no longer talking about drink garnish, but he was stoic enough that I couldn't be sure.

I walked us to an empty cocktail table, and we stood on opposite sides of it. Ironically, in the middle of the table was a full bowl of olives next to a smaller bowl for the pits. "Well, now I suppose your olives are safe."

"I get the feeling nothing is safe where you're concerned." Now he was definitely smirking.

I felt the heat creeping over my face and a lightning shock of adrenaline pulsing through my chest. I cleared my throat, which made him laugh.

"So… are you a friend of Chris's?" I asked. It was just a guess. Being new to LA, I didn't know all of Nikki's friends. Or his, for that matter.

"Nikki's. We knew each other in grad school and stayed friends." My brain started working through likely scenarios.

Nikki had gotten a master's degree in communications. He certainly could have studied at the film school there and gone on to an acting career. Or he could work in publicity like her or even be some kind of on-air reporter.

I realized I was willing him to be an actor, mainly with the— likely false—idea that actors were sluttier and better looking than regular people. I had no evidence to prove that assumption, just hope. But maybe the less actual information about the object of my hookup dreams, the better.

"Do you work in a similar field as Nikki?" I asked, immediately contradicting myself by asking for details that would turn a handsome slut into a real person. I couldn't help it. The conversation about condiment theory had piqued my interest. I hated small talk for the sake of filling dead air space, but I liked finding out the intriguing bits about people that they shared more willingly with strangers. We all had those moments of honesty that came from an innocuous question from someone who didn't know us well enough to judge.

"Eh, it's a party. I don't want to talk about work," he said, scooping our drinks off the table and handing me mine. He held his glass up for a toast. "To new friends."

I couldn't help smiling because I liked that he'd deflected the conversation about work. The last thing I wanted to talk about was my job when I wasn't at work. "To new friends. Or even just people."

"People?"

"Well, it may turn out that we're just two people having a drink at a wedding. Maybe we won't become friends."

"Ah, I like that you're specific."

"Of course, maybe we will, in which case your toast is apt. And even if not, I suppose your toast could just be in honor of other people becoming new friends. Or people being people in congruent spaces, enjoying some time together, and not ever becoming friends. In that case, the toast should just be in honor of people. So..."

He was looking at me like butterflies had just taken flight from my ears. I was used to that look. It happened whenever I started speaking in an endless flow of verbiage that made sense if you cared enough to follow my train of thought, but which made most people react like I'd just escaped the nut house.

Normally, my thoughts were rational and limited to well-conceived, relevant comments. It was why I made a good lawyer. I could remain calm even in the face of anxious clients, nasty opposing counsel, losing arguments, and hopeless causes.

Unfortunately, all that even temper went flying off to Saturn when I was with the tiny percentage of people who made me nervous. And this guy—with those eyes and that face—made me nervous. It was the good kind of nervous, borne of feeling unexpectedly intrigued by a handsome stranger, but still... nervous.

I did my best to avoid situations that put me outside my comfort zone. In my work life, I was good. With close friends—also good. But with attractive, mysterious men I didn't know well... not so good. Once I started yammering, it led to a slippery slope of more nerves and more absurd conversational gems from me.

"Well, in that case, I'd like to amend my toast because I'd like it to apply to us. You're absolutely correct that I've made assumptions. How about if we toast to making use of bars that no one else knows about?" he said.

"Um, okay." I felt suddenly calm, and my penchant for ridiculous blather had stopped in its tracks.

Oh. My. God.

He'd just taken my nervous crazy and... diffused it.

No one had ever done that before. Most people gave me a polite nod and made for the safety of the nearest rattlesnake den rather than risk possible contagion from my lunatic brain. But not him.

I was struck by a new feeling, something I'd never experienced before—I felt excited, happy, and... intrigued. Instead of slogging through the necessary small talk required to get him to take advantage of a hookup opportunity, I wanted to know him and understand him. And then kiss him.

So startled was I by his easy handling of my nervous blather that I didn't say anything at all for a few moments. I needed to process what was happening. He was different. He was quietly confident. He was also insanely hot. I had little to say, absurd or otherwise, so I clinked my glass against his. "I will drink to that."

He nodded, unperturbed by my nonsense. I sipped my drink, vaguely noting that it was strong before I'd downed most of it.

"Maybe we shouldn't wander too far from the bar," he said, leaning his elbow on a tall cocktail table and looking slowly over my face. "Given that we might want to toast again to people."

"Or even people at weddings."

He held up a hand. "That's awfully specific."

Yup, I liked this guy. He didn't seem inclined to wander anywhere, which was just fine with me.

# CHAPTER TWO

ANNIE

THE CACOPHONY of voices had died down before I realized that most of the wedding guests had gone inside. I hadn't noticed anything or anyone outside of our bubble because talking to Finn was actually... fun.

We meandered inside stood next to each other when Nikki and Chris had their first dance, and he obliged as my dance partner when the wedding party was invited to join them on the floor. Finn was a good dancer. A really good dancer. He moved with ease, he knew how to lead, and holy crap, he had moves.

"I like your dress," he said, his hand trailing down my arm to where he rested it on my hip. "Doesn't look like the usual bridesmaid fare." He'd put his jacket back on and the effect of the full suit made him look even better.

"Spoken like a man who's danced with a lot of bridesmaids." I draped both hands around his neck. It seemed appropriate and not overly familiar, though the feel of his hand on my hip elicited all kinds of other desires that I needed to keep at bay for the sake of decorum on a dancefloor.

"I've danced with a few." He didn't elaborate. I wasn't used to men of few words. Most of the people I worked with at my now-former law firm couldn't get enough of hearing themselves talk.

Finn was a relief.

The song was slow and romantic, and he wrapped one hand around my waist while taking my hand in the other. I had to look up to see his face. What I saw was a mask of stoic good looks which he seemed to wear when he looked around the room, but his gaze immediately softened when he looked at me. I liked the way it felt.

The way his expression shifted reminded me of the way I sometimes felt when I was in court arguing a case. I became a different person, putting on a mask to keep my inner self safe from the hard-edged litigator who made enemies if necessary. Starting over at a new firm added even more reasons to wear that mask until I found my comfort zone. I'd been wearing it since I arrived in LA, a fact I only realized because Finn made me feel like I didn't need it.

"What're you thinking about?" he asked, rubbing his hand lightly up my back and combing his fingers down through my hair. Then he did it again, and I felt the heat rise in my cheeks and a wild flutter in my stomach. His touch was intimate considering we'd just met an hour earlier, but I didn't want him to stop. I edged my body a little closer to his and ran my fingernails through the hair at the nape of his neck.

"Oh, just the real world creeping in for a moment. I had an unwelcome thought about the work I have to do tomorrow."

"What do you do?" he asked.

"I train sea otters." It was the first thing that came to my mind, and it rolled out before I could stop it.

"Really. Is there a big market for otter trainers?" He moved his hand lower, back to my waist. The song was still slow—something by Marvin Gaye—and everyone on the dance floor was moving at a lazy pace.

"Everywhere, really. They're unruly, so…"

"You don't want to talk about work either." He shrugged, and I relaxed.

"I'd just as soon avoid thinking about it as long as possible. It's bad enough I have to spend all day tomorrow on it," I said. It was a lie. I was perfectly content to spend my weekends working, but he didn't need to know that.

"Do you mind working on a Sunday?" He tilted his head, watching me. I didn't feel like he was judging.

"Honestly, not really."

We danced until the song ended, and the band launched into a set of pop cover songs. I pulled my hand back from around his neck, and we each took a step back, but he didn't let go of my other hand. We looked at each other, assessing whether the other wanted to keep dancing. I shook my head and he led me out of the room and back out to the garden where we'd been before. It felt unnecessary to verbalize that we both wanted to leave the crush of people and the loud music.

The sudden quiet on the lawn immediately washed over me. I was no longer thinking about work or trials or whether my drink needed refilling because I'd already finished two and I was pleasantly buzzed.

Finn wordlessly dropped my hand and took off his suit jacket, which he draped around my shoulders. "You'll freeze out here," he said, explaining the gesture.

"I was okay, but thanks." I wasn't used to kind gestures from men. I was good at taking care of myself, so I didn't look too hard for people to lighten my load. But it was sweet, and I liked that he did it without asking.

"Come." He led me through the garden and down some winding pathways between bungalows, some of which were larger than my San Francisco apartment. Finally, we arrived at what seemed to be our destination—the pool.

No one was sitting on the lounge chairs at that hour, but the tiny twinkling lights made the setting look like it had been designed for a midnight tryst. Finn grabbed a stack of plush towels and spread them out on the cushion of a lounge chair and tilted it to full recline.

"Wow, you get right to it," I said, sort of impressed that he was moving right to writhe-around-on-a-lounge-chair-and-make-out mode. He looked at me quizzically and proceeded to put towels on the lounge next to it. He tilted that one back as well. With an extended hand, he gestured for me to sit on one of the chaises, before taking the other one a couple feet away. Slightly confused, I looked over at him as he picked up my hand again.

He lay all the way back and after some momentary hesitation, I did the same, still unnerved because I'd thought we were on the same page. Didn't most normal single people hook up at weddings? Wasn't that where he was leading with his sultry stroking of my back and all the hand holding? And now we appeared to be gearing up to take naps at a great distance.

The thick cushions were comfortable, and I supposed I could think of worse ideas. Still, I couldn't help but feel disappointed. Had I read all his signals wrong? I'd felt sure he understood the rules.

"So, I take it from your comment you were expecting me to have my hand up your skirt by now?" he said.

"Oh. I mean, not really, but I guess… well, yeah."

He laughed. "Noted. And then, by corollary, I guess you wouldn't object."

"Um, yeah, sure. And who says, 'by corollary' in ordinary conversation? Are you on the debate team or something?"

"Or something," he said.

"Right. No talking about work. Fine."

"You seem disappointed in how this is going," he said, an amused smirk on his lips.

"No, not at all. I was hoping for a moon tan and lots of sober conversation during my best friend's wedding reception."

"I can always get you another drink. Don't want you to be disappointed."

"I'm not disappointed. I'm fine. And so… we're not making out, then. Just to be clear."

He turned toward me, and those green eyes burned into mine. "I'm not ruling it out." He yanked hard on my lounge chair and pulled it right up against his. The movement made a scraping noise on the patio and added to the brute strength of the gesture. It also sent a jolt of wanting straight between my legs.

"I'd be a damned fool if I got you alone and didn't do this," he said, leaning into me.

I leaned forward, feeling a magnetic pull toward him and whatever his instinct directed him to do. He reached toward me and cupped my cheek in his hand. His movements were slow and deliberate, and he locked onto my eyes as his thumb caressed my cheek. When he ran his fingers through the hair at my temple, I shuddered. Waves of intense craving shot through me at his touch. I scooted a little closer to him, still on my own lounge chair, still too far away, according to the urges of my body.

Then he tilted my chin up so I was looking directly into his eyes. I couldn't look away and I didn't want to. My lips were perfectly positioned just inches from his. I expected a tentative pass of his mouth against mine, but Finn was not a man who abided expectations. He kissed me hard with his delectably soft lips claiming mine in a generous, commanding sweep that had my heart pounding and my breath in my throat. He kissed me like it was necessary—like if he didn't give in to the impulse, he'd perish.

His tongue tamed mine into a sensual rhythm, just like his body had led me seamlessly on the dancefloor. He wasn't hurried or desperate, but he knew what he wanted and his lips melded with mine until I reached a state of fiery bliss I could barely manage. This was what a kiss was supposed to feel like. It put all the JV kissers in my past to shame.

My pulse was racing, and at the same time, I couldn't breathe, which I knew would lead to a backlog of some kind in my heart. Maybe I would die. If it was possible to kill someone with a kiss,

Finn could murder. He brushed his lips away from mine and lingered near my ear, breathing heat and fire that sent shivers down my spine and pooled low in my belly.

"But I also wanted to do this." He rolled away and onto his back and looked straight up at the sky. With the hope of more kisses like that on the table, I reluctantly looked up as well.

"Oh, wow." We had an unobstructed view of the sky, and it was a perfect, clear night. The moon was full and hung directly above us like a big, smiling grandpa face. And around it, I saw stars, tiny points of light in a dark sky that would never go black under the refracting lights of the city. "I didn't think it was possible to see a real night sky in LA," I said.

"Spoken like someone who doesn't think much of LA. Or who's from out of town?"

"Ten years in San Francisco," I said, planning to tell him about my recent move, but he interrupted my train of thought with a cool fact about the night sky.

"We're in a waxing gibbous, so the sky appears darker and the stars brighter." He leaned toward me, so our heads were practically touching, and guided my gaze to where he was looking. "Do you see that area that looks blurry? It's a star cluster, the Orion Nebula. Are you familiar with nebulae?" Ah, so he was an astronomer.

"A little. I think I've seen one."

He backed away, looking skeptical. "Not in San Francisco. It's too foggy, for one thing. And when it's clear in the city, it's generally too bright. LA is usually too bright as well, especially with the full moon and the inversion layer, but this time of year there can be decent visibility."

"I *have* left the city on occasion, taken some camping trips in the mountains. But this is… it's pretty magnificent." I stared up until the brightness of the moon started to hurt my eyes.

When I turned to look at Finn, I saw him studying me with a serious expression. I wondered how long he'd been doing that. He pulled me a little closer and I scooted toward the edge of my chaise. He did the same until we were pressed up against each other.

Neither one of us spoke. We just lay there, side by side, holding hands under the bright, white moon for a long time.

The intimacy of lying next to him in the dark, feeling his thumb trace circles on the back of my hand, made me feel connected to him in a way I hadn't planned on feeling, especially with a nameless hookup. It was unwise to think this nerdy astronomer seduction was anything more than his particular prelude to a kiss.

I pushed down the odd, swirling thoughts I was having about him in which I imagined what could happen after tonight. No, this was a wedding one-night stand. It didn't matter that my love-starved brain was working in matchmaker overdrive—"kiss him again, take him home, bear his children, engage in wifely duties."

I had to admit, my yenta brain had a point. In a matter of hours, he had me wanting things I'd never considered with a man before. I was fantasizing about seeing him again—about getting to know him—and feeling untapped emotions about where that might lead. This felt mature and real. It was as though all the brute force making out and perfunctory sex with okay guys since I was a teenager had been missing the point.

Finn made the folly of all my previous relationships clear: how could polite, perfunctory sex and good enough conversation have ever been enough? How could it possibly qualify as a relationship? Of course it didn't. I'd just never allowed myself to believe there was more.

And… maybe there wasn't.

Finn had backed away so completely after his initial torrid claim on my lips that I didn't know what to think. My mind whipsawed between desperate need for his tongue and his delicious lips to wondering if I'd just imagined the whole thing.

Maybe this was his game—giving and taking away. I wasn't in the mood for games, and I started to think that he'd only kissed me because it's what he thought I wanted. He was throwing me a bone.

I was not one to beg.

That's why I wasn't expecting it when he brought my hand to his lips and kissed each finger. And when he turned on his side to face me, I wasn't expecting him to do anything more than talk more about the sky or propose another arcane activity that no one did at a wedding reception ever.

I decided I could be good with that. Despite my initial shallow intentions, I liked him. He was different. And interesting. And not the kind of guy who was just looking for a piece of ass on a chaise. But he was still so reticent, I wasn't sure *what* he was looking for exactly.

"You'd be crazy to think I haven't been wanting to do this for the past two hours," he said, pressing closer to me, which had the effect of moving me over so both of us were facing each other on my lounge chair and the distance between us disappeared. Then his lips swept across mine, hinting at what I'd loved earlier but withholding it. He nipped at my bottom lip and sucked it gently before backing away. "I just didn't want you to think it was *all* I wanted."

"What else do you want?" I asked, surprised at how breathless I sounded after his kiss.

"Ah, babe, the list is long." He kissed me again, deeper this time, and I felt every part of my body shudder at his touch. I tugged his dress shirt free from his pants and ran my hands over his abs, which felt like they were etched from marble.

His tongue tangled with mine, and his hands were in my hair, brushing loose strands away from my face. But there was nothing frantic or hurried about his pace. He wasn't trying to get to a finish line. He was the frustrating sort who wanted to admire the view.

That had never been my priority. I was all about the accomplishment, the checking of a box, even when it came to sex. I wanted to know where we were headed, so much so that my body had gone stiff as my brain tried to exert control.

"Hey," he said, pulling away and focusing his eyes on mine. "Relax."

"I am relaxed."

He laughed and rolled his eyes. "You're not relaxed. The question I have," he said, running a finger over the contours of my cheek until the skin tingled with goosebumps, "is what it will take to get you there?" He followed the path of his finger with a row of kisses which ended at my neck. He followed that with his tongue.

"I... I could maybe get there," I mumbled, my brains scrambling and willing to agree with whatever he proposed. His breath was hot on my skin. His lips followed. He held my cheek in his palm and kissed my forehead, my nose, my chin. Finally, my lips.

He kissed with the same unhurried intensity that he employed when he talked about space. The passion behind his words—and now, his mouth—eclipsed reality.

"You are getting there. But you're still struggling a little bit." He kissed me again slowly, raking his teeth across my bottom lip and following with his tongue. My lips parted because I wanted more of him, and I was starting not to care how slowly he wanted to go and how long he wanted to kiss me before we did anything else.

I finally gave in to the idea that the kissing was enough. This, here, now. I lost my power to think about anything else.

"Yes, now you're relaxed," he said against my lips, not backing away enough for me to answer with words. I couldn't have, even if I wanted to. His kiss—the way he moved his tongue languidly against mine, the way his lips connected with mine like he was committing every contour to memory—reduced me to the most basic human drives.

Need. Want. Desire.

His lips traveled over the curve of my chin. I felt his tongue sweep along my neck and his breath caress my ear.

And I was gone.

~

THEN I WAS BACK.

"Shit." Finn pulled away from me and shoved a hand in his pocket. I assumed it was a panicked attempt to check for condoms.

"It's okay I have one in my—"

"Shit," he said again, only this time he'd pulled out the sexy nerd glasses and his phone. "I'm sorry. I'm so sorry. Shit, shit, shit. I can't believe I have to do this, but… I have to go. I didn't realize how late it'd gotten." He seemed perturbed and more ruffled than I'd imagined possible from a man who'd seemed so calm and thoughtful all night.

"It's okay. Can I do something?"

"No, no. It's fine," he said, backing away from me. "I'm so sorry. This was lovely. You're… enjoy your night."

He was starting to put on his jacket, then he apparently decided to abandon that instinct and grabbed it in his fist as he moved a few paces away.

*Enjoy my night?*

I wasn't used to being confused by men and Finn… he confused the hell out of me. That made me want to chase him for answers, but I didn't get the chance. He doubled back and pulled me to him. His lips crashed onto mine once more, and he kissed me like it was his last night on earth.

Then he turned and jogged—almost ran, actually—down the pathway and out of sight.

I could still feel his lips on mine, and a part of me felt so whiplashed by his abrupt departure that I had to do a double take to make sure we weren't still kissing. My fingers went to my lips in a futile effort to connect. They were still wet. I could still smell his aftershave on my skin.

I looked to where he'd been a moment earlier on the garden path. One last-ditch hope that he'd made a mistake. But he was gone.

# CHAPTER THREE

FINN

MY MOTHER HAD TAUGHT me to be a better man than that. Even at sixty, she'd kick my ass if she knew how badly I'd behaved with Annie.

*Enjoy your night?*

I should have my man card revoked.

As the only boy growing up in a house with a supremely talented mom and five empowered sisters, I was schooled early and often in the importance of always treating women with respect and honesty.

As the Uber drove me toward my house, I had ample time to think about how poorly I'd scored on both counts. I hadn't given Annie much relevant information about myself, and I certainly hadn't been honest about my early curfew and the reason for it, not that she needed to know. Talking about olives, otters, and nebulae was a welcome distraction from the rest of my currently-shitty life.

Besides, it was a wedding and she was the maid of honor. Drinks were being poured; twinkle lights were twinkling. It was hardly the time for long, sordid tales about arrest records and complicated excuses. No one wanted to hear that sort of stuff at a wedding reception.

Well, she might have wanted to hear it. Of anyone I'd met lately, she was the first who seemed to be fighting her instincts to have a deeper conversation and trying to convince herself that the better route was a meaningless romp on a chaise. I could see her struggle, and it interested me.

And because bright, shiny, fascinating things always lured me away from the straight path I was supposed to follow, I chased her and threw out all my rules for the evening. Of course, there had been rules. I was to attend the wedding ceremony, stay at the reception until I could have a face-to-face moment with Nikki, at which time I'd congratulate her and tell her she looked beautiful. Then I would ghost the party, and she'd be too busy dancing and mingling to notice.

The rules were made—by me—to avoid just the sort of situation I'd found myself in with Annie. I hadn't planned on talking to anyone, which was why I was lurking alone when I saw her trying to navigate the throng of wedding guests jockeying for a spot in line at that stupid ice bar.

I couldn't just leave her there in that morass when there was a perfectly good empty bar nearby. But I should have given her the necessary piece of advice and left it at that. She was a bridesmaid and she was beautiful. She'd have no trouble finding people to talk to at the reception. I didn't need to babysit her.

But I wanted to, and wanting things has always been a slippery slope for me. It was how I'd found myself in trouble with the federal government and ended up on leave from a job I loved.

Looking through the fogged backseat windows, I smirked at the stupidity of a Ferrari in the next lane over, revving its engine on Sunset Boulevard like there was the remotest possibility for a road race. In my years living in LA, I'd never gotten used to the cars, some of which cost more than three times the average American annual income. Not that I didn't spend money—just not on cars.

I rolled my eyes, but with the fogged windows acting like a mirror, I was rolling them at myself. Completely appropriate, I realized. I could smirk at cars all I wanted, but it wasn't going to distract me for long from feeling like a grade-A asshole.

Actually, it wasn't even anything as subjective as *feeling*. I was an asshole, objectively, and in all countries, territories, and jurisdictions.

"How's your night?" The abrupt intrusion of the Uber driver jarred me from my downward spiral of thoughts.

"Oh, okay, thanks. How about yours, Abe?" I noticed his startled expression in the rearview mirror when I called him by name, but his name was on the app when it confirmed my ride, so it only seemed like common courtesy to use it.

"Not bad, not bad. You at a party?"

"Yeah. Something like that." I was being vague so he wouldn't think he had to keep me entertained with conversation. In fact, I'd read several articles and internet posts about how rideshare passengers complained so much about drivers who made idle conversation that the apps had considered inserting a click button option to let the driver know to stay silent.

I'd have to remember to investigate the status of that option.

Even if I talked to Abe for the rest of the ride, it wouldn't blunt the ache in my chest. What kind of guy leaves a jaw-droppingly stunning woman—a woman who's clearly smart, a woman who's made it clear she wants nothing more than wedding night sex— and dashes away like a common crook?

Well, I suppose I am a common crook, as far as many people are concerned... maybe leaving with few words of apology sums up exactly the kind of person I am. The kind of person I've become.

"Abe, are you married?" I asked.

"No, sir. Two ex-wives, though."

I tried to get a better look at him by moving to the other side of the bench back seat. He looked younger than me, but with a few days' growth of facial hair and a hat pulled down over half his face, it was hard to tell. "I know, you're thinking, 'what kind of crazy-pants lady lets a guy like me walk away? Let alone two of 'em.' Am I right?"

"Seems like a crime." I willed myself to engage with him. I didn't want to be in my head. Maybe he could distract me from myself for a few minutes. "How long were you married?"

"Not long, either one. I'll tell you what, the first one, she was a white girl, loved me more than I deserved, but her parents didn't like the idea of her marrying an Armenian man. Wouldn't support us having a wedding. Drew a line in the sand about it. We eloped but that didn't sit well with them and they threatened to cut my bride off from her inheritance if she had mixed-race babies. Actually said it like that—made it clear it wasn't me they had a problem with. My *parents* were from Armenia. I was born here but that didn't matter to them. And she couldn't stand up to 'em."

"That's a shame people can't see beyond the labels."

"Exactly. Welcome to my world, man. I feel it on the daily, people thinking I'm Persian, not even knowing it's not the same thing. And not like it would matter anyway since they probably have assumptions about anyone who doesn't look like them."

"You're a hundred percent right, Abe. Some people can't get past what they see." It made me think about my own troubles and the fact that guilt seemed presumed in my case.

He turned around and looked me squarely in the eye, showing me a wide toothy grin in appreciation. The problem was he was still driving forward at forty-plus miles an hour. I felt my eyes unconsciously dart past his face to watch the road—because that seemed more important than our moment of connection. His head swiveled quickly around to the front, and he slowed the car a bit, which saved me from having to piss my pants.

"And you were married a second time?" I asked, hoping he'd keep his eyes on the road.

"Yeah, I married my girlfriend in Las Vegas after a Grateful

Dead show. We were high on a bunch of stuff I'd best not mention to you since you're trusting me to get you home."

He looked at me in the mirror, raising his eyebrows.

"Kidding. I'm stone cold sober now. Don't you worry," he said.

"I'm not worried." I was worried, but I was always a little worried when I got in the car with a stranger. Everyone should be.

"That marriage was more like a weekend thing. We got it annulled and then dated for another year or so. It was never serious. Still, I like to say I was married twice. Something to talk about anyway."

The few minutes of talking distracted me enough from the workings of my mind that I didn't notice we'd shifted off Sunset and started climbing into the hills above the famous Strip until we were rounding the bend at the top of my street. A few moments later, Abe deposited me beside the wall that wound around the front side of my house. "This is fine," I said. He looked uncertain because we were stopped on a wide curve in the road, and the wall didn't look like a welcoming entrance to anything.

"Yeah? Okay, man. Thanks for the chat." He held a fist out, and I bumped it before shutting the door behind me and watching his car churn up the hill.

I punched in the code and waited for the gate in my wall to swing inward. It was a good, solid gate in a good solid wall. I'd liked that when I first looked at the house. Not like I'm a privacy nut or anything, but if a person's going to have a gate and a wall, they might as well be sturdy. I've never understood the low decorative gates that don't serve to separate anyone from anything except maybe their pride if they trip when hopping it.

My penchant for extra security was also a product of having a family of women. I wanted them safe from the world if they came to visit. I couldn't help being a protective son and older brother.

I tried to ignore the impression I had every goddamned time I walked through the gate that I was entering a fairy kingdom, but it was impossible.

My yard was lit like the set of *A Midsummer Night's Dream*, courtesy of a landscaper who insisted on low voltage path lights and small upward spotlights on various plants, along with strings of bulbs and twinkling vines twining up the branches of various trees. On the plus side, as a result of her elfin touches, no one would ever get lost on the way to my front door. On the downside, someone with a pacemaker might die before ever reaching it from the strobe effect.

"I don't need lights twinkling out here," I'd told her.

She looked at me the way she'd probably looked at countless other clients whom she assumed to be lacking in their ability to visualize the landscape. "You do need them."

"I just need to be able to see. Anything beyond that is superfluous."

"You need to trust me. I'm doing my job."

I wanted to argue with her and tell her that her job was to outfit my yard with sustainable plants, which I wouldn't have to water and would be native to the Southern California climate. This was why I'd hired her in the first place. But eventually, I came to see her lighting schematic as the price I'd have to pay to make her go away. I figured I could always unplug them. And then I forgot.

The first thing I did when I got inside was double check the time on my phone and the clock in the kitchen to confirm that I had, in fact, returned home before my curfew. There was no reason for anyone to chase me down and accuse me of violating my Supervised Home Confinement.

I always built in a cushion of time to make sure that nothing—red lights, stubborn front door locks—kept me from getting home and in the door at the appointed time. I was nothing if not punctual, and I didn't want to see my probation officer any more than I had to. For fuck's sake, I still couldn't believe I had a probation officer.

The second thing I did was pour myself a healthy glass of tequila, the good stuff made for sipping. Not the crap they had at the wedding. I figured that was why Annie diluted hers with soda and lime, but I didn't want to sound like an arrogant jerk who thinks only certain tequila is good enough. But maybe I am because I do.

The wedding reception would be going on for another two hours at least, so I'd just toast the happy couple from here. And I wanted to drink something that tasted decent.

Then I wanted to forget this whole night ever happened. I wanted to erase the fact that I'd blown what was maybe my one opportunity as a free man to get laid. And I wanted to blot out the fact that my overactive brain had me more interested in talking to Annie than trying to get in her pants. I was an idiot in so many ways, and I wanted to forget each and every one of them.

Then I wanted to forget her. She lived in San Francisco, and I'd likely never see her again. There was no point in adding to the misery in my life by thinking about her anymore.

# CHAPTER FOUR

ANNIE

I DRANK another tequila and soda, this time with three limes squeezed into it. Was it in Finn's honor, in memory of the guy who gave me the best kiss of my life and ran away? A little bit of self-torture because my man-picking radar had failed me again? Maybe.

The band was still fired up and playing song after song, and Nikki hadn't left the dance floor. I wasn't all that surprised. She'd always loved to dance. Even back in college, we used to take the BART train into San Francisco and find some club in SoMa where we could dance all night. She wasn't ever interested in dancing with guys or meeting anyone. She just wanted to dance until her clothes were stuck to her back, and her hair was up in a ponytail out of necessity.

I felt a little guilty that I'd missed half the reception, but not that guilty. It had been worth it, even if my companion had vanished like Cinderella chasing a pumpkin coach. Nikki wouldn't care that I hadn't witnessed the cake cutting; I'd been there for the first dance and the toasts.

I didn't want to hassle her with questions about Finn on her wedding night, but I also really did. It was just so weird. The reception was still in full swing, and Nikki seemed glued to the dance floor. But Chris looked exhausted and sat out a few songs.

I could just as easily ask him what was up with my fleeing companion. He probably knew most of Nikki's friends by this point, at least friends who were close enough to merit an invitation to their wedding, so I pulled a chair over to his and sat down.

"Congratulations, Mr. Nikki," I said, kissing him on the cheek.

He smiled, watching new wife shimmying in her white dress. His jaw-dropping superhero smile shone even brighter for her. "You got that right. I definitely got the better end of the deal here."

"Oh, I'm not so sure about that. I'm pretty sure Nikki would call herself the lucky one." Marriage goals—they embodied them.

He smiled and I almost had to shield my eyes from his charisma. It was no wonder he could commandeer a movie screen. "You enjoying your night?" he asked.

"I am. In fact, I enjoyed a certain friend of Nikki's who I wanted to ask you about."

"Oh yeah? Ask away."

"His name's Finn. Do you know him?"

Chris didn't answer immediately. I turned and saw his gaze fixed firmly on his wife, who was now barefoot and dancing in a circle of friends. The smile on his face said more about their future together than any of their vows. And their vows had been beautiful.

When he finally tore his attention away from her, his smile had dimmed a bit. "Wait, you hooked up with Finn?"

"I mean… a little. Why, is he married? Lives with his mother?" My brain had already spun off and compiled a list of likely scenarios for why he'd left skid marks on the pavement. *CIA operative whose cover was blown? Parolee from an asylum?* I sure could pick 'em.

Chris looked at me strangely and started to answer but I

31

missed whatever he said because I was yanked by the hand onto the dancefloor by the bride who was grinning through her sheen of sweat and nodding at me that it was my time to prove my bridesmaid worth. A couple of exhausted-looking friends smiled at me with empathy as they kissed Nikki goodbye and made a run for it. She wrapped her arms around my neck and swayed her hips from side to side, the wide grin still on her face hours after the band had kicked off the dancing with a Kool and the Gang hit. "Thank you so much for being my maid of honor. I couldn't love you more," she said.

"I couldn't love you more," I told her. "And you look gorgeous."

"Thank you. So do you."

"You don't have to say that." It always seemed like people felt obligated to return a compliment. I always felt obligated to let them off the hook.

"I don't ever lie to spare your feelings, you know that," she said.

"Okay. Thank you for being brutally honest about how gorgeous I look," I said, smiling her because her joy was contagious.

I was about to bring up Finn and ask her for tawdry details, but then Chris wrapped his arms around both of us and grinned. "Mind if I dance with my wife?" And if I did possess any ability to turn him down, the smile obliterated it.

"Seriously? Tonight?" I said sarcastically.

"I know. He's so pushy, isn't he?" Nikki said, already letting me go and wrapping her arms around Chris's neck.

"He really is. You just mind yourself, buddy, you hear me?" I wagged at finger at him in warning.

Chris laughed and kissed me on the cheek. "Thank you for being a good friend."

"Okay, okay, enough thanking me already. You're gonna make me cry. I'm leaving you two now, so behave yourselves."

They looked at each other, pure love abounding everywhere. "We will."

My romantic life was going nowhere, so I could only encourage theirs. "Go on your honeymoon, have all the sex. And come back and I'll hang out with you every day. I'll be your third wheel. I can be like your practice kid until you have one of your own."

They were both laughing, and it bothered me a little that they didn't seem to think I was kidding. "I'm serious. I will haunt your doorstep," I said, pointing at them.

As Nikki was hugging me once more and kissing me on the cheek, I strained against the urge to ask her details about Finn. Ordinarily, she'd want to know everything. She'd expect all the dirt about whether he was a good kisser and what else we did on the lounge chair by the pool. Ordinarily, I wouldn't let her take three steps without telling me everything about the mysterious guy who had to run off without doing me the courtesy of leaving a glass slipper.

But these were not ordinary circumstances. It was her wedding night. And as much as I knew we'd have a big debriefing when she came back after her honeymoon, I'd be selfish if I pulled her out of her bliss just to satisfy my curiosity about a guy I'd never see again. Because he was a married astronomer on the lam.

So I kissed her back and told her to have the time of her life on her honeymoon in Anguilla. Then I went home and dug out my vibrator.

# CHAPTER FIVE

ANNIE

SUNDAY WAS A GREAT DAY. I was up by seven and out the door fifteen minutes later in shorts, a tank top, and running shoes. The condo I was renting was about a mile from the beach and the bike path was my new favorite running spot.

The sky was already blue and bright, unsurprising for July, but a little unusual for the beach, which had been fogged in the first couple weeks I'd been in town. It was a comforting reminder of San Francisco. I hated to think I was homesick already, but if I'm honest... I was.

For the hour I ran along the oceanfront, I sorted through my mental to-do list and decided how I was going to spend the rest of my day. I planned to grab some coffee at one of the cute places on Montana Avenue and get all the remaining work done on all the other partners' cases so I'd have a clean slate for my first solo case in the morning. I'd grocery shop. I'd nap. I'd cook something from my grilling cookbook.

I would cook for one.

As I passed a man pushing a jogging stroller with a cute toddler's arms and legs splayed over the sides, I affirmed my disinterest in entanglements. No men, no babies, no commitment, no heartbreak.

That mantra and my full day's schedule should have been enough to keep errant thoughts about Finn and his mysterious departure from spinning through my brain, but my errant thoughts staged a coup.

Running turned out to be the perfect milieu for obsessing over him and only him. As my feet hit the pavement, I rhythmically replayed every part of our conversation from the night before, trying to figure out whether I'd missed clues. Had he told me something that should have indicated he lived with his parents and had a curfew? Did he seem like a hardened ex-con running from the law? Did he seem like he was pretending to be someone he wasn't?

The answer to all my questions was a resounding *no*, and I considered myself a decent judge of people. He'd seemed conflicted about his desire to kiss me. Maybe that was him trying to take the high road since he knew he'd have to dash off in a matter of hours. Or maybe my man-judging meter was just broken.

There were already bikes and other runners on the path, but the sun had yet to peek over the palisade bluffs that divided Pacific Coast Highway from Santa Monica. It felt good to run. Feeling my feet land hard on the cement made me understand why people liked contact sports.

Before I realized it, I was already at the pier, marking my turn-around point. More bikes, walkers, and runners were on the path now, and I needed to get back before the beach became a madhouse of people dashing across the bike route to claim a spot on the sand.

Less than an hour later, I'd showered and walked up the block to a cafe with large picnic tables extending down the street. They were never close to full, even on weekends, so I ordered a latte and settled at one of the tables for a couple hours with my case files.

Working outside and drinking coffee made by someone other than me came pretty close to my personal nirvana. And the coffee at the Sandpiper was good. So was the blueberry scone I ordered with it. Lately, I'd been living on carbs. And meat. There was a good chance my body would revolt for lack of fiber or produce, but I wasn't about to pass up a scone.

The file folder I'd been carrying around for a week was stuffed with the odds and ends of various cases, tasks for the newbie to take on as a nerdy hazing ritual. I'd been working on everything that was thrown my way because the faster I could crank through the scut work, the sooner I could move on to my own solo case.

"I'm impressed with your experience in white-collar crimes and securities law," Tom Chavez, the managing partner, had told me during our Skype interview, before flying me down to meet in person. Then he hit me with the rest of that sentence: "But we expect everyone to work together in the interest of the firm. No lone wolves. Especially if you come in at the partner level."

"I will. That's the goal." If I'd had my preference, I'd be a lone wolf. I hated relying on other people. It usually slowed me down, and I didn't like asking for help. But I could be a team player if necessary, especially because Tom had said the word I'd been dying to hear for over a year now—*partner*. I'd join my new firm as a partner, and that was worth uprooting my life.

Tom didn't ask why I wasn't staying at my old firm. The head-hunter I'd hired had told all potential employers that I was moving to LA to be closer to family, which was sort of true. My parents still lived in the small Central California town where I grew up, and without traffic, it took about twenty minutes less time to drive out and visit them from Los Angeles than it did from San Francisco.

Law is a field of technicalities, and I was more than willing to exploit a technical misconception about distance to avoid the discussion of the issues at my old job. And really, there was just one issue. I'd been passed up—twice—for a partner position after being told it was practically mine for the taking. So, I signed up with a headhunter who zeroed in on firms where I could jump onto the partner track. I expected it might take a couple years to earn a partner spot at a new firm, so the offer to come in at partner level made the job and the move a no-brainer.

Tom also made it clear that he appreciated my single woman status, which meant he could load me up with billable hours and not worry that I'd be running home at six to put my kids to bed. I hated that he looked at women in the workplace that way, but it was reality. Men were viewed as safer bets because they didn't take time out for maternity leave or childcare issues. Neither would I.

The idea of a relationship lasting long enough for me to have kids was laughable—especially after my most recent almost-boyfriend, the overcooked burger to my underbaked bun, had dumped me to move to Hawaii with a nineteen-year-old yoga instructor who'd had a life-changing effect on his cobra. The position. Whatever.

They planned to open a *huloga* studio—huloga being her term for a hula and yoga hybrid she wanted to promote at fancy resorts.

"She's trademarked the name," he told me. "You're a lawyer; you know all about that." He was nodding and smiling excitedly like we shared a love for trademarks.

"I'm a criminal defense lawyer. I'd only deal with trademark law if someone profited on an illegally-obtained trademark by selling an enormous amount of stock," I said.

"Well, so you know."

"It's a stupid name. No one is going to do huloga. It sounds like a greeting from a dying goose," I told him.

"She's trying to start a trend." He looked as hopeful as a puppy eying an expensive shoe.

"Well, good luck to her." I didn't mean to sound snarky, but what did he expect when he let his cobra make decisions for him?

My most successful courtship to date had been the process of blind dating several firms and signing with Bristol, Chavez, and Greeves. That marriage had produced my first baby—a securities fraud case that I couldn't wait to dive into in the morning.

If anything could distract me from Finn's disappearing act, it was the anticipation of my new case.

Sipping my coffee, I noticed a petite brunette who looked about my age laughing at something on her phone with the guy next to her. She had one leg wrapped around him, her hand curled around the back of his neck. In her oversized sweatpants which I guessed to be his, she looked cute, happy, and smitten. The way they were leaning toward each other made me think they were still under the six-month mark of dating, having a morning-after-sex breakfast, charmed by each other, and shutting out the rest of the world.

I couldn't remember the last time I felt that way about a guy. Maybe I'd never felt that way.

Well, that wasn't entirely true. Oddly, my lingering feelings about Finn the astronomer had my stomach twisting in ways that surprised me. Especially given my sharply-honed ability to tune out anything when I was working. Was it wrong that I was plotting ways to track him down? I had search engines at my disposal. Maybe I could find him. And kiss him again.

*Focus, focus, focus.*

The couple at the other table wasn't helping the situation. They were making me crave a morning-after-sex breakfast, making me wonder if Finn and I had a special connection that could have gone beyond a fling.

I had to stop. He was gone and the best thing I could do was to find fascinating legal tidbits in other people's cases so I didn't spin off into an obsessive loop of thinking about Finn.

*What's wrong with me? I don't ever obsess over men.*

I was normally more like the guy to my right, doing the Sunday crossword puzzle and sipping his coffee slowly. He looked focused. With his shock of white hair and reading glasses,

I put him as older than my dad. And yet... I identified more with him than with the cute couple my age.

After another gulp of coffee had my brain buzzing with caffeinated pleasure, I looked back at the files in front of me. I had two briefs to write, where I'd set out the arguments of each case along with legal precedent for why our position was the right one. Then I needed to review a contract to make sure the client wasn't losing out on foreign royalty rights and the language provided by the entertainment company who hired him was typically convoluted. I loved red-lining these kinds of contracts and stripping out all the bullshit.

"Looks like you're working hard," said a guy to my right, peering over his iced coffee and sipping it through a paper straw. I never understood why that would be a person's chosen opening. If he really believed I was working hard, why interrupt me?

*I'm a pain in the ass. No wonder I'm single.*

"Yeah. I brought my office to the cafe today," I said, looking up briefly and returning to my pages to give him the idea I was too busy for conversation. Was I, though?

"Brought your office. I like that."

I looked up at him once more and smiled unconvincingly. He looked about my age and wore cycling shorts and had fancy mirrored sports glasses perched on top of his head. He wasn't bad looking—light brown hair and warm eyes, nice smile—and it's not that I was against the idea of meeting someone new at a cafe. It was probably what I was supposed to be doing if I ever hoped to go on a date. And I did. If Finn showed me anything, it was that my prior crappy relationships were a lopsided portrait of attraction.

And yet... I couldn't muster any amount of enthusiasm for the brown-haired biker. He seemed nice. It wasn't his fault. But I needed more.

*Well, maybe your fairy godmother will help.*

This would plainly not do. I couldn't move forward comparing every man I met to Finn, whom I'd probably never see again unless it was on a Wanted poster somewhere. I had to stop, so I looked at the guy again and tried to smile with more enthusiasm. "Yeah, well if I have to work on a Sunday, this isn't a bad way to do it."

"What kind of work do you do?" he asked, scooting a little closer, close enough for me to notice his shaved legs. I knew serious cyclists did this, but even that didn't make him much more intriguing to me. I stifled a sigh.

This was how it would go. Me, single, in LA.

I'd talk to this guy, ask about his cycling hobby, find out what he did for a living. He'd ask me about my job, work his nerve up to get my number, and we'd go on a date. It would be *fine*. It would be the way it always was, and if all went well, we'd have polite, ordinary sex. I could handle that progression of events. I was used to it. I could make it work.

"I'm a lawyer," I said, extending my hand. "Annie." I tried hard not to think about shaking hands with a very different guy the prior night.

I tried really hard. I almost succeeded.

# CHAPTER SIX

ANNIE

I WOKE up in the dark on Monday because I'd agreed to meet my co-counsel, Ben Jackson, at the ass crack of dawn so he could debrief me on my new case. He'd worked on it briefly before I'd been hired, but he'd made it clear he was happy to hand it over.

Getting to the office at six in the morning was early, even for a rooster like me, but Ben handled some of the firm's East Coast accounts and routinely arrived before five so he could be ready to talk to clients at nine their time. It seemed crazy to me, but it turned out I was crazier.

I might have been a little bit excited about my new case. I might have woken up at four and paced around my apartment for an hour before hopping in the shower. And I might have spent extra time blow-drying my hair and applying mascara because I had time to kill. If Ben noticed that I was overeager for my first solo case, he didn't say.

He towered over me, even when I wore my tall pumps, which were navy with a striped bow at the back and a three-inch heel. They matched the navy pencil skirt I wore with a rose-colored sweater. It was a more conservative outfit than I'd usually choose —the firm had a loose dress code if we weren't meeting with clients or going to court—but I wanted to make a good impression: competent lawyer, professionally dressed, ready to kick legal ass.

Ben had a Sterling K. Brown vibe, part scholar, part father, part serious badass. That morning, he wore his usual attire of dark jeans, button-down shirt, and a grey vest that matched the sport coat that hung on the back of his chair. I wondered what he did with all the pants that were part of the three-piece suits, but after knowing him only a couple of weeks, it didn't seem appropriate to ask.

We met in his office, where he was drinking a diet cola and eating potato chips at his desk. "It's practically lunchtime for me," he said when he caught me looking askance at his snack.

"Do you go to bed early?" I asked, taking a seat in one of the client chairs facing him.

He nodded. "I have a strange schedule, I admit. I leave here at five in the afternoon, go home, sleep, and then I get up at between two and three, depending on whether I want to ride."

"Ride? Like horses?" I asked.

"No, like cycling."

"You get on a bike at two in the morning?"

"Yeah, about three days a week."

"Aren't stationary bikes kind of loud? Don't you wake people?"

"I could. My kids are light sleepers. But I ride on the road," he said, biting into a chip and holding one hand under his chin to catch the crumbs, which he deposited onto a napkin on his desk. "Shall we get started?" he asked.

There was so much more I wanted to know. His kids were light sleepers? What kids? Did he have a wife? A husband? And what was this about riding outside at two in the morning?

"Holy hell, no. What do you mean, you ride on the road? In

the middle of the night, in the dark, you're out on a bike ride?" I asked.

"Yes. My bike has a light." He said it as though it explained everything.

"Still, aren't you worried about getting run over?"

He shook his head and bit into another chip, again catching the crumbs. "Nope. Interestingly, the hour between two and three has the smallest number of cars on the road of all hours in the day."

"Oh, so only a small number of cars will run you over?"

"I sense your sarcasm, but I assure you, it's perfectly safe out there with my bike light. Plus, you know, in the city it never really gets that dark because of the inversion layer."

Okay, that was strange. For as long as I could remember, no one had ever talked to me about the inversion layer, and now, it had come up twice in a matter of days.

It also made me think of Finn, something I'd been trying very hard not to do over the past twenty-four hours because every time the image of his face came into my mind, I felt a mixture of curiosity, regret, confusion, and longing. It was the longing that was proving most problematic.

I'm not too proud to admit that I'd used the legal databases and high-powered search engines at my disposal to see if I could learn more about him and his background but I only knew his first name and it got me nowhere. I looked at social media sites but came up empty there too.

Not like I blamed him for not being plastered all over the Internet. I wasn't on social media either. Setting up a profile and trying to project an upbeat image to the world felt too much like the dating sites which already exhausted the perky right out of me. The flailing I'd been doing on dating sites felt like necessity, but I couldn't handle a Facebook fail too.

After a few semi-targeted attempts to find people named Finn in and around LA, I searched for graduate school information in the communications school where he met Nikki. But I found no one named Finn or Phinneas in the logical date range. Eventually, I gave up.

It was stupid. Better to forget about him and his placid green eyes. Better to focus on my new job before it became my old job.

Jackson was staring at me, and I got the impression he'd asked me a question he expected me to answer. I raised my eyebrows and cocked my head like I was considering my reply. Then I nodded, hoping that would satisfy him.

"You didn't hear a word I said, did you?" he asked. There was no finessing lawyers.

I smiled, caught. "I did not. Apologies. I'm not a hundo p at this hour."

"Come again? Just 'cause I'm black doesn't mean I'm a rapper."

"Oh, see, I thought it *did* mean that. Jesus, Jackson. It's an expression. Hundo p. A hundred percent. My nephew texts it to me all the time. He's twelve and not a rapper."

"Great, is this what I have to look forward to? My twins are eight," he said.

"I'm afraid so. And as much as I want to ask you a million questions about your twins—and see pictures—I'm gonna limit myself to one pic, then we should talk about the case."

Jackson was already swiping across his phone screen, looking for a photo. And… still looking.

"Aren't they on your home screen? Isn't it a law or something that all parents have to use their kids' pictures as their screen saver? My brother does it, and like I said, his kid's almost a teenager."

He looked up and grimaced. "Fine. Here's the one on my home screen," he said, passing the phone to me. "I was just looking for the one from their first day of school because they were wearing matching dresses."

"Oh my God, Jackson, they're adorable," I said. The two girls were grinning through gapped teeth and standing on their tiptoes, each plainly trying to be taller than her twin.

"They are adorable. And if they start saying things like hundo p, I'm… I'm…" I could see a vein pulsing in his temple, and I refused to be the source of an aneurism in my first month on the job, so I patted his hand.

"They won't. I'm sure they won't." Just for good measure, I added, "And neither will I."

Jackson wiped his hand across his forehead, as though trying to smooth out the horizontal creases that had taken up residence there, but he was unsuccessful. "Okay, the case. Let's talk about that, so I don't have to think about my two angels growing up. Unrepentant criminal clients are always good for keeping my mind off my actual life."

"Ah, *unrepentant* gets me all excited. Tell me," I said, at the ready with a yellow pad in front of me and my laptop open. I wasn't sure which I'd need first but I was prepared.

Jackson slid a slim file folder across the desk to me with a flourish, as though he was imparting a gift. "Ok, the broad strokes are that our client was sued under the Federal False Claims Act by a whistleblower. Then the SEC filed suit as well. He made seven million dollars trading stock, timed perfectly with a busted merger."

"Who is this guy?" I asked. I couldn't wait to meet the client. Part of the reason I'd gravitated to white-collar crime was that the people who tried to get away with duping the government were generally smart, and they were usually either confident or arrogant. Both types posed problems, but I liked the challenge of breaking them down and making a case that could defend their behavior.

"College professor at California U. He's an economist. Smart guy, self-effacing, liable. But something's off. He made the money buying and selling stock in a couple telecom companies that were expected to get government approval merge. Only he bet against them, timed his sell-off almost perfectly and then shorted the stock of a different company. He made a ton when the merger fell through days later and the stock tanked."

"So he's either Nostradamus or he had insider info. Was there any discussion of a plea bargain?"

Jackson drank his soda and shook his head. "That's where I hand this off to you and say 'good luck.' This guy is a real piece of work. Totally in denial. Or rather he denies he did anything wrong."

"That's true of almost every white collar criminal I've represented. They all believe they're justified in whatever they did. Sometimes that helps me defend them."

"Glad you're not daunted."

"Not at all. So, who's the whistleblower?"

Jackson slid the file back over toward himself and had a look at the pages. "A colleague at the university. He consulted for the companies whose stocks this guy traded and called foul. He said the exact dates of the trades coincided with information only insiders would have."

"What's our guy say?"

"Nothing."

"What do you mean, nothing?"

"He knew his case would be handed off, so he told me it was a waste of both our time to go through everything. I got that much from him—he doesn't like to waste time. I haven't seen him since the arraignment."

"Yeah, that was what, two months ago?"

"Around that, yeah. The SEC filed its own charges, and that caused delays. But you know how it can be with a big case like this one. Other firms try to get a bite of it, see if they can swoop in and be the hero with the great idea. Maybe there was competition because of the whole Nobel Laureate thing."

I hated looking uninformed, so I tried to play it off. "Right. You mean how the timing of announcing the Nobel Laureates would have made it hard to—"

Jackson started laughing. "Sorry, I would have loved to let you keep rambling on, just to see what you were gonna come up with, but I'm not that cruel. The client was on the shortlist for the Nobel

Prize. Tom wanted his case. Even if we lose and he goes to jail, it's still a feather in the firm's cap to be his counsel."

"I'm not going to lose," I said.

"I like your confidence."

"Thank you. I know the whistleblower statutes and the relevant SEC cases, and I have a plan." My brain was starting to kick into gear now that we were talking about the legal system. I loved my job, and it somehow lit the fire under me that a thousand cups of coffee often failed to do. Actually, scratch that. I needed the coffee too, but it helped that I loved my job.

"Sounds good. I'm happy to wash my hands of this thing. And hopefully, you can settle without going to trial," Jackson said. "Gotta tell you though, I've been in white-collar law a long time, and I've never seen a case like this one," he said.

"Why's that?"

"It's just a little odd. The client didn't want to answer my questions. It was like he didn't trust me, and if you can't trust your own lawyer, who can you trust? Plus, he won't just pay a fine even though it would keep him out of jail. He's stubborn and he likes to do things his way." Jackson shook his head as if he pitied me for what I was about to undertake. I was undaunted.

"That's okay," I told him. "So do I."

# CHAPTER SEVEN

FINN

I WAS EMBARRASSED to admit that I was awakened on Monday morning by the sound of car tires squealing around the curve of the road in front of my house. Embarrassed because I'd overslept. I knew that car. I anticipated it every morning. It was a teenage kid in the neighborhood who had a habit of driving too fast and taking that curve like he was jockeying for the win in the Indy 500.

My goal was always to be in the shower by the time he came screaming around the corner so I wouldn't be tempted to run outside and shake my fist at him like the grumpy old man I feared I'd already become.

Wasn't I recently a teenager myself who drove stupidly fast because I believed I was invincible? Only if twenty years ago is considered *recently*. Apparently, it's long enough ago that fist-shaking is my go-to instead of cheering him on. Welcome to life in my mid-thirties.

Really, my main concern was that I lived on a relatively steep hill and the wall around my house tracked a fully one-hundred eighty degrees around a curve, so at the speed he drove, there was a decent chance of his car ending up on my front lawn one of these days if he wasn't careful.

I was not embarrassed to admit that when the screech of tires woke me, I'd been pleasantly dreaming of kissing Annie at the wedding. And in my dream, she was even more intent on getting her orgasm on than she'd been on Saturday night. She was downright insistent, and like the man I'd wished I'd been that night, I didn't disappoint.

I dreamed us right back on the chaise lounges by the hotel pool, her bridesmaid dress lifted over her head, a lace silk bra and panties an invitation for me to test their durability with my teeth.

My dream continued with her moaning and screaming my name so loudly that the guests at the wedding reception heard her over the rollicking band, and I was not at all apologetic. But then I was awakened and felt my shitty reality kick me in the face.

I'd spent the past thirty-six hours swimming in regret. For so many reasons. I hated the way I'd rushed out of the wedding without an explanation. She deserved more than an "oops, gotta run" excuse after we'd spent two hours talking and another good hour making out.

Even though I'd wanted to do better that night, I couldn't bring myself to ruin what had been a perfect three hours with a near-perfect woman by being honest. And no, I'm not calling her near-perfect because I noticed a single solitary flaw at any point during our time together. But no one is perfect.

The house full of women who raised me insisted I learn that at an early age. Not only does perfection not exist, it shouldn't even be a goal. My sisters schooled me early to make me understand that women grow up with unrealistic norms and expectations of how they should look, many of them self-inflicted because they're surrounded by unattainable images of beauty every day.

When I was in high school and I tried to explain this fact to guys I played football with, they let me know where I could shove my unattainable images. But the more they insisted their last priority was to discourage women from aspiring to unachievable ideals of beauty, the more I felt the need to prove my point. Sadly, for them, I liked proving my point. And I'm good at it.

By the time we graduated, our high school football team had won sponsorships from three women's product companies, all of which sought to normalize the way women feel about their perception of beauty. We even did a few national television PSAs and funded a scholarship program with the prize money we received for being forward-thinkers.

All of this is to say that I assumed Annie was imperfect, and I expected nothing else, but in the time I'd spent with her, I'd have wagered that if perfection did exist, it was this woman.

It made me feel like even more of an asshole for not at least getting a phone number or email or finding some other way to get in touch with her. I wanted to explain, even if she'd gone home and forgotten about me. I'd be sure to ask my friend when she returned from Anguilla—an apology two weeks late had to be better than none at all.

Grabbing my phone off the desk in my bedroom, I clicked the remote to open the shades on the back wall. As soon as the sunlight began to stream through the tall leaded glass windows, I felt better.

"Finn, what in God's name was that sound?" The voice was shrill and sounded annoyed, and I'd been listening to it for most of my life.

My sister, Becca, staggered into my room and with the light pouring through the glass, I could see her blonde hair in a knot on her head with wisps sticking out in all directions like the bride of Frankenstein. She was wearing one of my old football jerseys that I hadn't seen since high school.

"Why do you have that?" I asked, ignoring her question about the sound. I knew she didn't really care. The point was to let me know something had woken her up before her alarm.

"What?"

"That," I said, pointing at the jersey. "I thought Mom put that in the giveaway pile fifteen years ago."

"You thought wrong. I love this thing. It's the best for sleeping in when the weather's cold."

"Is it cold here in the summer in Southern California?" I asked. The last I checked it had been in the high eighties.

"In your house it is. Do you always sleep in a refrigerator?"

"I like it on the cold side."

"Which is why I brought the winter PJs. I knew this about you. Why are we even discussing it?" She seemed more aggravated than I remember her being in the mornings. Of all my sisters, she was the least capable of functioning before noon, so it made sense that she'd chosen a career as a night shift obstetrical nurse at the hospital in Oakland from which she was currently taking her vacation time.

"Want some coffee?" I gestured to the espresso machine and fridge in the corner of my bedroom next to the large zinc-topped desk.

She followed my gaze to the coffee setup, which I always kept stocked with several kinds of coffee, clean cups, and a jar of spoons. "Are you serious? You have a coffee bar in your bedroom? When did you become so bougie?"

"I'm not bougie. I just need to have coffee before I do anything else and having it in here makes it easy."

"Ah, so I stand corrected. Not bougie. Just lazy."

"I accept that."

Becca had arrived the day before, ostensibly because she felt like spending her week off sightseeing in LA. But given that she'd been here dozens of times and hated anything trendy or prone to crowds, I knew that wasn't the reason for her visit. Plus, she'd never accepted my invitation to stay at my house, and this time she told me she was excited to bond. This was my sister. If we weren't bonded after living in the same house for our formative years, there was something wrong with our glue.

She was visiting because she was worried about me and had it in her head that this visit might be the last time she saw me before I went to prison.

I couldn't blame her. I was worried too. I certainly didn't want to go to prison, but a lot had to happen—all of it going the wrong way—before that would be my fate. At least, that's what I told her. I made it sound like I had a plan, hoping she'd go back to the Bay Area in a week and report to the rest of my family that I was fine.

Plus, I didn't want to spend the precious time she was in town with her fussing around and looking at me like I was dying.

Becca yanked the hairband from her hair and the blonde mess fell down her back, sweeping the crazy strands along with it. Her bright blue eyes seized on mine. "I'll have a latte if you're not too lazy to make one."

"Coming up." I walked over to my coffee setup and started the bean grinder. "You still like soy milk?" I asked.

"Ugh, no. Now I'm into nut milk."

"That's appropriate."

"Shut up until I drink my latte and can think of a comeback."

"See? I'm not so crazy for keeping the caffeine in my bedroom. It's needed immediately."

As I was waiting for the beans to grind, I glanced at my desk, where I'd organized pages and pages of reports and models I'd been working on for almost ten years. That was the data that was going to set me free, if only I could convince people my motives were honest.

I fished around in the mini-fridge and found some cashew milk, which I poured into my frother. A couple minutes later, I handed off Becca's latte and grabbed my own double espresso, which I tempered with a sugar cube. "Hey, give me a couple minutes, okay? Then I'll make you some breakfast," I told Becca.

"You don't have to cook for me."

"It was a metaphor. We're having cereal."

"You're a loser." She padded out of the room, and I nostalgically glanced at the number eleven on the back of my old jersey, recalling days when life was simpler. No computer trails that lived forever, no text messages that someone who barely knew me could use to make a case for my supposed guilt.

All I wanted was the chance to apologize to Annie and explain why I had to run off so abruptly. It was crazy that I cared about it more than the meeting with my lawyers in a couple hours. She'd taken hold in my thoughts and I couldn't let her go. I didn't want to wait two weeks for Nikki to get back from her honeymoon to get information. I'd never been a patient guy.

So instead of getting in the shower, I took a stab at making technology work to my advantage.

Even with just her first name to go on, there was a decent chance I could track her down through social media. I'd insisted that we not talk about work that night because I wanted to live in the present, given my circumstances. But that resulted in me having even less information to parse through now. It wouldn't stop me.

Logging into the regular social media sites, I started with Nikki and looked through her friend lists for anyone named Annie. Or Anne. There was nothing. Instead of feeling frustrated, I found myself even more intrigued by this woman who seemed to have shunned social media. Or maybe Annie wasn't her name at all. Maybe her whole quest to seduce a man at a wedding had started with a fake name and a lack of identifying information. It made sense. She was looking for a one-night thing. Of course, she wasn't going to give me any real information about herself.

My search possibilities dwindled, but my interest only grew. Who was she? And if I did find her, could I ever make her understand what had happened to me? Would a confident, stunning woman like her even give me the time it would take to explain why I'd been arrested?

I carried that thought with me into the bathroom where I took a good look at myself in the mirror. I didn't look like a guilty man, but that was only based on movies I'd seen with Edward G. Robinson committing crimes and mob bosses who ordered hits on weasel-like men who crossed them. And just like in the movies, illusion was as important as reality when an audience—or a jury —decided on guilt.

I needed a shave, and I needed sleep; that was a given. But if I ever did see Annie again, I wanted it to be when I didn't have federal charges hanging over my head or the stain of accusation darkening my name. I needed to be free of the messes I'd found myself in as of late.

In other words, I needed a miracle.

# CHAPTER EIGHT

ANNIE

I RAN into my boss in the coffee room, where I'd planned to refill my cup before going to the conference room early for my client meeting. I had just enough time for some quick pleasantries, but Murphy's law had other plans.

"Annie, good morning..." Tom Chavez said. I was about to respond when he opened the fridge and we both caught a whiff of something that had apparently died over the weekend. "Oh my god, what the hell...?"

I leaned in, feeling it was my duty to take the bullet for the boss and deal with whatever vile food item was decomposing in our midst. I found the offending item—a microwaved broccoli quiche which had been loosely covered with foil—and held it up like a dead rat dangling from two fingers. "Broccoli. Barely good when it's not left festering for the weekend. Deadly after three days. I'll find a place for it," I said.

"Far away. Take it far, far away."

I busied myself with the rotting food, opening and closing drawers in the coffee room in search of a bag. When I couldn't find anything except a spare trashcan liner, I opted for that, unrolling the flimsy plastic from the roll and working against the laws of cling wrap to get the damned thing open. Then I inserted the offending broccoli dish, whipped the bag around a few times, and tied a knot at the top. "All done. Ready for the diaper bin. If you'll excuse me..." I said.

After racing to the lobby to discard the trash and taking the stairs back to our floor, I went back to my office to pick up the notes I'd compiled the day before. I felt ready, but now I was running late. All thoughts of Finn from the wedding were stuffed to the back of my brain where they belonged, and I was a sharp, capable lawyer by the time I left my office. Hundo p.

The conference room was at the end of a long hallway, and I race-walked all the way, aware of a sheen of sweat on my forehead.

Nothing a quick swipe with my sleeve wouldn't fix. I discretely leaned toward my arm while I pulled the conference door open and spun around to look for a seat in one of the ergonomic chairs that were pulled up to the long, grey glass table.

I had my coffee balanced on top of my file folder and notepad, and my eyes stayed keenly focused on the cup so it wouldn't spill before I had a chance to put it on the table. For that reason, I didn't immediately see my new client, but as soon as I'd deposited my armload of items, I straightened and made right for where he was sitting, extending my hand.

"I'm Annie Prescott. So nice to meet you."

It was then that I made eye contact and nearly recoiled. His eyes were very familiar. Of the childhood favorite marble variety.

*Holy shit.*

My mind raced through how it was possible that the man who'd had his tongue in my mouth less than thirty-six hours earlier was sitting at the conference table at my new place of employment, masquerading as my client. This had to be a joke.

And yet... it oddly made sense. The early curfew. He hadn't

wanted to talk about work. He'd checked a text on his phone and seemed concerned.

But then there was the other Finn... the one who talked to me about nebulae and kissed me in a way that made my skin heat as I stood looking at him. My hand unconsciously went to my lips the way they had when he'd left the reception.

For a split second, I saw a combination of emotions pass behind Finn's eyes—fear, guilt, apology, vulnerability—but only for a moment. Then he tucked everything behind a wall of stoicism and focused.

Even in this most bizarre of moments, he was different than most men I'd ever met. He didn't look down, eyes seizing on the V-neck of my sweater. Finn held his gaze steadily on mine as he took hold of my hand and shook it. "Norman Finley. Thanks for meeting with me today."

"I... yes, of course," I said. He was so good at pretending I was a stranger that I almost believed he didn't remember meeting me two nights earlier.

Tom nodded as we shook hands and gave us his a barely-there smile that he used whether he was annoyed or downright gleeful. "Excellent, we're all here. Let's get started. As Jackson mentioned, Annie Prescott will now be your lead counsel on the case. For all intents and purposes at the firm, you belong to Annie."

The expression on Finn's face morphed quickly from shock to embarrassment to a neutral veneer of approval. He nodded once and set his lips in a stiff line, while continuing to meet my gaze.

His stare had a distressing quality that was at once so smoldering and handsome, like he wanted to finish what he'd started on Saturday, mixed with the complicated story I still didn't fully understand about why he'd illegally traded stock.

I was faced with something I'd never had to deal with at work before, a man who made me fear I'd lose my shit in front of my boss. I didn't like that feeling at all.

"And it's your case that belongs under my purview, which isn't to say that you belong to me. I wouldn't own you or seek to control or dominate you in any way." The nervous flood of thoughts was coming hard and fast and my mouth was just the unwitting delivery vehicle.

*Shit, shit, shit. Where is the edit button?*

I started to sputter and wheeze, and I knew what would come next—some sort of nonsensical stream of consciousness prattle that would only serve to make Tom question my abilities. He'd recall the broccoli smell and associate it with my inane diatribe, and out I would go with my legal pad in hand, back to the headhunter.

The blather was threatening with furious force. I tried to have the conversation in my mind, silently, to avoid letting all the words slip out of my mouth. "Lead counsel is what I will be. I will give counsel. Or therapy if you prefer, but not really because I'm not a licensed therapist. Not that it has necessarily stopped others from giving out armchair psychological advice or even just normal unsolicited advice. I was once told by my dentist that I shouldn't wear long skirts because people will make an assumption that my legs don't look good in pants. What does that have to do with cleaning my teeth? Nothing. So I'm fully aware that giving out advice is viewed as conversational, but I'm saying now that I will not do that because I am not a licensed psychologist." I heard my voice in my head and tried to let that be enough without letting the words out into the world.

My face screwed up into a grimace at the unspoken words because they were ridiculous, and I needed to breathe and calm myself down. It was hard, though, because Finn was still staring at me, and he still looked every bit as handsome as he had at the wedding. And I was so, so angry at him for reasons I couldn't fully articulate.

"Anyway, you should feel confident in my abilities as counsel, but not as therapist, of course. I'm not implying you need one…" I was about to release all the crazy, but I heard Finn's voice quietly reply. "Thank you."

The sound of his placid response stopped me in my tracks.

I didn't dare look at Tom, but I could see his horrified expression anyway. He tried to repair the situation or keep our client from fleeing with a stern reply. "That is to say that as your lead counsel—"

But Finn interrupted with a response directed at me. "I understand. I appreciate that, Ms. Prescott. Unless I request your advice as a therapist. In that case, as lead counsel, you'll help me with that, correct?" he said, calmly.

"Um, yes. Of course." And for the second time in his presence, his quiet economy of words had the effect of stopping my verbal hemorrhage and calming me the heck down. I felt like I'd entered a spa and breathed in rosemary mint aromatherapy salts that set me at ease. "Will you be needing that? Therapy?" I asked.

"Not at the moment, but it's good to understand what's on the table."

"You're the client," Jackson said, in a sing-song way that made me happy he was in the room. He seemed to be the only one who wasn't unnerved.

"I am," Finn said quietly.

He was the client. *The client.*

I still didn't understand fully how it could be the case. I'd spent an hour talking to Jackson about the college professor and economist who was nabbed for insider trading. I'd pushed the mysterious man from the wedding far from my mind because it was pointless to obsess over a hot guy who vanished.

And at no point did it occur to me that those people were one and the same.

I tried to look at Finn now and meld those two personae into one in my mind. But all I could think was that he was wearing a tan sport coat instead of his dark suit and that his eyes were that gorgeous navy green. Apparently, they didn't change color depending on what he was wearing, and in the moment, my brain considered that the most crucial bit of information.

Tom began speaking. "As you know, Mr. Finley has been

charged with securities fraud through a qui tam. Mr. Finley, in case you're unfamiliar with the term, it means—"

"Qui tam pro domino rege quam pro ipso in hac parte sequitur. It means 'he who sues in this matter for the king as well as himself,'" Finn said. He didn't look smug or proud of his knowledge. He wasn't trying to prove something. He just knew what Tom was referring to because he was educated and he'd read things most people didn't bother to review.

Tom did a double take. "Yes. And actually, I've never heard the entire phrase quoted, to say nothing of the fact that most people have no idea what it means." A part of me wondered if Tom knew what it meant, outside of being a stand-in term for a whistle-blower suit.

I glanced at Jackson who was looking at Finn with curiosity. "Mr. Finley, I'll admit to being one of the people who's never heard the entire phrase before. I've always heard it referred to as qui tam and I'm embarrassed to say, I never researched the origins of the term."

Finn sparked at Jackson's admission like a professor who's been granted the chance to teach something to a student who's legitimately interested. "If I may..." Finn held up a finger, as though asking permission to interject more facts into the discussion about his own case.

"Please," Jackson said. Tom's mouth ticked down into a slight frown. I could tell he would rather have hurried the meeting along without time spent learning things.

"It comes from Roman law, from the days when private citizens were generally the ones to initiate prosecutions. And at the time, the criminal statutes offered citizens a part of the property forfeited by the defendant as a reward. That way, people were financially incentivized to turn in their neighbors when they'd committed crimes, just in case they weren't sufficiently incentivized by the idea of doing what was right."

"So interesting," Jackson said. Tom nodded out of bored obligation.

"There's more," Finn said, looking from face to face to gauge interest. Jackson's eyes lit up, and he motioned for Finn to continue.

"The Romans weren't the only ones to employ a version of qui tam. The English Parliament did it, too, as far back as the fourteenth century, but it was more about making sure localities weren't selling wine. That was the jurisdiction of the king alone. So they enacted legislation such that if someone sued someone else for selling wine, that person was entitled to keep one third of it with the other two thirds going to the king."

I took the opportunity to watch Finn as he spoke, unhindered by the need to limit my perusal of his face to secret sideways glances. He was speaking, and it would have been rude to look away. So I kept my eyes riveted to his handsome face, noticing details I hadn't allowed myself to see before, like the fact that he'd shaved since I met him at the wedding and his jaw looked more defined.

He spoke with the confidence of a person who knows he's right and isn't worried about misspeaking. His eyes lit up when he talked because he genuinely enjoyed imparting information. And when his lips formed words, small dimples danced on either side of his mouth.

I could imagine him standing in front of a lecture hall doing the same. It went without saying that the college women in his classes would be fangirling. I couldn't imagine taking a course from him and trying to focus on what he was saying instead of the plush pink of his lips when he spoke.

*Quit objectifying the client!*

Jackson shook his head when Finn finished his explanation. "Amazing. Hard to imagine there weren't a few incentivized wine lovers out there looking to rat out their fellow countrymen."

"As is the problem with qui tam in general," Finn said. He was right. The problem with rewarding whistleblowers was that they were incentivized to turn in their colleagues, which made the system ripe for abuse.

"Which is one of the ways I plan to challenge the whistleblower's claim against you. He has an implicit bias," I said. "I'll look to depose him next week. I'll also depose one of your colleagues who's a former SEC official—Darren McCutcheon—so he can speak to your character and act as an expert witness on how you used the information you had at your disposal," I said.

I forced myself to focus on the legal issues in which I was proficient. If I thought about anything else—like the taste of Finn's lips—I'd lose my mind. Jackson nodded in agreement, and Finn's eyes met mine. I immediately felt a flush warm the back of my neck because his gaze looked appreciative and not just of my knowledge of the law.

I debated how to handle the next part. I could sit through the rest of the meeting with Tom and Jackson and pretend I'd never seen Finn before and sort through my myriad questions when we were alone.

Or I could let Tom know we had a mutual friend and therefore a conflict of interest and back out as lead counsel. It would be cleaner. I could let another attorney at the firm—probably Jackson —handle his case. I could trust someone else to do the job I knew I was capable of doing and wait my turn for another great case.

I couldn't do that.

I also wasn't sure I could lie.

"Full disclosure," I blurted. "We know each other. We've met previously."

Tom looked confused. "You've already met?"

"Yes!" I said, wishing I hadn't finished my second cup of coffee because everything out of my mouth sounded like a declaration.

"Is that a euphemism for something else?" Tom asked.

"No!" I shouted. "I'm only saying that it's a fact. We've met."

"Um, okay," Tom said. Great. All in the open. Maybe that would be the end of the discussion.

Jackson jumped in. "How did you meet?"

*Dammit, Jackson.*

Finn's expression remained unperturbed as he turned from me to answer Tom and Finn. "We were at a mutual friend's wedding on Saturday night and we chatted. Serendipitous, right?"

If someone asked me for a list of words to describe what I was feeling as I sat across the table from him, *serendipitous* would have been dead last.

"Ah, well that is a coincidence, to be sure. It's also cause for concern. Before we go any further, we should discuss whether having Ms. Prescott on your legal team makes you uncomfortable, given your mutual friend. It's certainly not a problem from a legal standpoint," Tom said.

He looked at Finn, who I felt certain would take the opportunity to ask for any other lawyer the firm had—or even a paralegal or night janitor—instead of having to work with me every day and relive our disrupted time on the chaise lounges.

Plus, the more separation I could get from him, the more I could allow the tiny inkling in my brain to grow into a small belief that we might someday be able to finish what we started at the wedding. There was no way I could even entertain the thought of anything if he was my client, but if he wasn't, maybe...

"No, it doesn't make me uncomfortable at all. In fact, I wouldn't be satisfied with another partner, so let's just leave everything the way it is," Finn said, still calm. I started to feel wary of his ever-placid demeanor, in the way police investigators said that guilty criminals sat calmly when left alone in the interview room. Innocent people would be sweating and climbing the walls. I didn't need a one-way mirror to see that Finn was not at all bothered by the choice of lawyer. Which probably meant he was guilty.

It probably meant there would be nothing I or anyone else could do to save him. So what did it matter? Maybe he thought he could get a piece of ass in the process.

"I'm uncomfortable with it," I blurted before I realized I'd formulated an opinion on the matter. "On his behalf. It would be cleaner and better for him to work with someone who has no chance of reporting on the case to a mutual friend."

Three pairs of eyes turned to me. I looked from one pair to the next. Tom looked annoyed. Finn was smirking. And Jackson was looking curiously at me for the first time since I'd walked into the room.

"Oh. I was under the impression there was attorney-client privilege," Finn said, his eyes fixed on me and the faintest hint of a grin on his face. Two nights ago, that look was seductive. I didn't know what to think about it now when he cocked his head to the side like he was trying to solve an amusing puzzle.

"There *is*," Tom said, looking at me with the same expression he gave to the putrid fridge remains.

"Of course there is," I stammered. "Of course. I meant it more for your comfort level and your perception."

"My perception is that you're a professional and the fact that we have a friend in common would never prevent you from doing your job at the highest ethical standard," Finn said. He wasn't laughing at me. He looked serious.

"Yes, of course. There's no conflict on my end. Everything that happens between us stays in the vault," I said. Finn's smile ticked up on one side, and I stammered some more. "Everything you tell me stays between us."

"You will be in excellent hands," Tom said, standing up. Jackson did the same. They shook hands with Finn and wrapped up their time in the room with some pleasantries, leaving after a few minutes. Leaving me at the table facing Finn.

I didn't know where to begin. So instead of speaking, I glared at him with my head cocked to the side the way I imagined doing if I ever had kids. I intended my look to communicate their dire prospects, the gravity of their self-inflicted doom, the severity with which they needed to consider their next words very carefully. Because if they didn't, they just might be disowned. I did not plan to have children until I'd perfected that look.

"Hi," Finn said.

His reaction told me I had, sadly, not yet perfected it.

"Hi?"

"Well, we didn't get a chance for a normal greeting since you freaked out when you saw me and went from querulous to corporate lawyer at warp speed."

"Querulous?"

"Nervous."

"No."

"No? Do you always offer to dominate your clients?" He was smirking, rubbing a finger across his lips. I found the movement both distracting and enthralling.

"For the record, I think I said I would *not* seek to dominate you," I said.

"Correct. Accurate. I can already see you're an excellent lawyer. I made the right call insisting you stay on my case."

"I'm glad you think so, but—"

"No. Don't disagree with me. You're my lawyer; you've taken my case. Let's talk about that." He looked at my file folders and sat back in his chair as though he expected me to explain exactly how I'd go about defending him.

Then he was rolling his chair all the way around the conference table to the side where I sat. Nothing about him made sense. There were chairs on my side. He could have just stood up and taken one.

So I stood up and walked so that my back was to the glass walls of the conference room, needing to be able to move around while I thought. First, his name. How had I not put two and two together when I read his file? I opened it and scanned the pages.

"This is just... I don't know where to begin," I said. Instead of *querulous*, I was tongue-tied and having a difficult time sorting through all the questions I had for him.

He shoved his hand in his hair, which was slicked back the way it had been at the wedding. His movement had the effect of ruining his carefully-coiffed appearance, which oddly made me feel slightly better about him. "I know. I owe you an apology. I wanted to call you or reach out to you somehow, but I had nothing to go on," he said.

I shook my head at him and waved my hands. "No, no, no. I'm not even prepared to talk about that. I'm still trying to get my brain around the fact that you're the same person whose case I've been mulling all morning long." My voice was higher-pitched than normal and threatened to dip into hysterical-sounding.

Finn leaned back in his chair, as though he understood I needed to sort through some sort of process and had resigned himself to wait until I was ready.

"First off, your name. Your file talks about a college professor named Norman Finley. You said your name was Finn. It never occurred to me it was you, and that makes me feel very stupid."

"You're not stupid. Everyone calls me Finn. Finley, Finn. It's not much of a leap. You'd go by Finn too if your name was Norman."

"Okay. Fair enough. But on Saturday… there was time… we talked about the inversion layer and olives. There was time for you to tell me you were a criminal."

He let out a surprised laugh. "Yeah, that usually goes over well at cocktail receptions. 'Hi, I'm Finn. Are you a friend of the bride's or the groom's? Would you like a drink? Oh, better make it quick because my ankle monitor is about to go off.' Can you honestly blame me?"

I instinctively looked down at his ankle. "They gave you an ankle monitor?"

"No! It was a joke. Are you always this literal?"

"Maybe." I inhaled, realizing I hadn't actually taken a normal breath since I'd walked into the room and seen his face. No, I couldn't blame him. And I didn't. "No." My shoulders slumped.

How could I blame him?

I blamed myself and my eternal terrible radar for men. That wasn't his fault. Finn couldn't help getting swept up in my trawler net of bad fish. It had been in operation since puberty. He just happened to get tangled on the path to order a martini.

The truth was, I had a job to do, and he was my client. The fact that I had a momentary desire to rip his clothes off after my friend's wedding was irrelevant now. I would treat his case with the professionalism it deserved. I just wouldn't look too hard at his eyes because they contained depth that made me want to talk to him for hours about anything and everything except his case.

"Okay, look. My inclination is to be furious with you for not being honest, but because you're charged with a federal offense, I don't want to add to your problems. Let's move on, shall we? You wanted to apologize. Consider it accepted. I wanted to freak out because I'm surprised you turned out to be my new client. Consider me less... freaked out. Let's just both agree to be professional and get to the facts of the case."

He raised a finger in the air. "Yes, speaking of being honest... didn't you tell me you lived in San Francisco the night of the wedding? Was that an intentional obfuscation?"

I loved his vocabulary. Before I collected my wits and formulated a response, I realized I was grinning at him like a linguistics groupie. "I don't recall intentionally trying to lead you to believe I was visiting from San Francisco. But I can fully believe that I wasn't clear. I'd probably had a few drinks by then."

"I recall you said you'd lived in San Francisco for the past ten years. Maybe I assumed you still did. Maybe that was my wishful, wedding fling brain taking charge."

Oh boy. I'd done pretty well so far *obfuscating* our Saturday night activities. Now he was erasing every trace of my willpower by bringing it up. I knew I needed to brush the comment aside and only think of him as a client. "Wishful?" my traitorous mouth said. Clearly, it hadn't been briefed on the plan.

He closed his eyes for a long blink, giving me a momentary respite from the continual draw of his gaze. "I apologize. I know we need to keep things professional. I shouldn't have said that."

He looked at his watch, which made me notice it. Unlike most people I knew who used their phones to tell time, Finn wore a nice tank watch with a leather band. In fact, he hadn't so much as glanced at his phone during our entire meeting. I couldn't recall the last time that had occurred with a client. "Wow, time flies, huh?" he said.

"Are you having fun?"

He studied me for a moment. Then he was silent again. Of course, he wasn't having fun. He was facing potential jail time and major fines from the SEC, not to mention he'd been put on leave from the job he loved, and his tenured position was probably in jeopardy. What a stupid thing to ask. "Sorry. I know this can't be fun for you."

After looking through the conference room glass for a moment, he nodded. "Actually, it is. But only because I haven't been able to stop thinking about you since we met, and now that I have the pleasure of your company, it makes me happy," he said.

"Wait, what?" I felt just as giddy as I had at age fourteen when a boy I'd been crushing on for months asked me if I'd mind paying for his slice of pizza after a high school football game. This was pre-cheerleading, to be clear. After I made the squad, the fourteen-year-olds paid for me. Mostly.

"Was that not clear? I can't stop thinking about you. I've barely thought of anything *but* you since we met. And given that I'm charged with insider trading and facing jail time, I find that significant."

"Oh."

"Oh?"

"I mean, that's… ordinarily, it's exactly what a woman wants to hear. But now…"

"Now that you know I'm charged with insider trading?"

"No, now that you're my client. You insisted on being my client. I gave you an out, and you insisted. So now you get lawyer me, not Saturday night me. That was your choice," I said. It was my turn to look through the glass because I couldn't keep gazing at him without repercussions.

"I wasn't aware you were two different people. For the record, I like both," he said with a smile.

"You don't get both. That's not how this works." I turned toward my notes, hoping he understood that recess was over.

"I'm the client. Don't I get to dictate how things work?" he asked.

"No, you get to be the client. You answer my questions, and you behave yourself so I don't get fired or disbarred. I feel like you weren't listening when I just explained all that."

"I was listening. I just chose to ignore it."

He was frustrating. The fact that he was hot in a nerdy chiseled-jaw professor way was also frustrating. I needed to get control of the situation. Looking at the stacks of books on the conference room shelves, I saw nothing to give me direction as to how to handle the situation.

*They should make law books for this. Or self-help books. Any guidance would be welcome.*

I needed to get out of the conference room and back on my own territory. Maybe I'd feel more in control behind my hulking partner desk. It would give us a physical barrier, if nothing else.

"I hate these big rooms unless I'm talking to a crowd. Would you be okay moving to my office?" I asked, immediately worrying that it sounded like I was inviting him upstairs to my apartment. I smiled stiffly and didn't elaborate.

Finn nodded and gathered a pile of pages sitting by his feet, which caused me to notice it for the first time. "What's all that?"

"Research, evidence. All the stuff I've pulled together that will help you understand how I was able to make legal trades without insider information." There were piles and piles of pages.

I nodded slowly, intrigued anew by this man. Something about my expression must have given him pause because he stopped gathering his documents and looked at me.

"What?" he asked.

"I'm just... I think this is the first time since I started practicing law that a client brought research and evidence to help me make my case, at least not without my asking for it first."

A small smile spread over his face. "I'm an academic, so I live in research and evidence. I just figured it couldn't hurt for you to have all the information I have."

I gestured for him to follow me down the hall. As we walked, him with his load of papers and me with my files, I stole a look behind me at his face. "What?" he asked, again.

I shook my head. "Very few people surprise me."

I was praying it wouldn't be a problem.

# CHAPTER NINE

FINN

WELL, that was embarrassing. And unexpected, which made it even more embarrassing.

I was not used to the unexpected.

My career was based around running analyses of all situations as a matter of training and habit, so it was an unfamiliar feeling to be unprepared.

I hadn't been prepared when I met Annie on Saturday night, and I'd been unprepared again at her office. It wasn't lost on me that this woman had unnerved me twice in thirty-six hours for different reasons and the last time I could remember feeling that way was... never.

When I'd spent the day yesterday going through the possible scenarios in which I might see Annie again, all kinds of ideas came to mind. I thought I could wrangle a dinner invitation to Chris and Nikki's house sometime when Annie was visiting from San Francisco. I imagined getting a few more details from Nikki and giving her a call if I was up at Berkeley for a meeting.

However, in none of my imagined scenarios did I picture her

coming into the conference room at my lawyer's office and signing on to be my new counsel.

And then trying to back out of having anything to do with me or my case.

I wasn't sure I liked it. I mean, granted, it was great to see her again and it solved a lot of my problems, like how I was going to track her down... but in the fantasy I'd had in my head about our eventual reconnection, I'd planned to explain the issues with the SEC as I saw them, not as they'd been written down by a court stenographer at my arraignment.

"I'm innocent," I said because it was important for her to know at the outset.

I didn't know what I expected. Maybe I thought she'd be relieved that I wasn't a white-collar criminal. Maybe I thought she'd thank me and say that I'd made her job so much easier.

I wasn't expecting her to laugh.

"Finn, I've defended dozens of client in white-collar cases and none of them were innocent. It's sweet that you want me to believe in you. But it doesn't matter."

Sweet? It wasn't sweet. It was fact. I wanted her to acknowledge the facts of the case because they were material. They were reality. "What do you mean it doesn't matter? Of course it does. How can you defend me unless you know whether I'm guilty or not?" I asked.

"Because I'm building the case I'll present to the judge based on the persuasiveness of arguments. Your actual guilt or innocence has little bearing on how I litigate on your behalf."

"My actual innocence has bearing to me." I liked her, but she was pissing me off. She was in full lawyer mode, which meant she was sexy as hell, sure, but also wrong-headed because she wasn't listening to me. "I don't want a lawyer who doesn't believe I'm innocent," I said.

"Why is it so important to you what I believe? I assure you I've more than competently argued the cases of unapologetically guilty people. And managed to get their sentences reduced or exonerated them at trial. Actual guilt or innocence isn't the point here."

"It is to me. I am innocent."

"Okay," she said, wearing a mask of stoicism.

"Okay." And that was the end of the discussion. For the time being. She was right, however, that my innocence or guilt barely mattered when it came to keeping me out of jail.

I'd done my research, and without convincing evidence, it was hard to beat insider trading charges. I couldn't provide convincing evidence. Unless Annie's legal skills included pulling rabbits out of hats, I was probably going to jail. So I might as well enjoy myself with her until then.

She began to make a numbered list on her whiteboard as soon as we entered her office. I put my research on her desk and stood next to it while she wrote on the board. "The issue here isn't whether you were explicitly told the merger would fall through. If you were given other information that pushed your thinking in that direction, it's still considered a violation of Section 17(a) of the Securities Act of 1933."

"I'm aware of that. No one gave me information," I said.

"Maybe not directly, but there are all kinds of areas where you may have received insider information without realizing it: knowing about executive changes at a company, knowing about a new product launch, potential lawsuits or settlements that would cost the company money, the award or loss of a big piece of business." She tapped the whiteboard with her pen.

"None of that. I was told of none of that information by the companies," I said, watching her face to see if she believed me. Most people didn't. Maybe she was different.

"Let's talk about the worst-case scenario if none of this goes your way. The maximum sentence is twenty years and the maximum criminal fine is five-million dollars. But since your colleague filed a civil suit, the maximum could be much higher." Wow, she was all business.

"I'm aware. Let's avoid the maximum, if it's all the same to you." I said.

She looked at me warily, perhaps deciding whether I was a fool or a hopeless dreamer. "Sure, Finn. Sounds like a plan." I detected sarcasm. Then she cracked the tiniest inkling of a smile and that was all I needed. She was trying so hard to wipe all traces of Saturday night from her brain but I wasn't wrong about the chemistry. So I met her gaze and smiled back at her, which caused her face to brighten almost against her will.

God, I liked this woman even more now than when she was trying to get me to shove my hand up her skirt. It wasn't lost on me that I was enjoying talking about my possible incarceration with her. She was fun to talk to.

"I wanted to make sure you knew my priorities," I said. She pressed her lips together as though trying to block her real thoughts from escaping. Then she turned back to the whiteboard and started making a numbered list. I couldn't deal with lists right now. All I could think about was her in a peach-colored dress on a perfect night that I blew all to hell.

"Annie..." I said.

"Yes?" She didn't turn around. She was copying some godforsaken list of standard defense tactics from a yellow legal pad. I didn't care about any of that.

"Will you look at me?"

She finished writing item number two and turned to face me. Then she almost dropped her legal pad. Her eyes fixed on mine and immediately grew dark and hazy. My brain went fuzzy with how much I wanted her, and I didn't dare blink.

"Hi," she said, the banal greeting making me happy because for one second she wasn't talking about case law.

"Hi," I said, feeling the hint of a smile on my lips.

"What's on your mind?" she asked, still standing with a dry erase pen in one hand and the notepad in the other, but doing nothing with either of them.

I blinked a couple times, leaned back, and cracked my neck from side to side. "I think we should talk about the other night."

She looked panicked. "What? Why?"

"It feels like the elephant in the room, and that's not good when we have important work to do," I said.

"Okay... What do you want to talk about?" she asked warily. She still hadn't put the cap back on her pen but she turned away from the board.

"I... want to say that I... enjoyed getting to know you," I said, choosing my words carefully. I knew this was weird for her, but I needed her to know I wasn't the douchebag she assumed I was.

Annie slumped against the whiteboard and I worried she was in danger of getting covered with ink. But she seemed to realize it and capped the pen, went back to her desk chair, and swiveled around to face me. "I enjoyed it too, but Finn... we can't relive that. We need to keep this professional."

"I'm not sure I can do that." Because I didn't want to do that.

"Well, given that I'm now your lawyer and given that you insisted I not pass your case off to someone else at the firm, you're gonna have to."

"Really?" I asked, leaning an elbow on her desk.

"Really." I could tell she was trying to level me with some kind of stern schoolmarm expression, but her attempt was half-assed at best.

"There are some things I'd like you to know," I said.

"See, that's where I think we get into trouble. You wanting me to know things, me wanting to know things, me getting myself fired..."

"I'm not suggesting I take you on your desk right here and now. I understand that's not allowed."

"Oh, good. I was afraid you thought that came with your retainer fee," she said. I loved her sarcasm.

"What I mean is, I'd just like to clear the air. I want you to understand what I was thinking that night and what I'm thinking now. I just want to talk."

She nodded. I hadn't prepared a speech or anything, especially given that I wasn't expecting to have this conversation at my lawyer's office, but I did the best I could with the errant apologetic thoughts racing through my brain.

"I'm disappointed in myself. I should have been honest with you. I should have taken the time, even if it meant missing my curfew," I said. Jesus, I sounded like a robot.

Annie shook her head and held up a hand. "No, you were right to be respectful of that. It's important not to jeopardize your case."

"But it wasn't respectful of you," I said. Maybe it was the weight of my honesty, but she slumped forward on her desk like a noodle. When she looked up at me, her expression was sympathetic.

"I already told you I forgive you. Your circumstances were... unusual." She nodded as if thinking about just how unusual they were. She wasn't wrong. "Actually, hang on. If you were under house arrest, how did you even get permission to go to the wedding?" she asked.

"Your colleague Jackson made a very strong argument to the judge, whose daughter was recently married herself. He had a soft spot for me attending the wedding of a dear school friend," I told her.

"And that's another thing. Dear school friend? I'm a dear school friend. How close are you and Nikki?" As soon as she said it, her eyes went huge and she clapped a hand over her mouth. Then she waved her hand like she could erase what she'd just said. "Sorry. I didn't mean to sound so accusatory. It's not like I have a monopoly on her friendship. Really, please try to forget I said that." She was blushing. She was so goddamned gorgeous I almost climbed right over the desk and kissed the fuck out of her.

Instead, I leaned back and nodded. "It's okay. I understood what you meant. We were close during grad school, actually, but it's funny how life gets in the way. I still consider her part of my inner circle, but we probably talk four times a year and rarely see each other even though we live in the same city," I said.

"I get how that is. I think Nikki and I stayed closer with me living in San Francisco because we made an effort to see each other and get on FaceTime regularly. I'm hoping now that I live here we won't get lazy."

Her face softened and I caught a glimpse of the relaxed side I'd cajoled out of her at the wedding. I wanted to see more of that side. I met her eyes and for a moment it was there, the unquantifiable connection that made me believe in something bigger.

Then her eyes narrowed suspiciously.

What had just happened? "Why are you looking at me like that?" I asked.

"Like what?"

"I don't know. Like you don't trust me."

"Ha. It's not you I don't trust. I don't trust myself," she said.

That surprised me. I raised an eyebrow. "How so?"

She rolled her eyes like this was a conversation she didn't want to have. But she brought it up, so I wasn't letting her off the hook.

"Ugh, maybe you're right. Maybe it's best to get this out in the open. I'm doing my best to be professional and only look at you as a client, but I have to admit, I'm struggling."

I smiled at that. "How do you want to think of me?"

"It doesn't matter, does it?" She looked defeated, but I was intrigued.

"Everything matters. And I'd like to know." I shrugged, but I wondered if she planned to mete out a punishment or a negative assessment. It wasn't that I didn't care about my legal troubles, but I'd been thinking about them and my potential jail time for months. Flirting with her was a welcome reprieve.

She opened her mouth, then closed it. Almost like she was giving her brain—or maybe her mouth—one last chance to regain control over the situation and keep her thoughts to herself. I really hoped she wouldn't do that. I hoped her brain and mouth wouldn't agree to toe that line.

"Fine. I liked talking to you. I liked kissing you. I found you intriguing and intelligent. And different. And hot. There I said it. Now that it's out there, hopefully we can bury it in the past where it belongs. No more tension."

I couldn't help but grin like a school kid who'd just earned a gold star. I may have even smirked. "Oh, sure. Knowing all that will go a long way toward reducing tension," I said. She might as well have stripped right there in her office for all the tension it was going to reduce.

"It should," she said.

"It doesn't."

"Try harder."

"You found me hot?" I asked.

"Oh God, that's what you focus on? I thought you were all about not objectifying people. I also found you interesting and smart," she said.

"I'm sorry. I'm fixated on the hot part."

"Great. Have at it. Fixate away. It doesn't change the fact that now I find you supremely annoying, cocky, and difficult."

Now I was definitely smirking. "That's better. I'm used to that."

"I'll bet you are." But she couldn't help it. She was smiling at me too. There was hope. Then she shook her head. "I still can't figure you out at all. What is your deal? You're a professor who's able to mind read the general public's intentions and therefore game the stock market?" she asked.

"Exactly. I also count cards when I play poker."

"That's against the rules."

"I know that."

"You really do that?" she asked.

"No. I do not. You don't have much of a radar for sarcasm, do you?" She made me laugh. I had never met anyone more literal, except for the times she was saying something sarcastic herself. She didn't seem to see it.

"I guess not when it isn't coming out of my own mouth." She looked exhausted and defeated. The glimmer of relaxation was gone, replaced by worry lines as she held a wrist against her forehead.

I wanted to help. "Do you need a glass of water or something?"

"No! I do not need a glass of water." I was pretty sure she needed a glass of water. I was pretty sure I needed one too. Or possibly a cold shower.

"I have an idea," I said, deciding we needed to put an end to the innuendo and the tension and the flirting. At least for the moment.

"Ideas are good. Pertaining to what?"

"Our situation."

She raised her eyebrows, suspicious. "I wasn't aware we had a situation."

"This," I said, gesturing between us. "We need to resolve the tension if we're going to work together, otherwise I'm going to keep making inappropriate advances and you're going to keep turning that adorable shade of pink. Not that I'm complaining in any way. But I know you want to be 'lawyerly' and such." Yes, I air-quoted it.

She nodded, maybe a little too enthusiastically for my taste, but at least we were in agreement. "Okay, I'd like to discourage the inappropriate advances that will get me fired, so let's hear your idea," she said.

I really had no idea, but I knew how to think on my feet. More than a few times, I'd been lecturing in front of two hundred students and lost my train of thought and needed to make something up. With Annie, I stood up and paced a circle around the room. I did some gesturing, some hand waving, some explanatory pantomime as I outlined my idea. "We need to get everything out in the open. Talk about all the unmet desires from the other night.

Paint a vivid picture. Dispel the mystery. I think that once we do that, we'll get it out of our systems. A last hurrah, so to speak."

"So, kind of like breakup sex but without the sex."

I had no idea what that meant and I had even less of an idea how to pull it off in her office. But, hell, I was game to try.

"Exactly. Let's have breakup non-sex," I said, gesturing for her to get comfortable. "Shall we?"

# CHAPTER TEN

ANNIE

CLEARLY, I'd lost my mind somewhere between the discussion of obfuscation and my agreeing to breakup sex. During the workday. In my office.

On the other hand, nothing about my interaction with Finn had been exactly normal, and I needed some way to stop thinking about him as anyone other than a client important to my new firm, where I wanted to keep my job.

So, I agreed.

Even though we had a desk between us, I pulled at my skirt, trying to cover as much of my legs as possible. It's not that I thought he was trying to sneak a peek. I wanted to discourage myself from crawling across the desk and straddling him.

He shoved a hand in his hair again. He'd already reversed the effects of whatever hair product he'd used, and his hair no longer looked so perfectly slicked back. The waves were going in different directions, but the overall effect was still handsome AF. I tried again to look away, in a last-ditch effort to keep my cool.

I failed. I studied his angular jaw, his tousled hair and the intensity of his eyes and actually started to salivate.

He cleared his throat and cast a glance toward me. His eyes moved from my lips to my throat to the open neck of my sweater. He didn't say anything. He didn't have to. The look in his eyes told me what he could do to my bare skin with his tongue and mouth and teeth. I felt the heat creep over my neck and enflame my cheeks. I had an urgent need for a fan.

Maybe this was what we were going to do—have a sexy staring contest.

Well, two could play at that game. I fixed my gaze on his face and studied his features. I'd spent so much of my time trying to avoid looking at him directly that it was a relief to give myself permission to see him.

I took in the shape of his mouth, which could have graced the cover of a men's magazine. Or his face could have been the enticement for a car or liquor ad. Whatever it was, I'd find it impossible not to buy it. His lips were deep pink and full, and it looked like he'd spent time liberally applying lip balm to keep them soft. I found myself wanting to move closer to him so I could see his lips a little better. Or maybe to put myself into closer proximity in case he lost his balance and happened to fall against my lips.

When I could hear my own heart beating in my ears, I wrenched my gaze away and moved over his aquiline nose. I never knew what an aquiline nose was. For many years I'd read books where the most exquisite people were described as having such noses, so eventually, I'd become curious and looked it up. It meant his nose had a slight curve to it, which made it imperfect, because it wasn't straight and regal looking, but damn if it didn't work with the rest of his features. Nose, check.

I was almost afraid to look again at his eyes. They'd already mesmerized me and if I didn't trust myself around Finn's lips, I'd need a straitjacket when I allowed myself a peek at his eyes.

They. Were. Just. So. Incredibly. Sexy.

The noise I heard startled me out of my reverie. It sounded like a gasp or even a pre-orgasm moan, and I found myself a bit confused about where it had come from since there were only two of us in the room.

When I focused my attention back on his lips, I saw that he was smirking again at me. Because, of course, I was the source of the panting and gasping, and of course, he heard it loud and clear.

"Um, so what did you have in mind with this breakup thing? How do you envision it working?" I asked.

"I don't really know." He raked a hand through his hair, which was bordering on messy, and I loved it even more. I was an unstoppable train of libido in serious danger of crashing. "I've never had breakup sex before."

"You've never...?" I couldn't finish my sentence because I was busy cataloguing my emotions. I must have had a strange expression on my face because he started chuckling quietly.

"That seems to surprise you? Or trouble you?" he asked.

If Finn had an otherworldly ability to calm me out of my run-on sentences of thought-jousting, he also had the power to incite them. "Um, I was thinking that I liked that. I like that you haven't had breakup sex. It makes me appreciate you more as a person because you're not the type to have a final meaningless night with someone when you know there's no future. That takes maturity."

I could have stopped there. I should have stopped there. But my brain had other thought grenades it couldn't help launching. "Also, I don't like it because I imagine you only having fantastic meaningful sex which is something we won't ever do, which is expected and accepted and by design, of course. But also a little sad. At least as I'm imagining it."

"I find it a little sad too," he said.

I took a deep breath and looked at his chin. That's right, I focused on his chin because it had been made clear to me that his lips were dangerous, and his eyes put me in flat-out criminal territory. His nose sat between the two, which made it too tempting to glance up or down, so the only choice left was his chin. "I think this was a bad idea. We should end our meeting, shake hands, and move on," I said.

"Oh, okay."

"Really?"

"No, Ms. Oblivious to Sarcasm That isn't Her Own."

"Fuck!!"

Finn's eyes went wide as I continued yelling profanities into the ether. I too felt shocked. I also felt concerned that one of my colleagues would come running.

After waiting for a silent minute and listening for footsteps, I relaxed a bit. "Sorry," I said. "But you're frustrating."

"I'm aware."

"So why do you do it?"

He shook his head, impish like a kid who's pretending not to have an obvious wad of gum in his mouth. "I don't know. Habit, I guess."

"Okay, clearly we need an adult in the room, so I'm going to be it. This is how it's going to work. You're going to sit there and tell me—in detail—everything you think would have happened between us on Saturday night. You'll leave nothing out. Paint a picture of the best one-night stand we could have ever had. Then I'll do the same. Then, curiosity satisfied, we'll move on. Agreed?"

He looked surprised at my sudden command of the situation. For a moment, he glanced around the room. Maybe he was imagining surfaces he might invent for his virtual sexcapades. Who knows? But then he nodded. "I think that's a fucking great idea."

I hadn't expected him to agree so readily, but I was relieved we had a consensus. I felt exhausted. Leaning forward on my elbows to support myself, I flicked a hand in his direction. "Great."

"Do I go first?" he asked.

"Sure. All yours."

"Okay," he said, looking around the room once more, as if for inspiration. I wondered if his fantasy would include a credenza and a laptop. "Close your eyes."

"What?" That made me nervous. "Why?"

"I want you to picture it. You can't do that if you're looking at your desk blotter or focusing every bit of your will to keep from looking me in the eye." I hated that he knew. But as long as he knew, I could stop pretending his chin was extra fascinating.

"Okay, fine." I closed my eyes and immediately felt vulnerable. My eyes shot open, and I checked to make sure he hadn't moved from his chair.

His calm expression met my hysterical one. "Lean back in your chair. It's okay. I'm not going to hurt you. Or even touch you. I promise."

"I know, I know. I just have a hard time when someone tells me to close my eyes, and I know I'm being watched."

"I'll tell you what. I'll close my eyes too. I'll even do it first. Then we'll be on even ground. Okay?"

I decided I could live with that. I watched as Finn closed his eyes, noticing how long his lashes were when they fluttered shut. I looked at his face longer than I should have, knowing I had unfettered access to stare. He really was so beautiful, but seeing his eyes closed, I realized how much of his attractiveness came from a light that resonated from within. I didn't know enough about him yet to understand its source, but I wanted to know more, and I tried to convince myself it would help me defend him. The truth was that I just wanted to know him.

I let my eyes drift shut.

"As I said, you've been on my mind since I saw you. Not when I called you over with my lame excuse to check out the other bar, but earlier, when you swept down the aisle in your peach-colored dress. It was almost like you were floating. I thought you looked like a dessert, like something I'd savor if I was lucky enough to get a taste."

"Finn…" I opened my eyes.

"Yes?" His eyes were still closed.

"This isn't going to work."

"Why not?"

"Your metaphors are lovely, but this is weird." I studied his face, the calm over his features. He didn't seem troubled. I had the wherewithal to notice the irony that the person in the room facing possible prison time was more zen than me.

"You have trouble hearing people say nice things about you?" He opened his eyes as if he knew I was staring at him.

"Maybe that's part of it."

"That's why I told you to close your eyes. It's easier that way."

"You know this from experience?"

"No, but I think I'm starting to know you. And I want to tell you the way I'd have preferred the night we met to have gone. Please. I hated that I had to leave like that. Let me make it up to you by painting a picture." His voice was quiet and sexy and I didn't have it in me to fight him.

"Okay, fine." I closed my eyes again, squinting at first and not at all relaxed. He didn't speak, and I knew he was waiting for me to settle down. I took a deep cleansing breath and tried not to focus on the possibility that Finn was sneaking a peek at me.

"Like I said, you took my breath away, and that was before I'd even heard you speak. I wouldn't have been halfway as attracted to you if I hadn't found you funny and smart. I'd hoped that would be the case, but of course, I had no way of knowing. Hope is something you hold in your hand like a sand dollar, praying you can carry it home without breaking it."

I felt myself shiver at his words, and I was tempted to open my eyes to make sure his were still closed, but I fought the impulse, instead sinking harder against the back of my chair and letting my head rest. I might have sighed.

"I recall vividly that you were the most stunning woman there, and I found myself jockeying for position to get close enough to you to say something. And I was almost beside myself, looking around in the garden because it seemed like just my luck that you'd already be with someone, nibbling on another man's olives, so to speak."

I pressed my lips together to keep from grinning at the memory.

He went on. "Anyway, once I mustered the nerve to talk to you, it became clear you were the one hell-bent on stripping me naked, seducing me, and screaming my name when I brought you to your fourteenth orgasm."

"I was not hell-bent on that!"

"Hey, quit driving the bus. I'm in charge of this fantasy, and in my version, you were hell-bent. And in my version, I was charming and commanding. I lulled you into relaxation under the stars and pulled those sexy stiletto heels off your feet. After hours of standing in those shoes—and I'd have followed you anywhere in those, by the way—I had a feeling your feet needed to be massaged."

I sighed again at the idea of a man who gave foot massages. I imagined Finn reaching under my desk and taking off my pumps, which I found gorgeous but a little too tight.

"I don't take such things lightly, and I don't rush. Each of your feet would have received its due time and attention. I'd have worked on each tendon, each toe. And as much as I like a woman in a pair of thigh-highs, I was delighted that night that your legs were bare. Which meant your feet were bare, so when I'd worked them free of your shoes, I'd have had access to each of your lovely toes. Do you like to have your toes sucked?"

I inhaled a heady breath. "Mmm hmm." No one had ever sucked my toes before. I probably wouldn't have allowed it, had it ever been suggested, because I'd have worried about my feet being sweaty or smelling bad. But the way Finn described it, he made my feet sound beautiful. I'd have let him do what he wanted. I slouched down in my chair and listened like he was telling me a seductive bedtime story.

"I'd like to think I've got a fair amount of willpower, but you were testing it every minute you lay on your lounge chair looking at the stars. I wanted you to see them because I believe that seduction starts in the mind, and I wanted you to feel something. It was romantic on those lounge chairs, wasn't it? No one was around; the air was warm and balmy. It felt so still, and I wanted you to sense the stillness, so any movement, any brush of my hand against your skin, would be earned. I was trying to get you to slow down."

How had he known that about me? If I hadn't felt so swept away by his words, it might have unnerved me that at a wedding reception on a night when I had all kinds of warring thoughts interrupting my peace of mind, he had noticed. He'd wanted to pull me out of my own head. I wanted to ask him, but I was also desperate to hear more.

"It worked," I said, surprised at how breathless I sounded.

"I know," he said, his voice low and quiet. "I liked being there with you, watching you in a moment of peace. I sensed it might be a unicorn moment, and I felt lucky to share it with you. But it was also painful because I wanted you, all of you. And I don't just mean that in the hooking up sense. I mean, sure we could have torn each other's clothes off and it would have felt incredible to feel your naked body against my skin, but I didn't want to rush. Even if we were ever only going to have one night together, I wanted to savor it, which is why I ran out of time. But don't think about that. In this scenario, we had hours."

I was so swept along by the fantasy picture he was painting with fine strokes on the canvas of my imagination, that I almost forgot it was only a fantasy. I imagined I was under the stars at the hotel pool with him touching my feet intimately, sucking each of my toes. And I realized how much I wanted him to suck my toes.

"You have gorgeous legs; I imagine you know that. I wanted an intimate tour of those legs, starting at the curve of your Achilles above your heel and continuing higher, using both hands to savor the taut skin of your legs. I'd have rolled you toward me, pulling you onto my lounge chair so you could straddle my hips. That way I'd be able to watch your face while my hands traveled the length of your legs, stopping mid-thigh."

"What if I didn't want you to stop?" I asked without thinking.

"Then I'd know I was doing something right." I could hear the smile in his voice. I almost opened my eyes to look at him, but the drowning pull of sensation was too great. I didn't want to dull the sound of his words by involving another of my senses.

"You're doing everything right," I said, again surprised that I was answering him as though his fantasy was actually taking place somewhere outside of my imagination.

"You're so beautiful," he said. "And incredibly intelligent. I wish I'd told you those things, but I was caught off guard by my reaction to you and I didn't say everything I should have. I found myself having urges that surprised me. It wouldn't have been enough to touch your skin—I don't think it would ever be enough—but I'd have gladly lowered the straps of your dress down over your shoulders, so when you leaned forward above me, your dress would inch down, just slightly, just enough for me to slide my tongue along your throat and down across your sweet skin."

I was fully in the moment. There was no question I wanted him to do everything he said.

"Finn…"

"Yeah? Too much?"

"No. It's good. I just wanted to say your name."

He laughed quietly. "Oh baby, I'll get you to say my name, don't you worry." His voice was still lilting and quiet, like the provider of the world's hottest bedtime story.

It sounded like he'd shifted in his chair. I popped one eye open and saw that he was moving to the couch. He laid back on the pillows and clasped his hands together over his chest. He looked over at me, and I closed my eyes again.

"I didn't want to stay on my pool chair, but I resisted moving to yours because I wanted you to be aware of wanting me closer to you. I wanted you to crave my touch, so when I finally did reach for you and slide my hand across the bare skin of your shoulder, appreciating the heat and every curve of your body, you'd be desperate for it. I wanted you to need my touch, so when I slipped my hand lower, into the cup of your bra, it would almost push you over the edge."

I slid lower in my chair, imagining his gorgeous assault on my skin.

"I wanted to taste your skin, to roll my tongue over your nipples until they grew hard and firm. Your dress would have had to go. Neither one of us would have had any patience for layers of fabric. I'd slide it up over your head and let my eyes take in your body in what I'm imagining was a lacy bra and panties."

"I'll never tell," I said.

"In my version, they were lace. Or satin. I like red satin."

"Noted. I'll put that in your file."

"Do that. Then take them off."

"Finn…"

"I mean, that's what I would have said to you. And you'd have told me to do it for you, and I'd have gladly acquiesced. There's something so seductive about uncovering a woman's most intimate places slowly, and I'd have taken my time with you. First, the bra would go. And I'd lavish attention on your breasts with my tongue, then my hands until you had chills and a moan on your lips. You'd have had your hands under my shirt, again clothing getting in the way, so I'd unbutton my shirt. You'd be working on my belt and my pants. Finally, it would just be you and me on one lounge chair, each of us only in our underwear. And I'd have all the time in the world, not even limited by the ending time of the wedding, only limited by maybe the cleaning crew at the hotel arriving at daybreak to put out new towels. Long before then, I'd have peeled off your lace or silk panties, and you'd have pushed down my boxers. Then I'd ask you what you like. You'd tell me, and I'd do everything on the menu."

I startled at that and froze. Finn didn't notice because he must have had his eyes closed, but suddenly, I was out of the trance he'd put me in with his words. Men had asked me in the past what I liked in bed. Generally, I'd answered by telling them that whatever they were currently doing was just fine. It was perfect. "More of that. Thank you."

The truth was I had no idea what I liked. In the years since I'd first had dates and boyfriends, no one had ever done anything so profound that I found myself asking for it again. Or for a replay with someone else. No one had knocked it out of the park, so I had no idea what it would feel like if someone did.

I was momentarily glad Finn and I had been stopped by his curfew because having him ask me what I wanted would have set off alarm bells of abject panic. I didn't know what I liked.

But I wasn't going to say that now. Finn wasn't asking. He continued with his virtual seduction, and I listened.

Unfortunately, I'd been in my head for the past few minutes, and I missed what I felt certain were vital sensory gifts, but I let his words bring me back to some semblance of rapture. It wasn't hard. "With the taste of you on my lips, I'd work my way back up your lovely body, hungry for your kiss."

And goddammit, I'd missed him going down on me thanks to my overactive brain.

Then there was a loud clattering of noise. My sated senses barely interpreted the noise as a person knocking before my door was cracked open and Jackson's face peered in.

I sat up straighter in my chair and tried to wipe away my orgasm face, but I was unable to form words.

"Hey. I was hoping you weren't at lunch yet," he said, peering around the door to where Finn sat on the couch as nonchalantly as if we were discussing securities law. "Oh, perfect, you're still here. I was just researching more about the historical origins of qui tam. You got my intellectual juices flowing."

He didn't seem to notice anything out of the ordinary between Finn and me, despite the fact that my juices were definitely flowing.

"Oh yeah?" Finn asked, eyes dancing at the potential imparting of information. Maybe it even thrilled him more than dirty talk. "What'd you find?"

"Laws enacted by King Henry VII to prevent whistleblowers and defendants from colluding, which apparently was a known

practice, and a bunch of things having to do with religious trans-
gressions."

"Naturally. Always a good religious transgression to be
found," Finn said.

"Anyhow, sorry to interrupt. I'll leave you to work," Jackson
said, gleeful over his information.

And he was gone.

I expected Finn to abort mission after the interruption. Were
we crazy, doing this in my office? With the door unlocked? "I,
um..." I had thoughts but I couldn't articulate any of them
because Finn had my virtual panties around my ankles.

"Close your eyes," he said, going to the door and locking it.

"What?" Was he kidding? He couldn't keep going.

"Close. Them," he said.

"Um, okay..." I put a hand over my eyes and tried to relax,
which was near impossible. And Finn continued.

"Maybe I'd let you regain your composure, but maybe not. I
think I'd want you to be feeling the full force of a shattering
orgasm when I kissed you again. So I'd take my time. I'd enter so
slowly." He didn't say anything else and I felt a growing desperation for him to continue. I needed him urgently. Entering slowly
wasn't working for me.

"It would drive both of us mad. I'd be teasing you at first,
brushing my erection against you gently, with just a hint of what I
could give you. I'd let you respond to the sudden lack of sensation. Then I'd touch you again, more insistently but still withholding what I knew you wanted. I'd watch you. I'd want to see
the desire build in you. To see that you were feeling the same
desperation to be touched as I'd feel, needing to touch you."

"Then I'd stop. Not to play games but to give your desire a
chance to build again, so when I returned, it wouldn't just be to
satisfy you, it would be to fill you. To own your trust and your
desire. Would you trust me to do that?"

"I'd trust you," I said, breathless. I wanted him to do everything he was saying, so much so that I was having a hard time

sitting idly in my chair, one hand on my chest as if to keep it from exploding with desire and the other hand creeping between my legs. It would be too weird to touch myself. Right? He was doing crazy things to my body and my brain, and I could only slouch down and try not to moan at his suggestive tale.

"I'd trust you too. I'd trust you to know that I didn't want to own you like a possession or plaything to be dominated. The way I'd want to own you is all about surrender because I know you hold on tight to responsibility. When you'd come, you'd let go of everything. You'd dive in. And I'd want to give that to you. So when you'd come—again, harder this time, with quivering abandon—you'd be completely transported."

I was transported.

Finn was silent for a moment, letting the afterglow of his words hang in the void.

"So... yeah. If we only had one night together, the way I'd have wanted it to be, something like that. I'd have left you unable to articulate any legal arguments. Hell, I'd have made you forget your own name. And anything else that had filled your brain before we met. I'd have left you completely satisfied. Well almost completely satisfied. If I did it right, you'd very likely be begging me to do it again. And being a fool for a beautiful woman in a pretty dress, I doubt I'd have said no."

The longer I heard his voice, the more I started to believe that maybe he could be the first one to do something so profound that I'd be screaming his name and asking for more.

I'd never know because he was my client and there were boundaries, but it was pleasant to think about. Finn was quiet again, and I stayed reclined in my chair, unable to move or speak.

He'd destroyed me, and he hadn't been within ten feet of my body.

Finally, I opened my eyes to find his lazy smile aimed in my direction, a smile that came more from his eyes than his lips. "How was that?" he asked, as though checking to see if I was satisfied with a takeout burrito I'd eaten for lunch.

I nodded, still having a hard time articulating much of anything. "Good."

I didn't know what I was expecting. A two-minute description of him flipping me over on the lounge chair, pushing my panties aside, and grinding on me until we both felt sufficiently turned on to climax together, before cleaning up and reappearing at the party before anyone knew we'd been gone? That would have been my version, which I couldn't possibly share with him now.

Holy mother of all things made of cheese. I wanted his version. I'd certainly spend many future nights dreaming of his version. But I couldn't possibly be expected to come up with a scenario that in any way approached his fairytale of sexiness. No way in hell.

So I nodded at him and let my eyes connect one last time with his beautiful green gaze. And I told the first and only lie I ever planned to tell my new client. "My version would have been a lot like that one."

I couldn't do more. I was done, reduced to a puddle of want and need, and I had to dismiss him from my office before I begged him to take me in all the ways he'd just described. If I didn't get a little time and space away from him—physically and mentally—I was going to implode like a black hole of permanent orgasm.

And as much as I wanted *that*, I wanted to preserve some shred of dignity more.

Finn was nodding at me like we were in agreement about how cleansing it felt to get all that out in the open. I didn't feel cleansed unless the damp puddle in my panties counted as a Mop & Glo shine.

"Anyway. That is what should have happened on Saturday night," he said.

I was still breathless when I responded. "I'm… sorry it didn't. Although I might not have recovered."

"No?"

I shook my head. I wasn't sure I'd recover from the lust I was currently feeling, and he was still across the room.

"Then I guess it's a good thing my curfew came crashing in like an uptight chaperone because now we can work together like professionals. Boundaries restored. All tension is gone."

"Gone," I barely managed to say, agreeing because I had to agree.

"Great," he said, collecting his things. "I feel much better, don't you? We got it out of our systems."

"Um, sure, uh huh."

I was so much worse. So lost for him. So full of shit, but he didn't seem to notice. He seemed jolly and cured of any residual temptation, which was even more baffling to me.

"Fine, then. I'll be in touch and we can figure out when we should meet next. I know you have stuff with my colleague and the other lawyer, so maybe in a few days?" He started to reach out to shake my hand, but maybe he thought better of it because he raised his hand in a small wave instead. I was slumped over my desk, limbs limp. I simply nodded at him as he made his way out my door and turned down the hall toward the lobby.

As soon as he was out of earshot, I let out the sigh I'd been holding in, and my head dropped to my forearms on the desk.

The tension was far from gone. It was not great. And I didn't feel better. If anything, I knew I was in deep, deep trouble.

# CHAPTER ELEVEN

ANNIE

IF I'D QUESTIONED EARLIER whether I was in over my head, by the time Finn left my office, I was sure of it.

The effect he had on me was crazy. I was a self-possessed person in control of my emotions. I was determined to do well at my job, and I knew that required single-minded focus. I'd never had issues with that before.

Damned Finn. He was going to be the death of my career.

No. I wouldn't allow that. Where was my drive and determination when I needed it?

*And boundaries. I need boundaries.*

I had to pull myself together and remind myself why I'd become a lawyer. It wasn't to abdicate responsibility the first time a handsome man walked into my office.

The best way I knew to divert my focus was shopping for something wildly expensive I had no business buying. But I needed a friend to join me, and I hadn't gotten around to making any.

Yes, fine, I admit it. I'd made zero effort to meet people. To be fair, I'd been focused on getting up to speed at my job and running around doing bridesmaid things I couldn't even recall at the moment. Or maybe I'd just been avoiding reality—I needed to make friends, and I was bad at that.

I wished I could be the kind of person who made friends on airplanes or in line at the supermarket, but I knew in my heart that I was an introvert, a friendly one, but an introvert, nonetheless. I hated talking about myself, and the effort it took to get to know someone felt daunting.

Except for Finn. Talking with him hadn't felt daunting at all. I could have talked to him all night long on Saturday and again today. One more reason that thoughts of him kept fluttering back into my brain.

I looked out the window, over the Century City high-rises toward the ocean. I could take a pile of work with me and go home. That was my safe place—head down, working.

No. I could do better. I would be better. So instead of packing up, I wandered down the hall to where my colleague Janelle was sketching something out on her whiteboard, and I knocked on her door.

She looked startled, and I immediately second-guessed my idea. Then she gave me a welcoming smile. "Hey, sorry. I was lost in a thought," she said. "Come on in."

I hesitated, not wanting to intrude, but she waved me over to a grey sofa against the wall. I quickly took in the decor of her office, which had bleached wood furniture and large, abstract prints framed behind her desk. Her office had no windows and I immediately felt lucky to have an office with views. "I didn't mean to interrupt. Are you in the middle of trial prep?" I asked.

"Actually, I was trying to remember the name of a case I worked on a couple years ago where the plaintiff owned a bar and was being sued for trademark infringement... It's not a big deal. I can look it up in my files."

"Boldt Freight versus Eichengreen?" I asked.

She froze and studied me. "Yes. That's exactly what it was. How in the world did you know that?"

"I reviewed all the firm's cases after I took the job. Just... to get up to speed."

"*All* of them?" She looked incredulous, and I sort of knew why. The firm had over a thousand cases in the past four years, and it had been a bit of work to read through everything. But I was new, and I didn't want to embarrass myself by not knowing firm business. Turns out, I'd embarrassed myself by being an overachiever and a fast reader.

I must have looked uncomfortable because Janelle smiled at me and shook her head. "Girl, I am impressed."

"I'm a nerd, I know," I said.

"Well good on you. That'll come in handy around here." She made a couple notes on her whiteboard, then turned back to where I was sitting. I shifted and recrossed my legs, feeling conspicuous visiting her in her office when I barely knew her. "So what's up? You need help with something, or is this a social call?" she asked, laughing as though a social call was a ridiculous thought.

"Um, honestly... completely social."

Her eyes lit up. "Aw, now I love you even more." She came over and sat in one of the burgundy velvet wing chairs in the corner, facing me at an angle. "Are we gossiping? Please tell me we're gossiping." Her smile spread wide, which made me feel a little less uncomfortable with my bold social move.

"I'm not sure I know anyone here well enough to gossip."

"Eh, that doesn't matter. You can make stuff up. I'll take anything," she said.

"I was thinking about braving the mall and looking at shoes. Would you be up for that?" I asked.

"Oh, now you're speaking my language. And if we include a cocktail, I'll do the gossiping and tell you what you got yourself into with the folks here. Deal?"

"Only if you let me buy the first round."

"Not gonna argue with that. Give me an hour to finish up, then I'll swing by your office. Does that work for you?"

I nodded and practically launched myself off the sofa. "Perfect. See you in a bit." I wanted to get out of her office and into the hallway before she could see the creep of blush crawling over my neck. I felt like I'd just been asked on a date.

For a friendly introvert, it was a good start.

AN HOUR LATER, Janelle and I were standing in our underwear.

We'd worked our way through Nordstrom and several of the smaller stores in the Century City mall, and we were sharing a large dressing room in a French clothing shop that had long velvet curtains wrapped around the space and a small stool in the back. We'd each selected a few items—dresses, skinny jeans, camisoles —and the other of the two dressing rooms was occupied by a mother and teenage daughter arguing about why the daughter needed to own at least one dress.

So we'd agreed to share a dressing room. It could be said that nothing bonds two women more than seeing each other in their underwear, but I don't think that's exactly right. I'd say nothing bonds two women more than one of them crying over something she didn't know was bothering her while the other one offers solace. I'd been both of those women at different times in my life. This time, I was the one offering unexpected solace.

Melody, our perky sales associate, had told us to call for her if we needed different sizes. "Otherwise, I'll leave you to it," she'd said, winking and pulling the velvet drapes closed around us.

Janelle was focused on finding a pair of jeans that fit the way she wanted and a blazer she could wear with them to work. I didn't much care what category of clothing I tried on. I loved clothes, especially the kind I could imagine myself wearing some-place fancy and cool. My fancy and cool invitations were few and far between, so I took delight in wearing stiletto sandals with jeans and impractical bell-sleeved sheer tops over camisoles with my de rigeur pencil skirts at the office.

Janelle, who verged on six feet tall without shoes and whose black skin was flawless, looked gorgeous in any color she held up in front of her for my opinion. "What do you think of blue?" she asked.

"Yes," I said.

"Red?"

"Yes."

"Violet?"

"Yes," I said with a little less conviction. Sigh... I was beginning to get a complex, having not realized I was going to be sharing a dressing room with a woman who looked good in everything. Except for jeans, that is. She'd squeezed into her third pair and was looking despairingly in the mirror. They were tight across her thighs, generous around her hips, and overall unflattering.

"What the hell is wrong with my body?" she asked. "I should be able to fit into a pair of pants."

"It's not you. You know that, right?" I said, certain she must know that. No one had an easy time finding a good pair of jeans. That was why I'd worn my last perfect pair practically into dust, hung onto them until the shredded fibers would no longer cooperate. Then I turned them into denim cut-off shorts.

"No, it's my thighs and booty. Jeans just don't look good on me."

"Bull. Shit. You need to find a better pair." I felt strongly about this.

"Eh, maybe I just need to face facts and wear more skirts. They hide a multitude of sins," she said, but I could see from her expression she was fighting disappointment at what she saw.

"Uh uh. No way. This is the fault of the jeans and some fit model who had bigger hips than you. Or a designer who wanted the pants to hang a certain way on one specific type of body. Lady, there's more than one type."

She still looked disappointed, but she began nodding at me as she wrestled the jeans down over her thighs. Meanwhile, I'd put on a waistless, flowing knee-length dress that was swimming on me. The fabric was gorgeous—tiny red and purple flowers on a two-layered gauzy fabric. But it was a no go. "Like this. I look like I'm wearing a nightie. This would look stunning on you with your long legs, but I need something with a waist, or it looks like a tent."

"You could do better," she admitted.

"Yes, I think so. Even wearing a grain sack would be better. They're cut more for the female form," I said.

She laughed, which led to her wiping her eyes, which led to me realizing she was, in fact, trying to stop herself from crying. "Wait, did I offend you with the grain sack comment? I wasn't suggesting—"

Janelle saved a hand to stop me from analyzing myself. "It's not you." She fanned her eyes as if that would quickly dry the tears, and she half-laughed at herself but continued crying. "I'm sorry."

"Never apologize for crying. Never. Cry, I command you."

So she did. Her tears flowed for a solid minute, and she wiped them away with her knuckles while I searched my purse for the tissues I knew I didn't carry. I did find a folded eye mask in plastic wrap from the last redeye flight I took, so I unwrapped it and offered it to her to dry her eyes. If she thought it was strange, she didn't say so.

Finally, she sighed and blinked away the last of the tears. "Wow. Okay. I didn't see that coming."

"Again, if I said something…"

"No, it's… I… had an upsetting conversation right before we left the office. I thought I'd successfully stuffed my feelings away, but I guess not," she said.

"Oh. I get that. I think I've escaped emotional fallout and it creeps up on me later. I guess there's no escaping it when something bothers you."

She nodded. "It's not anything serious. I have a... challenging relationship with my father, and he happened to call me right at the end of the day. I should have let it go to voicemail."

"Ah, parents can ruin a day, easy. They know us too well; it's not a fair fight."

"He just knows how to push my buttons. 'You making decent money yet?' 'You make the Hollywood Reporter top entertainment lawyers list yet?' Sometimes I honestly think he's clueless, and other times I decide he's just cruel."

"I'm sorry. That's pretty shitty," I said.

"Yeah, well, over a drink—or ten—I'll tell you stories. He's a prickly cactus. You wouldn't believe."

She stared at the pair of jeans on the floor, and her eyes met mine in the mirror. At the same moment, we both seemed to realize we were standing in our underwear in a dressing room full of clothes and started to laugh.

"Okay, this is a little absurd. I guess it's fair to say we're officially friends now that I've cried in my underwear in front of you."

That pretty much fit my definition of friendship, so I suggested we wrap up our shopping expedition and find a place to get a cocktail. "You can save me from myself if you get me out of here before I decide to buy this beautiful shapeless dress," I said.

"Deal. Are you buying the other one though? That looked great on you."

"Oh yeah, I'm still spending way more than I should in this store. I'm buying the teal skirt and the dress with the belt. And those embroidered pants, even though I have no idea where I'll ever wear them."

She was nodding at my choices and gathering a couple hangers with blazers that looked great on her. "All those jeans can go to hell."

"Agreed."

"Okay, then, let's go spend our paychecks and find a bar."

"Preferably one with decent food. I'm suddenly craving a burger," I said.

"Ooh, I know the perfect place."

AFTER TWO BURGERS and four lemon drops between us, life was looking a lot better.

I'd opted not to ask Janelle anything about her father, if only because it seemed like she still felt pretty raw from the conversation and didn't want to ruin more of her day thinking about him. If she felt like venting, she knew where to find me. It turned out that not asking was the key to her willingness to talk about him.

"So, I was telling you about my dad earlier," she said, swirling the dregs of her second drink and looking into the glass longingly. I normally stop at two drinks. I have a strict policy about that because nothing good ever seems to happen after a third drink. I also break that policy when necessary. Janelle's unleashing of emotions had all the markings of necessary drinking.

After signaling to our waiter that we'd like refills, I focused my attention on Janelle, unsure whether we were starting a long serious conversation or finishing a short one.

"Don't worry, I'm not going to cry again. He's not worth the tears. I feel much better than I did a couple hours ago. Thanks," she said.

I held up both hands in a gesture of surrender that I hoped conveyed that I didn't mind wherever the conversation went. "You're welcome to cry. I won't judge."

"Nope. Done with that. Like I said, he just knows how to push my buttons and he never misses an opportunity to gouge me right where it hurts."

I nodded, fully understanding. I had my own issues with my parents, but I wasn't about to detract from Janelle's need to vent with my own. "I get it."

She pointed a finger at me. "Yeah, I didn't forget you said that earlier. I'm gonna ask you about it later, make no mistake. But as to my own dad, let's just say he suffers from insecurities that manifest in disparaging others."

"That sounds awful," I said. I'd had boyfriends who'd done the same thing.

"I've been dealing with it my whole life. You'd think I'd be used to it by now, but I still have this little kid need for affirmation. I'm a sucker for it. So even though I know I'm going to get slammed in the end, I keep going back for more, hoping for a different result."

"There's some psychological term for that, but I can't remember what it is."

"Yeah. Insanity."

That made me laugh. "I'm not sure that's it, but yes."

"I'm pretty sure it's the textbook definition. Trust me, I've been in therapy. I know I need to get past it, but it's hard. He and I have clashing neuroses. I need and constantly seek approval and he gets his jollies on withholding it."

The waiter showed up with our third round of drinks. By then, Janelle's was empty and mine was halfway gone. I slid the new colder one in front of my plate and let the waiter take my half-finished one away and replace it with a glass of water. "Make that two waters," Janelle said. "Anyway, probably doesn't help that I went into the same field as him."

"Oh, he's a lawyer too? What kind of law does he practice?" I asked.

"Entertainment law, contracts, and negotiation. Same as me." She didn't seem to think it bore examining that she'd chosen the same field as her ultra-competitive father. Was she a masochist? I decided to leave some of that for her therapist. It was too complicated for a post-shopping meal.

The effects of the lemon drops coupled with the mental whirlwind of my day suddenly had me feeling wiped out. I checked the time and saw it was after nine, which meant I'd made it to a respectable hour when I could go home and spend the rest of my time alone without feeling like I lacked a social life. Mission very much accomplished.

"You look sleepy," Janelle said, her own eyes glassy and at half-mast. I needed to make sure she wasn't planning on driving home. Yes, she was an adult, and no, I didn't need to act like a mother hen all the time. But maybe I did. It made me feel better if I knew where everyone in my life was going and how they planned to get there.

"I am sleepy. Early morning and a busy day," I said.

"Got it. Should we wrap it up?" she asked, fishing in her purse for her wallet.

"I think I need to. Is that cool?" I felt eager to end our evening before she asked me to unload details about my relationships or my parents.

"Totally." She checked her phone and typed a text message.

"Are you taking an Uber? What's your plan?" I asked.

"Nah."

"You can't drive. Not after three drinks. You can share with me if you want."

"No, I'm good. My dad should be getting done with work about now, and he'll give me a ride. I live on the same street as my folks."

Mentally, I did a double take. After all the complaining, she was going to hit up her dad for a ride? I decided it wasn't my fight. Sometimes people needed to steep in their habits until they became so uncomfortable that escape was the only option. In Janelle's case, it didn't seem like she'd reached that point.

I also didn't tell her about Finn or our meeting or my conflicted feelings.

At that juncture in the evening, I wasn't looking for opinions or even commiseration. Given that I was still learning the ropes at our firm, I didn't see any reason to complicate matters by admitting how bizarre my first case had already become. And I still didn't know Janelle well enough to fully trust her.

All outward signs pointed to her being a new friend and

potential confidante, but I wasn't going to be transformed into a trusting, open book overnight. I'd been burned too many times before—burned by law school friends who said my oral arguments were good enough and then slamming them in mock trials; burned by boyfriends who pretended I was good enough and then moved to Hawaii.

Now I avoided all signs of fire, even if they looked like the kind I could easily control. In my experience, those often ended up being the most dangerous kind.

# CHAPTER TWELVE

FINN

I ARRIVED home to find not just Becca haunting my kitchen but my youngest sister Tatum as well. The siblings were multiplying like rabbits, and I still had three more back home in the Bay Area. I wondered if I'd have a houseful of women inside of a week.

They were halfway through a bottle of rosé that I hadn't bought, so sometime between the landing of Tatum's plane and my return from the endless lawyer meeting, they'd shopped and even cooked.

There was no way I'd complain about that. The kitchen smelled like roasted garlic and fresh bread, although the baker in the family was still in the Bay Area, as far as I knew. I needed details.

Tatum was standing at my butcher block island tearing butter lettuce and slicing cherry tomatoes into a salad bowl. Becca was sitting *on* the butcher block, ankles crossed, sipping her wine and dipping pita bread into a bowl of hummus. Nowhere was there evidence of garlic or fresh bread. I wondered if I was starting to lose my mind and imagine phantom smells.

"Tater Tot, welcome to the homestead. Did you tell me you'd planned a trip and I forgot?" I asked before giving her a hug. For the record, I didn't forget. I don't forget information that's told to me, but I suspected Tatum had come because she felt sorry for me and I wanted to save her having to say it. I also wanted to save myself from having to hear it.

"No, it was a last-minute thing. I got a few days off work, I knew Becs was here, and the weather's already crap at home, so I hopped on a plane."

"Nicely done. There's a second guest bedroom upstairs with fresh sheets and everything. It's all yours."

I poked around the kitchen, where I spied a saucepan on the stove with bubbling bolognese sauce. That solved the garlic question. I went to the oven but found no bread.

Tatum popped a cherry tomato in her mouth and talked around it. "Already found it. And when you say fresh sheets, you're not kidding. The pillowcases still have creases from the packaging. Has anyone else used that room?" she asked.

I shook my head. "I don't have too many occasions where multiple guests come at the same time."

"Yet, you still have two guest rooms," Tatum said, raising an eyebrow.

"What can I say? Wishful decorating."

Becca piped in from her perch in the kitchen. "You could have made it a gym or a screening room or something. That room is gigantic."

"Well, I'm more likely to have two guests than I am to screen a movie, and I have a full gym downstairs."

"You do?" Becca asked. "How have I not found this in the two days I've been here?"

"Prolly because your lazy ass hasn't looked," Tatum said. Of all my sisters, she was the most into physical fitness, but not just for the sake of working out. Tatum was an athlete and had always gravitated toward team sports, starting at a young age. When I was on a little league team with other twelve-year-olds, three-year-old Tatum was at our practices, shagging balls in the outfield.

At the time, I didn't figure out that my mother just needed ways to occupy all her kids, and having the rowdiest one chase fly balls was the best solution.

Becca was religious about swimming and belonged to two different gyms, one with a large outdoor pool and a second with a smaller indoor pool in case of inclement weather, but she didn't exercise if it didn't involve water.

Becca glared at Tatum and I got ready for another round in a fight that had been going on for years. "I'm hardly lazy. I did a two-and-a-half-mile pier to pier swim last month."

"I know. I got the email blast, the social media pics and I saw the skywriting announcement," Tatum said.

"Funny. You're one to talk, since you're still telling people about how your college softball team won the championship. Eight years ago."

I was never willing to play referee between them, partly because doing so had only gotten me into trouble in the past, and partly because their battles amused me to no end. I was also elated to have the conversation focus on anything besides their worry for me and their fear of my impending jail sentence.

Tatum poured me a glass of wine, making sure to fill it past the halfway mark as she always did. "Glass more than half full. Cheers," she said, clinking hers with mine and continuing to slice tomatoes.

"Cheers. What smells like bread? Or is it just me? Maybe I'm having a stroke."

"That's when you smell toast, not bread, you dope," Becca said. She pointed to a bag on the counter. "Isla sent that along with Tater. From the bakery this morning."

"Ohhh, tell me this isn't a terrible joke at my expense. Isla sent bread?" I asked.

I went over to where the fat paper bag was sitting on the counter and lifted it, expecting its heft. My sister baked whole grain loaves with olives and rosemary or asiago cheese. These were no fluffy white dinner rolls. She'd made a career of baking for restaurants in San Francisco and had just put out her second cookbook. I unrolled the bag and dipped my nose in and inhaled.

"That's the stuff. I can't believe it's been in a suitcase and traveled on a plane, and it still smells this good," I said.

"It was in my carryon," Tatum said. "I cradled it like a baby chicken through the security line and kept it on my lap so it wouldn't get blasted with cold air in the overhead bins. I know how to treat bread on the lam."

I loved my sisters, and if one visiting me was good, two were better. However... I didn't love that they were at my house out of pity or obligation. And carting bread on a plane was a sure sign that my sisters were worried. "Tater, I hope you really are here to work on your tan, because if you think it's your last chance to see me before I get hauled off to jail, you wasted a trip."

"Yeah, why's that? You feel that confident?" she asked.

"I feel better than I did last week, so that's something," I said. It was true that my meeting with Annie had made me feel better in all kinds of ways, but I wasn't sure if any of them were related to my case. I had no way of knowing anything definitively, but I couldn't have them worrying about me.

Tatum moved on from cutting tomatoes to gathering ingredients for salad dressing. With the speed she was moving around and grabbing things, a person would think she was the one who set up the kitchen. Even I forgot where I'd stored things sometimes, but she'd pulled open the exact drawers where I kept spices and gone to the right shelves in my pantry. It was a little disconcerting.

"Do you have salad ESP or something? How do you know where everything is when you've never been here before?"

She looked at me like I was daft. "Seriously?"

"Yes, seriously. Did Becs send you a kitchen blueprint before you came?"

"No, but you did set up your kitchen exactly like mom's.

Exactly." She and Becca nodded at me simultaneously while I considered whether they could possibly be correct.

I thought about our childhood home, where our mom still lived. I couldn't even picture which wall the refrigerator was on, let alone whether there was a spice drawer. "Well, if I did, it was unconscious."

"Oh, you did," Becca said, hopping off the counter and going to the fridge for a second bottle of wine. She opened it with a wine opener I didn't even know I had. I didn't say a word. I didn't want to think about the symbolism of my kitchen.

"Maybe it's just because I put everything in the most logical place, as did Mom," I said. I took a sip of the wine, which was cold and seemed suddenly very necessary, even though my drink of choice was not pink. It wasn't bad. And after the craziness that was my day, I had no doubt we'd make it through the second bottle.

Becca settled at my kitchen table and waved her hand around like a game show assistant. "This kitchen is fabulous. When I grow up, I want to live in a kitchen like this."

"When do you plan to grow up?" Tatum asked. Even though she was the youngest, she had a mothering quality and always lorded it over my other sisters that she'd been the first to start a business—at age sixteen—and the first to travel abroad. "And are you serious that you'd live in a kitchen? Or was that just your poor grammar kicking in again?"

"Finn, will you help me plot her murder and make it look like an accidental fall from her majesty's pedestal?" Becca asked, coming over to hug me around the waist. "Then I'll come and live in your kitchen."

"No murders. How can I help with the food?" I opened my fridge to check the contents. As I suspected, they'd stocked it with two types of nut milk, sparkling water, wine, and fruit. I never understood how they could live on essentially that. I was glad that at least they knew me well enough to understand I needed a normal dinner, and I was even more glad that they hadn't stocked up my fridge like I was in need of full-time intervention.

Tatum shooed me away. "I've got this. You take a load off, and once you've finished your first glass of wine, you can tell me about what happened with the lawyers. And for the record, I agree that you have an awesome kitchen."

My kitchen was great; I won't lie, but I couldn't take a bit of credit for it. The prior owners of the house were interior designers, and they'd used the house to photograph their work for their website. The kitchen was tiled in Carrera marble with grey painted cabinetry and a terra cotta floor. I don't know much about design or architecture. I just knew that when I walked into the house, I wanted to live there.

Every surface material had been hand-picked from limestone quarries and stone cutters, every sconce sourced from an atelier in Europe, and all the rooms had natural light pouring in through tall windows, skylights, and perfectly-angled stained glass.

I made an offer the day I saw it, before it had officially gone on the market, and I didn't leave until the owners had accepted my bid. I'd made money in the stock market over the years, and by the time I was thirty-three, employed in the career I intended to have, single because I hadn't met anyone I could handle for more than two months of dating, I decided to buy a house that made me happy.

It never bothered me to wake up there alone. I had classes to teach, colleagues and students to see all day long, and a string of blind dates who were constantly pushed my way by well-meaning yet clueless friends. It is never a good idea to set two people up when the only thing they have in common is that they're both single.

But I digress. I never minded being in my house alone until Becca—and now Tatum—had come and reminded me that I do like people. I like waking up and having conversations with people, even if they're moody larks who'd rather not be woken by bad teenage drivers.

It sounded like Becca and Tatum would be leaving at around the same time, which meant that in a week I'd feel the dearth of companionship twice as much.

"So how'd it go today?" Tatum asked, nodding at Becca who refilled my empty glass. Tatum had moved on from the salad and was boiling water for pasta. Her efficiency in the kitchen was impressive. Becca was twirling a tendril of her hair and not doing much of anything to help with the food prep. That was also impressive because she loved to boss Tatum around. Maybe my sisters were maturing.

"The meeting was… interesting." I couldn't begin to describe it. I hadn't mentioned anything to Becca about meeting Annie at the wedding. What was the point? But now, I filled them both in on the woman I'd been obsessing over for two days who was now my lead counsel.

Becca squinted her eyes at me and shook her head. "This doesn't even seem possible. What are the odds?"

Tatum held up a hand. "No, no, don't ask an economist that. He'll actually tell you, and then he'll factor in population growth over the last century and explain how the standard deviation from the mean makes the whole thing invalid."

"I think you're confusing economics and statistics. But fair enough," I said. "What I will tell you is that I'm hopeful. For the first time since a federal officer walked me off campus and read me a list of bogus charges, I feel something other than dread."

"Is that your big head talking or your little head?" Becca asked.

"Jesus, Becs. Have a little decorum," Tatum said.

"Yeah, Jesus, Becs. *Little?* I'm insulted," I said.

"Oh my God. You two are so immature," Tatum said, moving away from us as though our humor was contagious. She was the most serious of my sisters and always believed 'that language,' as she called it, belonged 'in the bedroom.' She would whisper the last part as though just talking about a person's bedroom was akin to copping a feel. Her prudishness had been a running joke in our family, and my sisters never missed an opportunity to try to shock her delicate sensibilities.

For her part, Becca shook her head and continued her line of questioning. "It's a valid question. Are you excited because she's a good lawyer or because you want to get in her pants?"

"Becca. Seriously. He could go to jail, and you're acting like he's only interested in one thing." That was the closest she ever came to spelling it out.

"Oh, grow up. Human beings talk about sex. Why are you such a puritan?" Becca asked, shaking her head.

"It's just inappropriate. I don't want to talk about it, and I'm sure Finn doesn't want to either."

Becca squinted her eyes at her sister. "Oh, we're gonna talk about your issues for sure, just not right now. But your attitude smacks of a person who needs to get laid, and I want to know who stole your vibrator?" At that, Tatum turned the shade of a beet, and I realized that maybe Becca was right. Her seeming distaste for talking about sex had all the markers of a problem she was having *in the bedroom*.

We would get to that.

In the meantime, I did want their advice on how I should handle my future interactions with Annie. Even though I'd told her it was a given that she'd be my lawyer and I'd have no problem putting Saturday night out of my mind, it was only sort of true.

"You need to be honest with her," Tatum said. "If you lie to her, you're done."

"Especially since she's still getting over the fact that you lied by omission about your situation," Becca said, gesturing toward me from head to toe.

I looked down at myself to make sure there wasn't some situation I was unaware of, like an open fly.

"You know, leaving out the felon part when you were boning her at the wedding," Becca explained.

"Okay, first of all, I didn't 'bone her.' Second, we're well past that. She knows more about my case than I do at this point. She's deposing the whistleblower to try to discredit him. And she got the judge to suspend the house arrest so I'm free to go places other than my lawyer's office."

"Man, the Feds really mean business, don't they?" Becca said. For the first time since she'd arrived on my doorstep, I saw the flash of deeper concern cross her face.

I put down my wine glass and summoned the two of them to the kitchen table, where we could sit facing each other and hash through everything they'd been afraid to ask me. "Let's get all your fears and concerns out into the open, shall we?" I asked. "Ask me all your questions. I know you two are concerned about me, and there are three more of you. Should I expect to find a new sister per day showing up at my house? It's going to get a little crowded by Friday."

Becca rolled her eyes. "Not in this house. Finn, I can't believe it's taken me this long to come see this place. When you said you had room for guests, I didn't know you meant you meant thirty guests."

I cast a look past the entryway into the den, which was a high-ceilinged wide open space. But that was the only room visible from where we sat. That was another thing I'd liked about the place. From the outside, it was a nondescript wall. Inside, it was a winding set of rooms that rolled out to the garden on one side and ascended up a hidden spiral staircase on the other. A sprawling loft space with two guest rooms and en suite bathrooms were all but hidden from the rest of the house. It was tasteful and modest. There were just a lot of places to go on several stories, along with gardens that crawled up a hill in back and ended at an enclosed pool.

No question. I was lucky to be able to afford the place. Then again, I'd spent years studying industries, companies, and market trends. I didn't make my stock picks lightly. After a few years, I'd had so much success with my choices that my financial planner tried to woo me to work for her. I said no, but I knew she was surreptitiously piggy-backing on some of my trades for her clients, not knowing why I'd made the choices I had, but knowing my track record was better than hers.

Owning this house was important to me. I was the lone male in the family, my father having died of a brain tumor sixteen years ago, and I felt the responsibility to look out for everyone. Even though my mom and sisters were smart and self-sufficient, I'd always wanted to provide a fallback for them. I never said as much, but I trusted they knew that if they ever went through a financial downturn or a tough relationship, they'd have a safe haven here. It was something I'd promised my dad when he got sick.

I'd been only twenty at the time, but my dad trusted that I'd do it. His confidence convinced me he was right, so when I'd seen an opportunity to begin using some of my econometric models to make money in the stock market, I went all in.

"Honestly, Becs, if I'd known getting arrested was what it would take to get you to stay here, I'd have robbed a bank a year ago."

"Haha. This is serious, Finn. You shouldn't joke," Becca said.

"I absolutely should joke. Joking isn't going to make my fate any worse, but it's sure as hell going to make me feel better about it."

"He's got a point," Tatum said, reaching for our wine glasses and bringing them to the table. She was my chance to get the whole family to lighten up. If she went home and reported back to my mother and sisters that the charges were a scare tactic and a chance to make an example of someone, they'd stop worrying.

I couldn't have them worrying over me.

"Now that you see I have room for you, will you visit more?" I asked.

"Hells yeah," Becca said. "And I'm bringing friends. So you'd better not let the Feds seize this house." She tried to be cavalier but the worry behind her eyes persisted.

Tatum had been quiet, but she looked less concerned and more relieved now that we were addressing the elephant in the room. "No one else is coming... unless I tell them they should," she said.

"I love you all, but you don't need to circle the wagons. I'm not going to jail."

"And you say this because of the new lawyer you're so smitten with? Is she worth putting all your faith in? I'm... worried." Tatum had the most steady demeanor—almost to the point of bossing the rest of us around half the time—but I could see she was freaked out.

"What is it going to take for you to believe that I will come out of this unscathed?" I asked.

Tatum perked up a bit at the question. "I can tell you exactly what it will take. I want to meet your lawyer and make sure she's up to the task. I want to look her in the eye and have her convince me."

"Convince you she's up to the task?"

"Convince me she can win your case and keep you out of jail," Tatum said.

"Ooh, I'd like her to convince me of that too," Becca said. "It didn't occur to me we could meet your lady friend, but I'm all for that."

"She's not my lady friend. She's my lawyer. Let's get that clear. She understands boundaries, unlike some people in this room."

Becca threw her hand at me dismissively. "Ugh, boundaries. I hope she doesn't understand. Don't you think she'll do a much better job defending you if she's got the hots for you?"

Tatum glared at Becca again. "Now I really need to meet her. She can think you're handsome, fine, but if she's at all distracted, I want you to find someone else," she said.

"So you two want to meet my lawyer and evaluate whether she's sufficiently attracted to me to be interested in my well-being, but not so enthralled by my manliness that her brains will fall out of her ears? Is that what I'm hearing?"

Becca and Tatum nodded in unison. "Pretty much," Tatum said. "Now who's hungry? I think my pasta's ready."

# CHAPTER THIRTEEN

ANNIE

ON WEDNESDAY, Finn called me to come down to the lobby of my office building instead of meeting me upstairs. He made it sound like the guard was giving him trouble. But the guard wasn't even at his desk when I came down and saw Finn standing by the glass doors to the building holding a large shopping bag.

"Let's go," he said, holding the door open for me to walk through.

I didn't budge. "Go where?" He didn't answer, instead silently inclining his head out the door. After a minute, I realized I was blocking the entrance, so I moved out to the sidewalk. But I was still no more willing to follow Finn wherever he was headed until he explained.

"We're going to have a meeting."

"And that's not possible in my office, like a normal client?"

He started walking briskly down Century Park East, so I trailed along after him because he was talking and pointing. "Do you ever go to Roxbury Park?"

"Do I... no, I don't even know what that is," I said when I'd caught up. Why was he walking so fast?

"That's right, you're new in town," he said, raising an eyebrow and leading me to think the place we were headed was anything but a rolling green space. I almost turned back for lack of further explanation but Finn must have sensed my hesitance, so he grabbed my hand.

And dammit, that changed everything.

His touch sent a warm thrill through my body and I immediately felt the heat rise in my cheeks. And yet, despite the fact that he was my client and I knew better, I didn't let go.

We walked in silence for a few minutes, turning on Olympic and heading away from Century City. I had so many warring thoughts in my head—*where are we going, why am I going along with this, is my hand too sweaty?*

Finn stole a sideways glance at me and smiled. "This is hard for you, isn't it? Not knowing the plan?" he asked. When I looked at his face, I realized one of the things that had been so hard about our first meeting in my office. It had been almost painful to look at him and not be able to touch him. Forget almost painful. It had been damn near torture.

"I'm alright."

"You're so not. You're dying to know where we're going and why."

"So why don't you tell me? Are you trying to torture me? That's not very nice."

Finn was silent again, still smiling. I pointed to the white shopping bag he was swinging in his other hand. "What's in the bag?" I asked.

"Change of clothes."

"Something tells me I don't want to know."

A few minutes later, I could see the outline of what looked to be an ordinary park up ahead, so I felt a small sense of relief that I hadn't missed out on some sort of park-as-metaphor inside joke. He didn't seem inclined to tell me what the hell we were doing at a park instead of meeting in my office, so I opted to follow along —at least for a few minutes—to find out the rest of the plan.

When we reached the park, Finn guided us toward a small building that had bathrooms and two "changing lockers." He handed me a wrapped bundle from inside the shopping bag. "Here's your outfit."

"I have an outfit? Finn, I'm afraid I need a little more information."

Just then a petite woman with white hair cut in a pageboy and round, black-framed glasses came over and hugged Finn around the waist. She was a full foot shorter than him and dressed in pressed white pants and a white button-down shirt. "Finn! I've missed seeing you here. Who's your pretty friend?"

"Esther, meet Annie."

Esther took both my hands in hers and kissed me on both cheeks. "I bet you'll give this one a run for his money, eh? You a good bowler?" she asked.

"I'm um… okay?" I was really confused as Finn led me away from Esther and the crowd forming at a kiosk to explain to me that we would be spending the next hour lawn bowling.

"I thought we were discussing your case."

"We can do that too. There's downtime."

*Oh good, there's downtime. Downtime? From what?*

"What is lawn bowling?" I asked because honestly, I had no idea.

Finn led me over to a low chain-link fence that surrounded a neat grass rectangle marked with lanes. "It's a bit like bocce ball. Have you ever played that?" My questioning stare must have given him his answer. "Shuffleboard?"

"I've played shuffleboard."

"Okay, it's a little like that, in that you're rolling balls and trying to knock other people's balls out of the way. I'll explain more when we start." He was saying all of this like it was completely normal to be lawn bowling instead of having an office meeting about his case.

"And why are we doing this?" I asked.

"Because you need to get out of the office more and I've stood up my buddies in the league for the past two months. It's time to get back."

"Wait, you're in a lawn bowling league?" I asked, shocked that such a thing existed, and even more shocked that Finn was a member, given that he single-handedly brought the average age down by two decades. The lawn bowlers I could see were chatting amongst themselves, mostly grey-haired, all wearing white outfits, all adorable.

"I am," he said.

"I see." He continued to surprise me. And I really liked that, which continued to be a problem. Finn gestured with a tilt of his head that I should go change.

In the changing area, I unwrapped the bundle he'd forced into my hands, anticipating correctly that it contained something white. But wasn't just a white T-shirt to throw over my existing clothes to make me sort of blend in. Under the layers of tissue paper, I found a pair of white capri pants, a long-sleeved white T-shirt with a cotton sweater I could wear over it. It was warm so I tied it over my shoulders and slipped on the white oxfords he'd also included. It was all my size. I had no idea how he knew.

When I stepped back outside, I saw Finn wearing his own pair of pressed white pants with a white oxford-cloth shirt and a belt with tiny turtles on it. His pants were rolled at the bottoms and he wore white Converse All Stars.

He took in the sight of me in my lawn bowling attire and nodded. "You look perfect. You should join the league with me."

"No way, buddy. I'm only here because we have work to do and you're stubborn as hell."

He shrugged. "Whatever it takes. Come."

He led me over and introduced me to a few of the other members of the league, not one of them under seventy years old. After handshakes and more kisses, Finn explained the basics of the game to me. "The first player rolls the white ball. That's the jack. Then the other players build the head around the jack." That made sense but when he started explaining the forehand and backhand bowls and draw shots versus run shots, he lost me.

"Okay, forget the explanation. Let's just play," I said. How hard could it be?

It turned out it was harder than it looked. I should have paid more attention to the explanations of the small and large ring and bias because my bowls were ending up all over the place and nowhere near the jack where they were supposed to be.

As I stomped away after another horrific bowl, I found Finn sitting on a lawn chair laughing his head off. "It's harder than it looks," I said, well aware that the octogenarians I'd dismissed as feeble competition were kicking my ass.

"I know. I'm not laughing at you."

"Oh yeah? What are you laughing at?"

He pressed his lips together in a futile attempt to keep a straight face. Which turned out to be impossible. He was laughing again, and there was no question he was laughing at me. I leveled him with a semi-successful glare and punched him in the arm.

"Hey, no violence allowed at lawn bowling." He grabbed my hand and kissed it. I was about to yell at him for inappropriate client behavior, except that I lost my balance and fell toward him. On him, actually. Finn broke my graceless plunge by shifting so I landed on his lap, my face inches from his. It put me in dangerous territory because all thoughts fled my brain outside of the urgent need to kiss him. I wanted to lick the strong line of his jaw and bite his luscious bottom lip.

My eyes met his and we stared at each other, first in unspoken acknowledgment that we both had unfulfilled desires. We'd been interrupted at the wedding, we'd been interrupted in my office. Couldn't we just... once...?

No.

I saw it in Finn's eyes the second he saw it in mine. We couldn't. I had to be a better person than that. He needed my legal help and I needed to keep my pretty white capri pants on.

"So... we should record our scores before the next round," Finn said.

"Yes. Let's do that."

I reluctantly untangled myself from his lap and his limbs which had so naturally wrapped around me, marveling at the injustice. The first guy I actually wanted was the one I had to let go.

~

AN HOUR LATER, we'd finished the match, and thanks to Finn's practiced skill and my haphazard bowling mojo, we managed to come in third in our group. I took that as a big, fat win.

The other bowlers had gathered around tables having drinks and snacks, and Finn shepherded us over to a spot under a tree where he unfolded a plaid blanket and spread out turkey sandwiches, chips, and bottles of iced tea from the magic shopping bag.

"Finn, this doesn't seem ethical," I said, pointing to the picnic blanket.

He cocked his head and looked at me. "I have an unethical blanket?"

"It feels like a place people on a date sit, not a lawyer and her client. We should go back to my office," I said, checking my phone. We'd already been gone for over an hour and we hadn't talked about the case once.

"I see. Okay, let's nix the blanket." Finn folded it up and moved everything to a table. "How's this? It's just a table. Is it the kind of place you can sit with a client? Think of it as a lunch meeting without the corporate dining room."

I couldn't tell if he was being facetious or trying to help soothe my neuroses. It was just a table, after all. I could use it to turn our field trip back into a client meeting. "It's fine." I sat down and unwrapped one of the sandwiches.

"Listen, Finn, I know you know this, but you're crazy not to pay the fine and be done. You could likely avoid a trial and all of this by paying a fine. It might be a couple million dollars, but wouldn't it be worth it to make this go away? Your legal fees could be nearly that much if this drags out in court," I said. He had to know that, right?

But he was shaking his head before I'd finished talking. "Not a chance. I have an academic reputation and I didn't engage in insider trading. I either want to be vindicated or thrown in jail."

I was afraid he'd say that. "Okay, then. Moving on. Explain to me how an economics professor beat the stock market and made seven million dollars legally."

"I'm glad you asked," he said. "Eat your sandwich first. From what I know of you, you'll want to take notes and I'd hate for you to get mustard on your legal pad."

"It's yellow, Finn. Start talking."

# CHAPTER FOURTEEN

FINN

I WAS PACING on the grass. I'd been going in circles for ten minutes—literally—and so had our discussion, with Annie trying sixteen different ways with sixteen different phrasings of her questions to get me to answer the first one in a new way, but I wasn't going to lie to suit her or anyone else.

Let's start from the beginning. Tell me about your job consulting for Blink Telecom and Cellcom. Why did they ask you do that?"

"You mean why do economists consult for private companies?"

"Sure, start with that."

"Well, ever since the big trust busters broke up Ma Bell, companies have been merging, buying up other companies. Phone companies own entertainment companies, internet providers, and so on," I said, looking at Annie to make sure she was following along. She nodded.

"And each time there's a merger valued at over ninety-six million dollars, the government needs to approve. So the companies come in with research to convince the government that their merger is good for the economy and good for consumers. They hire economists to come up with the models, and obviously they'd like to show that the mergers are very good for consumers. They're paying a lot of money, so economists might feel pressure to give the companies the results they want."

"Did you feel pressure?" she asked.

"I did, which is why I haven't consulted in five years. It feels unethical."

I leaned down and shuffled through the shopping bag until I found the consulting agreements with the two companies. She took the documents and read through the key parts. "Five years? Did you use any information they gave you—anything about product development or future plans—when you traded in their stock?"

"No. Is that what they're saying?"

"That's part of what the whistleblower is saying—that your knowledge of the companies put you in a position to know insider information."

"That's not true."

"It doesn't look great that you were a consultant for the same companies whose stock you sold," she said.

"I'm sorry." I noticed that there wasn't a single fallen leaf on the grass. Granted, it wasn't autumn yet, but I couldn't help but think that the maintenance crew at this park must work awfully hard.

"So your colleague Craft consulted for the same two companies, and you made seven million bucks when their merger fell apart?" she asked again. Sharing my observations about the leaves would probably frustrate her so I kept my thoughts to myself.

"Yes."

"Well, I can see why that might annoy him," she said.

"So, fine. Be annoyed. But don't sue me and get the SEC involved. The guy's a prick."

"Did he tell you anything while he was consulting?" she asked, spinning her pen on the back of her hand. Some of my friends in grad school used to do that but I'd never gotten the hang of it.

"Nope. Already told you that."

"Then why does he think you had information?"

"He's making an assumption. Connecting dots that aren't connected. He can't believe I made my trades without knowing what only people inside the company knew."

That was the problem. The evidence everyone chose to see didn't conform to what I knew to be true. People made judgments based on surface perceptions. So maybe my guilt lay in a lack of creative thinking.

Annie shook her head. "I feel like a rat in a maze," she said finally.

"Yes."

"Any idea how to fix that?"

"I can put up a logical argument, but I'm not sure it's worth your time to listen."

"If you pay my hourly rate, you can ask me to do anything you want," she said.

I laughed. "I'm sorry, but as much as I'd like to take *full* advantage of that offer, I think you should rephrase, Counselor."

And again, her face turned a charming shade of pink. "Being your lawyer is going to be my certain death. I'm giving you one more chance to work with another attorney at this fine, fine firm. Please. For the sake of my boundaries and my sanity."

I hadn't imagined it was possible to get a hard-on from a woman telling you to find another lawyer. "Not a chance. I want you." I meant it in all the ways it could be interpreted, and I stopped talking so she could think about how many of those ways interested her.

From the hazy look in her eyes, it seemed like she was on board with them all. That made me smile. It was getting bad, my affinity for her. I'd tried to mask the intensity with lighthearted banter and innuendo but I was losing the fight against falling hard for her. Maybe that was okay if there was a minute chance she felt the same way. Her eyes told me I shouldn't give up.

But then... she composed herself.

"Fine. You can have me." She grimaced and closed her eyes, clearly not meaning it the way her words came out. "Not in that sense. You have me as your lawyer, which is what I meant."

"That's what I understood your meaning to be. Get your mind out of the gutter, Counselor."

I reeled my heart back in from its dangling position on the ledge of my sleeve. Maybe I wouldn't convince her today, but I believed I was still on the probability curve.

She ground her lips together and lowered her voice. "I swear Finn, if you make this harder than it needs to be, I'll send you back to Jackson, and you can flirt with him all day long."

"You will not do that. I'm the client, and I choose you." I liked saying it almost as much as I liked watching her reaction to me saying it.

Annie stared at me like she was still deciding whether or not to send me to death row. I sat patiently because I knew her well enough at this point to know she had to come to her own conclusions when she was ready.

"Okay, are you ready for the logic?" I asked.

She nodded, but her skeptical expression told me she was expecting a trick or more innuendo.

"The money companies pay economists for consulting gigs varies, but it can be a couple hundred thousand or even a few million for a specific project. Then upwards of tens of millions over time. Clearly better than what most of us make on the tenure track," I said.

"And over time, if you'd continued to consult on these giant mergers, you could have earned what, a hundred million?" she asked.

"It's likely, yes. But I turned it down. I wanted to test my stock market theory instead."

"Earning seven million in the stock market is peanuts compared to a hundred million in consulting fees. There's a hole in that logic, Professor."

I felt a surge of delight that she saw the point. "Ah, and there's the proof. If I was just after money, why would I say no to tens of millions, only to turn around and cheat the system to make less money in the stock market?"

"That's the defense you want me to use? Backwards logic?" she asked, laughing.

I shrugged, unsure it was worse than any other defense. "I wanted to make money legally by investing in the stock market according to theories I've been working on for ten years. And because of that decision, I'm being charged with insider trading, whereas I could have continued consulting and made a lot more money, legally. Ironic, isn't it?"

Annie looked like she wanted to murder me. But I was overjoyed because she was starting to see what I needed her to understand.

# CHAPTER FIFTEEN

ANNIE

LATER THAT WEEK, I discovered the downside to making friends at work—sometimes they wanted to hang out when I preferred to go home and eat a pint of salted caramel ice cream.

I couldn't say no to Janelle, especially after she'd unloaded all her insecurities about her dad. I'd seen her father leaving her office a few days after she'd opened up to me about their difficult —if slightly strange—relationship. So when she sent me an interoffice text and asked me to swing by her office, I did.

"Oh hey," she said when I knocked on her door frame. Her door was already open, and even then, I waited for her to respond before barging in.

She asked if I wanted to do something with her in an hour or so, after work. "Something healthier than shopping and cocktails."

Her words, not mine.

"Not too healthy. I still want it to be fun," I said.

"Have you ever tried cryotherapy?"

"No. Bawling my eyes out does not sound fun."

"Not crying therapy. Cryotherapy," she said. "You go in a freezer to relieve inflammation and increase your blood flow."

I knew what cryotherapy was, and I kind of thought it was a crock. "I was kidding. I've used ice baths a few times when I had tendonitis from running, but I've never done the freezer thing."

Janelle donated a shallow laugh to my attempt at humor. "Want to stand in a freezer next to mine? Maybe it will clear your mind, and you'll have new focus or something."

"I thought it was supposed to be for the body. It's a mind thing too?"

"I have no idea. But I bought a Groupon, so I want to use it."

"Ah, the truth comes out." I'd heard worse ideas than freezing my tail off in a box for ten minutes. Not a lot of them, but at least a few. "Fine. I'll do it. Then, we'll find a place to grab food. If I have new focus, I'll need to fuel it with a burger."

She threw her hand out toward mine to shake on it. "Done. It's on Wilshire in Santa Monica. Meet you there after work?"

Janelle didn't wait for an answer. She looked down at her desk, indicating she was done with the conversation. Her desk was impossibly neat for someone with cases and files, so I wasn't sure what she was looking at, but I admired her austere inner sanctum.

I went back to my office and spent the next hour trying not to think about Finn.

Obviously, the breakup sex idea had backfired. And the lawn bowling just made me want him in a fantasy wearing white. I was more confused, confounded, and distracted by him than before, and I hadn't thought that was possible.

I had the choice of accepting my lust but not letting it show when he was around, or I could make sure I was never alone in a room with him until the case was settled. The second idea might work. We could convene behind the safe barrier of email or text. I could busy myself with depositions and work on the case without seeing Finn at all… or at least for a few days. That might dry out my panties.

It also helped to have activities, so I enthusiastically embraced the idea of cryotherapy without really understanding how awful it would be to stand in a meat locker wearing someone else's socks.

A couple hours later, I found out.

Janelle and I filled out paperwork that essentially signed away our rights to sue the cryo place if we ended up freezing to death. "You know this isn't enforceable," Janelle said to the heavily pierced teenager behind the desk. He had one earbud in, and we could hear the tinny beat of the music coming from the one that was dangling over the front of his black British invasion T-shirt.

"If you don't sign it, you can't do a session," he said. I didn't know why Janelle was wasting her time arguing about the legality of a form he didn't create, but she was right. It was unenforceable. Nonetheless, I hoped neither one of us died, even if we could later sue over it.

We were ushered into a changing area and told to get naked except for a pair of wool booties and mittens. I was starting to see a pattern in my outings with Janelle—they all involved taking off my clothes.

When we'd stripped down and bootied up, we each climbed into what looked like a shower booth with our heads sticking out.

"I'll give you time checks every minute," the guy with the earbud said. "Feel free to move around, go in circles, dance, whatever you want."

I didn't envision myself dancing in the box with no music, but sure enough, after a minute in thirty degrees below zero temperatures, I was shaking my naked bits in a manner that probably looked a lot like huloga.

In an attempt to make the time go by faster, I ended up filling Janelle in on the huloga story, which led her to tell me about her last boyfriend who dumped her after a month. And as my brain froze and I lost all sense of appropriateness, I told her about my wedding hookup with Finn and my daily struggle with wanting to climb him like a tree when I should be calmly looking for legal loopholes.

She laughed, I gasped, and we collectively lost all feeling in our extremities. "I need to meet this man," she said.

In the freezing air, her laughter sounded more like hiccups, and I started to wonder if that was because I was dying.

"Janelle, I'm going to f-fucking k-k-kill you," I said, shivering and not understanding why I was subjecting myself to freezing my ass off at thirty-five dollars for ten minutes.

"I'm s-s-soorry. I thought it would be cool."

"B-b-bad joke."

We jumped and danced, and I swore a blue streak. Finally, we were released from the arctic winter and I gratefully put my clothes back on. "Don't you feel like you're glowing?" Janelle asked.

"Only because I'm regaining circulation in my limbs. You owe me a drink—a big one—and I don't care if it's unhealthy."

"I'm not arguing. But it can't be tonight. My dad promised to help me with a case." She pushed the door open and went out onto the sidewalk. I'd lucked out and parked in a spot right in front, but I didn't see her car.

"Nice. Do you work on a lot of stuff together?" I asked.

The cold front must have temporarily frozen her brain because she looked at me with terror in her eyes. "Oh... um, I mean, not a lot." She seemed panicked.

"Janelle, it's okay. I'm not going to say anything to Tom. Is that what you're worried about?" I put a hand on her arm. She seemed really upset.

She started biting her lip, and I worried I might need to throw her back into the cryo booth if she didn't calm down. "Just, yes. Don't say anything. I don't want people to know he's helping me with stuff," she said.

"Do you think anyone would care?"

"Um, yeah," she said. "He's a partner at a competing firm."

"But he's your dad. It's not like he's going to screw you over."

"You don't know my dad."

"So why are you showing him your cases?"

Janelle rifled through her purse until she found her keys. "Because he's a better lawyer than I am, and if I want to make partner someday, I need to impress the bosses."

Nodding my understanding, I reached for Janelle and gave her a hug. Then I promised I'd take her secret to the grave and said goodbye. "I'm swearing you to secrecy on my client crush too, so we're even," I told her.

"Okay, deal. You've got to keep me posted on that," she said, raising an eyebrow.

When she walked around the corner to where she'd parked, I released a sigh I'd been holding in for what felt like an hour.

Hanging out with her was stressful. Maybe that was because she was such an open book with her feelings. I wasn't used to that in new friendships, but I kind of liked that she got right to the messy stuff and didn't pretend she was perfect. And it was nice to have a friend at work.

I went home intent on making myself a vanilla milkshake and getting a good night's sleep. I would not think about Finn.

Okay, I would only think about him as it pertained to his case.

Fine. I would think about him a little bit, but only because my brain was still partially frozen and the thought of him always warmed me. It was pure medical necessity.

Also, I couldn't help myself.

# CHAPTER SIXTEEN

FINN

I COULD TELL Annie was avoiding seeing me in person. Being the pushy client, I called her assistant and scheduled a meeting, but I'll admit to having ulterior motives. She needed to get out of the office more often and relax. I'd managed to drag her to the park, but I'd have to be a little more creative if I wanted to keep up my shenanigans and still allow her to dutifully work on my case.

*What am I doing? Why is helping her relax more important than staying out of jail?*

Maybe I'd already accepted the fact that I couldn't win against the Feds. It's not that I didn't think Annie was doing important work on my behalf, but I had to withhold the one piece of information that she'd need to exonerate me. And she was missing too many sunsets. I knew that about her the first night we met.

So we convened in her office. I tried to keep my focus on the meeting, but it was damned hard with Annie walking back and forth in a short skirt and high-heeled pumps. I did my best to stay focused on the words she was saying and her obvious brain power. And I know it made me an objectifying asshole that I was thinking of her in any way other than as accomplished lawyer with a job to do, but spare me. I'm a man, and I'm not going to lie about the effect she had on me.

It wasn't just her toned legs under her skirt and hint of cleavage at the neck of her bohemian top. It was the woman's big sexy brain that had me fighting a hard-on during the entire meeting. What can I say? I'm a sucker for intelligence wrapped in a gorgeous package.

It's not like I thought I'd seduce her and crush her body against the credenza while hiking up her skirt and pulling down her panties.

Nope, that thought never occurred to me.

"I didn't commit a crime. I promise you," I said for what felt like the millionth time since I'd been charged.

"Finn, the sad fact is that it's not about your promises. It's about proof beyond a reasonable doubt. Now, I can get the criminal charge thrown out because it's a high burden of proof. The SEC would have to show that you, 'knowingly or with severe recklessness appropriated material, nonpublic information for trading.' In other words, that you intended to break the law. But for the civil case, it's a little harder, so I need you to tell me everything about when, why, and how you decided on your trades," she said, sitting behind her desk with her laptop screen partially blocking my view of her.

Her face creased with concentration as she typed but I could tell from the way her eyes were squinting that she was straining. "Have you ever thought about glasses?" I couldn't help asking.

"I'm sorry?"

"For the computer. To prevent eye strain. It looks like you're squinting. I'd wager there's a non-zero probability you could benefit from computer glasses."

"Non-zero, what?"

"Sorry. It's an economic term. It means there's a decent chance I'm right."

Annie made a point of raising her eyebrows and otherwise

stretching out the creases in her face. "I don't think I have eye strain," she said.

"Do you get headaches? After working a long time?"

"Sure, but doesn't everybody? That's just what happens when you're at a computer screen for hours."

"Not necessarily. I used to get terrible headaches when I was writing articles for academic journals. Of course, in part, that was because I'm a slow-ass writer. Some of my colleagues crank these things out in a couple hours. It would take me a couple weeks."

"Maybe you're just extra-thorough," she said kindly.

"I'd like to think so." The truth was that I needed to look over every piece of research and run all my own calculations, instead of trusting the work of other people. That slowed me down a lot. But I couldn't help it. I had to know how all the data fit together, and that required seeing it and working with it myself. "In any case, the eye strain would get pretty bad and finally I couldn't take it anymore. My eye doc gave me a pair of blue light glasses with a tiny bit of magnifier in them, and I'm telling you, it saved my bacon."

"All the better to use as a martini garnish," she said. Then she froze. "Sorry, forget I said that. Stay focused, Annie."

"It's okay, isn't it? If we acknowledge that we have some familiarity with each other?" At that, a blush spread from her cheeks to her chest and I backpedaled. "I didn't mean it like that. I'm not picturing what's under your skirt, if that's what you're worried about," I said.

"Finn! Shh. You barely know what's under my skirt so you can't very well picture it."

"Well, I'm picturing it now, and the longer you talk about it, the more vivid the picture gets."

"See? This. This is exactly why we can't talk about bacon," she said. Her voice was still a loud whisper and it was charming.

"I agree. Why would anyone want to talk about it when it tastes delicious? I'd much prefer to eat bacon instead of thinking about it."

"Stop it!"

I couldn't help it. I was all about her bacon.

She did her best to divert the conversation by looking back down at her computer like she was concentrating hard, but she had yet to type anything else. Finally, she looked up. "Computer glasses, eh?

"You might want to try them, is all," I said.

She nodded. "Okay, thanks for the tip."

"No problem. Happy to look out for your bacon."

Then I think she actually growled at me. "Finn. You are under indictment for three counts of securities fraud. This is serious stuff. And I bill in seven-minute increments. Do you really want to spend your money talking about bacon? Mine or otherwise?" I had an answer all ready, but she put up a hand. "No. Don't answer that."

In my mind, the whole explanation was simple. I grabbed a napkin from my bag and drew her a picture. "Look. The markets shift every day. It's not illegal to profit when companies do unexpected things. I just happened to expect the unexpected. And I did it intentionally."

"It's not that I don't see what you're saying…" she said, looking at the napkin where I'd drawn supply and demand curves. "I'm pretty sure I learned this when I took Econ 101 in college. But I got a B in Economics when I thought I understood everything, and I hate that I feel dumb now."

"Don't feel dumb. Stop that. It's complicated stuff and it involves a certain amount of faith in data. This is why I asked you to trust that anyone could have done what I did with the same information. Use my data," I said aware of the innuendo.

"I can't just use your data, Finn."

I smirked. "Oh, how I'd love for you to use my data. Don't feel guilty about using it and throwing it away when you're done. It's here for you and your transitory enjoyment," I said.

"Finn, stop it."

"Stop what?"

"You promised you'd behave like a client."

"I did? When did I promise that?"

"When I agreed to be your lawyer," she reminded me.

"Right." I pulled out my glasses to read some pages and saw her eyeing me appreciatively. She liked the glasses. "I am behaving like a client. I find it hard to believe your clients don't want to date you. So I'm behaving like them."

"My clients do not want to date me."

"Then your clients are idiots."

"Finn."

"Sorry." I scribbled out everything I'd drawn on the napkin. "Look, forget the supply and demand curves. You understand well enough what that means. Some people want to buy stocks, and other people want to sell stocks. That's what makes the securities market hum." I waited to make sure she was onboard with the concept.

"I get that part. I get that you wanted to buy stocks at one price and sell them at another. For an enormous profit. And you're saying you did it legally. I can't just ask a judge to take that on faith."

"Right. I'm trying to explain that. In addition to the buyers and sellers, there's data, lots of data. All the time, from all different sources, inputs are being received and all that data affects the price of a stock. All I did was see an inflection point in the data that no one else saw."

"Oh, is that all? Well, we're cool, then. That's all I have to tell the SEC. What they're going to wonder, however, is how you were the only one to see this inflection point, seven million dollars' worth in the weeks before a merger fell through."

I shrugged. "It's what I do. I study this stuff."

"So do other people."

I threw up my hands. "What can I say? Maybe I'm doing it better. I input every piece of data and analyze possible outcomes. Does one of my scenarios look exactly like what a person with insider information would know? Yes. Is that illegal? No."

"Seriously? That's what you think is going to keep you out of jail? That explanation? No. One. Will. Believe. You."

"How is that my fault?" I asked.

She looked at me the way people had been looking at me for the past two months. In utter incredulity. I'd gotten used it, but I liked the look a whole lot less on her face. "Finn, please tell me the truth. I can't defend you if you don't tell me how you timed your trades to make all that money," she said.

"I'm an economist. I figured it out."

She looked on her computer and studied some papers on her desk before shaking her head. "How is that a legal defense?" she asked.

I shrugged. That was the seven million dollar question. I took a lap around the room. Annie had encouraged me to pace because she said movement freed up the neural synapses and would help me make connections I wouldn't make sitting down. I happened to think she was correct, so I'd been pacing around for the past hour.

I watched her pick up a stress ball from her desk and start working it in her hand, but I squelched the impulse to verbalize an observation. Her office was sparsely furnished with a couch against the wall and two chairs on the opposite side of her desk, facing her. Boring and uninspired.

The desk didn't look like something she'd choose. It was too big for the space, for one thing, and it was old and heavy. It looked like something left over from the Mad Men days of mostly-male firms, heavy dark wood furniture, and Scotch passed around at a meeting after five in the afternoon.

The art, on the other hand, looked like her. There were three large aerial photos of exotic-looking beaches someplace in Europe—Italy or France, someplace with greenish-blue clear water—and from the distance at which the photos were taken, all that was visible were tiny dots of people under striped umbrellas scattered across pale sand.

"Did you pick these out?" I asked, pointing to the tryptic of photos.

She looked at them, and a small smile formed on her lips. "I did. I thought they seemed appropriate for LA. Beachy."

"But the desk… this doesn't seem like you."

She shook her head and grimaced at the other furniture in the room—the antique credenza, the empty curio cabinet, the dark wood bookcase. "Nope. That was here… It's fine. I don't care where I work, as long as the chair is comfortable."

I looked at her chair, which was an ergonomically designed modern blip in the crusty environment. It looked comfortable.

"Let's get out of here."

"Finn… we need to work," she said.

"And we will. I have an idea for a way you can win my case. I'll show exactly how I used information legally to make seven million dollars," I said, moving toward the door. An idea had just struck me and there was no question it could work. But I needed her to trust me.

She looked skeptical. "You have a way to show me that? What have you been waiting for?"

I shook my head. That wasn't the point. "I will show you. You need to trust me. Do you trust me?" I extended my hand to her. She seemed reluctant, but she took it and warmth spread in my chest. It had only been a few days since she'd toppled onto my lap at the park but I missed touching her.

"I trust you," she said.

"Good."

# CHAPTER SEVENTEEN

FINN

THIRTY MINUTES LATER, we'd parked in a lot on the Santa Monica Pier and were walking toward the carnival games. I looked from the pop-a-shot basketball to the beanbag toss and tried to decide where to begin.

"Finn, this is an amusement park," she said, looking around like she'd never been to the pier.

"True. Have you not been here yet?"

"I just moved here, remember? I've jogged down here but I've never come up from the boardwalk."

That made me even happier. The pier was pure magic as far as I was concerned. All a person had to do was stop and listen to the screams of joy from the rides and grab some junk food and life was transformed. I bought us some tickets and asked which games she liked to play. "This is going to help me win your case?" she asked.

"On my honor, yes. You said you trusted me, right?"

She nodded, rolling her eyes simultaneously. "Don't make me regret it. I like the bowling ball thing and the water gun."

I cast a glance at the bowling ball game and dismissed it immediately, at least for a possibility of winning, but it would make a good lesson.

"Have you ever won at one of these bowling games?"

She shook her head. "I think I demonstrated at lawn bowling that bowling is not my sport."

"Let's watch for a few minutes," I said, dragging her over. The bowling ball was sitting on a pair of metal rollers that extended up to a hump in the middle and sloped upward at the end. The object was the push the ball hard enough to make it over the hump, but not so hard that it rolled up the slope and back down fast enough to return over the hump. The ball had to land in the trough in the middle in order to win a prize. It looked simple.

"This game is near-impossible to win," I told her. "It's part of the design. Pushing it with the right amount of force requires exactitude which can't be gamed. It's either the right amount of force or it isn't."

We watched as ticket after ticket was handed over and countless unsuspecting contestants tried in vain to win. None did. It looked easy but it was secretly hard.

"Finn, I see that you're right, but I'm not seeing how this has anything to do with your case."

I expected as much, but I wasn't finished. "Give me a sec," I said, dragging her over to the water gun booth. "Let's just watch this one," I said. In that game, contestants had to shoot water from a gun into the mouth of a clown. If they aimed well, a balloon on the clown's head filled with water. The first of the six contestants to pop the balloon won a prize.

"What's different about this one?" I asked once the fourth contestant had walked off with a pink teddy bear.

She considered the game with a serious expression that melted my self-restraint. I pulled her to me in an embrace. "Annie, relax. You're not being graded. It's just a question." Under the insistence of my arms, I felt the tension seep from her body. She folded into me and dropped her head to my shoulder. I fought the fierce impulse to run my tongue along the slope of her neck and bite her earlobe.

I felt her exhale and she pulled away. "Okay. Here's what I see. First, someone wins every time in this game."

"True. What else?"

She studied the setup of the six guns. "Not all the guns seem to shoot with equal power."

"Ah, now we get to our stock market analogy. You're exactly right. But there's more." I hung an arm across her shoulder and pointed to the other data I saw in the game. "So many variables. One gun handle may be stiff. One may be warm from the person who used it last. One may have less water pressure. One balloon may be slightly smaller. The calibration of the whole game may advantage one position. And that's to say nothing of the players."

She was nodding. "One may have better aim, one may start shooting slightly earlier, one may have poor eyesight."

"Exactly. All of those are data points. And it might take a while —many years of study—but eventually, the data would start to create patterns. And anyone who studied this game would have access to the same data. Some might even use it to win the big prize," I said, pointing at the elusive jumbo dolphin at the top of the prize board.

"I get it. Your data, your stock market picks. You gave me your data. It's all available to the public. But you studied it and found out how to win. I can work with this, Finn." Annie's face broke into a giant grin. So I grinned back and we stood there smiling at each other like a couple of loons.

Then she leaned in and whispered, conspiratorially, "Let's win the dolphin."

Those four words cracked my heart right open. "Let's do it."

We loitered around the game for another hour or so, dutifully recording the results of each game, which gun was the most successful, which contestants didn't have a fighting chance, what we could learn from watching the balloons inflate. Finally, Annie decided she was ready.

"To win the big prize, I need three games in a row. First, I'm starting at the left because it's been reliably better. Probably the water pressure. I've also noticed a lag time with some of the guns before they start firing. At first, I thought it was random, but now I think there's a pattern. I'll have to hope for the best because I don't know what it is. Something seems to change with each new game. Position four has the most wins overall, so I'm going there next. Then I'll use the second gun at the end. Good water pressure coming from the left, but less strain on the machine from the prior games."

"Don't forget about the other players. Watch them before they start. See what you can learn," I said.

Her strategy sounded good to me. Granted, we hadn't been watching nearly long enough to have good data, but if she was a decent shot, she had a chance at winning even without the data.

"I'm ready," Annie said, handing over three tickets for the games she intended to win.

The bell rang, signaling the start of the first game and Annie aimed for the clown's mouth with the kind of precision that made me wonder if she was a trained marksman. The balloon inflated, then it lagged. Annie eyed the other players and pumped her gun, at which point the stream started inflating her balloon again until it popped. She turned around with a look of glee at her first win.

She raised an eyebrow. "One down..."

Two more easily followed.

At her third win, Annie jumped from her seat and charged into my arms. She hugged me hard and I dipped my lips to the top of her head before she backed away and her familiar air of restraint returned. How long was she going to keep this up? How long could I?

Those would be questions I'd have a chance to debate with myself long into the night. Alone. Or with my sisters, which was arguably not much better.

But I felt like we'd hit a breakthrough. She was starting to believe me. And that was key.

～

WALKING around the pier with Annie and an enormous stuffed dolphin, I felt like I was the one who'd won a prize, just by getting her to stroll with me in the pretty afternoon light.

"Oh, I should warn you, two of my sisters are in town and they really want to come to our next meeting, make sure you're up to snuff to defend me."

"I didn't know you had sisters."

"Five of them. Only two are in town though."

She shrugged. "Sure, bring them. I'm cool with concerned family members."

We grabbed a couple slices of pizza and sat at a table for three, the dolphin holding court over everything. Annie was staring at me, which I ordinarily liked very much. I liked seeing her eyes. But the way she was studying me made me a little uneasy. "Are you still trying to figure out if I'm a criminal or not?" I asked.

She didn't look away. "No. That's not it."

"Then, what?"

"I'm trying to decide if you're arrogant or just confident."

This interested me. "What's the difference, in your experience with clients? Why does that matter?"

"In white-collar law, if a person is arrogant, it tells me that there's a certain disregard for the rules. The law. Confidence is different. Confident people base their thoughts and behavior on knowledge, but they don't assume the rules don't apply to them. If anything, they're more confident because they've figured out how to work within the rules to achieve maximum advantage."

"Again, why does it matter?"

"It's harder to defend someone who's confident."

That surprised me. "Why is that? I'd think it would be harder to defend the person who thinks he's above the law. He makes bigger, bolder choices. Commits crimes. The confident person is working within the law, by your definition."

"An arrogant person, generally speaking, is compensating. He knows he's cheating the system, but he's got the balls to think he'll get away with it because he's stupidly full of himself. That's why he gets caught, and that's why he ends up making a deal, giving up a co-conspirator, anything to save himself and make himself feel like he won. The confident person, on the other hand, believes he's right because he's working within the rules. He'll never concede to doing anything wrong. He'll duel to the death rather than take a plea."

I nodded. She needed to know which camp I fell into. It would make her job easier if she knew what she was up against in trying to defend me. The problem was I was both arrogant and confident and neither one explained how I'd made my stock forecasts.

"You think you can tell if I'm arrogant or confident by looking at me?" I asked.

"No, not at all," she said, her eyes not leaving mine. "That would be silly. I'm basing my assessment on what I've seen of you so far."

"And what's your assessment?"

"Finn, you're smart. Really smart. Which means you think you can get out of the trouble you're in just by being yourself. By saying you saw a way to make a profit by looking at the market a new way." She chewed her lip and appeared distressed at the thought.

"And you don't believe that's a viable strategy?"

She looked sad, her face creasing in all the wrong places. "I just don't know."

I grabbed her hand again because I liked doing it and she had stopped objecting. "Come," I said, walking us away from the food area and toward the rides.

"Where are we going now?"

"Let's ride the roller coaster. Do you like roller coasters?"

She sighed. "Lemme guess. You're going to tell me that the velocity of a roller coaster car has some bearing on the stock market." She was walking faster.

"Um, no. We should ride the roller coaster because it's fun."

She stopped walking and looked at me, as if waiting for an additional explanation. I had none. I just really wanted to hold her hand tightly and see if the *velocity* of the roller coaster might drive her body onto mine.

A slight breeze kicked up and blew a few strands of hair into her face. I resisted the urge to brush them away because I'd already pushed my luck on this field trip and I was trying to be respectful, but fuck it. I reached over and tucked them behind her ear. I saw the heat build in her cheeks. Her eyes grew hazy and I prayed she wouldn't smack me if I moved a couple inches closer and sunk into her gorgeous lips. She met my gaze and blinked heavily, tilting her face to match the angle of mine. I felt her move infinitesimally closer.

Then she withdrew. "Finn, we can't."

I closed my eyes and nodded. Right, if she said so. I had no idea what I was doing anymore. My boundaries had collapsed completely. I briefly debated telling her to hand my case back to Jackson and carrying her to my bed like a caveman. But I couldn't mess with her career like that.

I needed to behave. I could do that. I would. Even if it killed me.

# CHAPTER EIGHTEEN

ANNIE

DARREN MCCUTCHEON'S office was a tidy box of space in a tall building on the California University campus. The first thing I wondered when he ushered me in and offered me a seat on his navy blue couch was whether office size was the kind of thing professors got competitive about. "Apologies for the mess. Can I make you a cup of coffee?" he asked, gesturing to a coffee maker on top of a grey file cabinet.

"Oh, thanks, you're sweet to offer. I'm good." I noticed the comfortable clutter of binders, books, and papers on his desk. Next to the couch where I sat, McCutcheon had a vintage Snoopy lamp on an end table. Two of the walls had bookshelves loaded with volumes of academic journals and textbooks, some of which had McCutcheon's name as a co-author. The color in the room came from the purple and gold of a framed Pau Gasol Lakers jersey that hung on the wall behind his chair.

"You sure? Only takes a sec. I'm going to have one, if that sways you... peer pressure..." He laughed at that and busied himself selecting two cups from behind the coffee maker and opening a sleeve of pods.

"In that case, sure."

"See, this is interesting. I've compiled stats on how often people refuse a cup when offered, but when I say I'm having coffee, eighty-six percent of people acquiesce." Having spent time with Finn, I wasn't at all surprised that Professor McCutcheon had studied it.

"What do you attribute to the fourteen percent refusal rate? Do those people have a stronger sense of boundaries? Not susceptible to peer pressure?" I asked.

He shrugged. "I always assumed those people didn't like coffee."

"Wait, that's it? What about people who don't like caffeine late in the day or people who only drink one cup in the morning or something? Have you analyzed your data with that kind of thing in mind?"

He looked at me strangely, then smiled. "Actually, no. Because I'm an economist, not a psychologist, and the proclivities of coffee drinkers don't interest me as much as other, bigger questions."

It was nice to spend a little time with another economist to put Finn into perspective, and what I concluded after my sample size of two was that I couldn't and shouldn't pigeonhole economists as behaving a certain way. But they were an interesting lot.

"So, you're a basketball fan?" I asked, gesturing to the jersey.

He glanced at it and nodded. "I'm a Lakers fan. I used to watch a ton of NBA games as a kid, and somehow I latched onto the Lakers."

"You from LA?"

"No, eastern part of Washington state. My parents were mortified I was rooting for an out of state team, but they got over it eventually."

A minute later, Professor McCutcheon put the two cups of coffee on a small tray and pulled his desk chair around his desk, so it faced where I sat on the couch. We were close enough that our feet almost touched on the carpet. He handed one cup to me and took a sip from his own. "This keeps me going all day. I was worried at first that having a machine in my office would compel me to drink too much coffee, but it turns out I can self-regulate."

"Probably nice to find that out about yourself."

"I'd suspected, but yes," he said, adjusting the sleeves on his sport coat so they covered the cuffs of the white shirt he had underneath. I studied him while he took another sip of his coffee. Dark-haired with some grey in his goatee, he had small, serious eyes that darted around the room when he spoke. I wondered if that was a byproduct of lecturing to rooms full of students and trying to make eye contact. I put his age at about fifteen years older than Finn, judging by the greying and the series of teaching awards on his shelf. He'd been at it for a while.

"Anyway, thanks for taking the time today. I know you're busy," I said.

"Of course. Anything for Dr. Finley."

The title startled me. I knew Finn had a PhD, but I hadn't heard anyone call him Dr. Finley. "How long have two worked together?"

He stroked his goatee and looked around the room again. "About ten years. He came out of MIT and started here straightaway. Youngest tenured professor at the university, not to mention department chair and shortlisted for the Nobel Prize, as I'm sure you know. Just a matter of time before he wins the thing with this theory he's been working on. It's revolutionary." I struggled to keep my jaw from hitting the floor as Professor McCutcheon rattled off Finn's list of accomplishments, none of which Finn had mentioned.

"He's a smart man," I said.

"Very much so. Smart enough to outsmart every other big player in the stock market."

"You believe he made the trades based on his own knowledge, not insider information."

"Absolutely."

I was still processing the information. "Tell me about this revolutionary theory."

"General economic equilibrium theory? It's used as the basis for analyzing markets, kind of the gold standard in thinking about these things now. That's why I believe he made his trades legally. If anyone is capable of predicting market activity, it's Dr. Finley."

McCutcheon was looking at me patiently, waiting to answer whatever questions I had. The problem was that there was so much I didn't understand, and I wasn't sure what to ask to clear up the confusion.

"Okay, I'm going to be honest with you. I know you and Finn are close. He told me he trusts you more than anyone else in the department, and you're the only one who truly has his back."

"I'd like to think that's true. I mean, I'm sure there are others who think highly of him and would go to bat for him, but are they friends? No. But he and I, yes, we're friends," he said.

"Why? What's unique about your relationship with him? Why are you the only one? From what I can see, he's a gregarious guy. He doesn't seem like he'd have a hard time making friends."

McCutcheon stroked his goatee some more and sipped his coffee. Then he rolled his chair back around to the other side of his desk, came over, and perched on the edge of the desk, facing me. "He doesn't trust anyone in the department. He likes them fine, but that's not the same thing, is it?"

"Why doesn't he trust them?"

McCutcheon spread his hands out in front of him. His eyes went wide and he looked directly at me. "Well, you can see why he'd have good reason not to. Look at what happened."

"But it sounds like he didn't trust people before that."

"True. He's been working on something for a very long time, something that no doubt will win him a Nobel in economics, as I said. And there are unscrupulous characters out there. You never know who it will turn out to be, so it's better to trust no one. You only need one person to bounce ideas off of, and we have each other. It works."

I knew it had been years since McCutcheon had worked at the SEC, but his former job would still carry weight with a judge if he could help explain how Finn's information was obtained legally. "You mentioned you could show how anyone could access the information Finn used to make his trades. Will it stand up to scrutiny with the SEC?"

McCutcheon grabbed a folder from a pile on his desk and opened it to show me its contents. "Yes. This is the information any public citizen could have accessed before the mergers fell through. If you can show the SEC how it could lead a person to do exactly what Finn did, you'll have reasonable doubt. Just between you and me, the SEC has a lot of cases and they're lazy—draw a roadmap, and there's a good chance they'll follow it."

I wanted to hug him. Instead, I smiled. I could see why Finn trusted him—there was no bullshit in his repertoire.

"Okay, just one more question. If Finn doesn't share his research with anyone except you, how would a whistleblower—Dr. Craft—know enough to allow him to file a claim?"

He looked around his office, and I almost felt like he was wishing some students would appear so he could make eye contact and find answers in their returned stares. He tilted his coffee cup to his lips and drained it, then wiped the residue from his upper lip. "Look, I'm an economist. We make assumptions, and we follow the string out on what will happen based on the best starting assumption we can make about what's likely to be true. My assumption is that Finn didn't say anything to a whistleblower or anyone else. That's based on my knowledge of Finn, the kind of academic he is, the kind of person he is, and the kind of brain he has. And what follows from that assumption is that a lot of what's being alleged is made up."

His idea gave me pause. Because what if he was right? I'd need to beef up the case I was making for why Craft would fabricate the whole thing. To do that, I needed him to stop postponing our deposition.

But McCutcheon wasn't done. "On the flip side, however, is

Dr. Craft's assumption. It seems to be a 'where there's smoke, there's fire' assumption. You'll have to lead the SEC away from that logic."

And I was back to square one.

# CHAPTER NINETEEN

ANNIE

"OKAY, how crazy is this that Annie and Tatum both has Ms. Carroll for sex ed?" Becca asked Finn, who had been getting his parking validated and had missed the beginning of the conversation.

"Who?"

Tatum explained. "You probably don't remember this because you were already in grad school, but I had this sex ed teacher who was a loon. She had all these old wives' tales about things it was dangerous to do."

"Relating to sex? Like if you masturbate your penis will fall off?" Finn asked.

"No, weirdo. Tell him, Annie."

He looked at me, uncertain why I was designated as the story-teller. "So she worked at my school... I guess before she moved to Oakland. And she told me I shouldn't jog because it would make my feet flat and I'd never be able to wear high heels, and she felt certain I was running away from demons."

"And she meant actual demons," Tatum said. "She was nuts. But super nice."

"I wish I'd had her," Becca said.

"Trust me, you don't," Tatum told her.

I liked Finn's sisters. And it was clear how much they loved Finn.

Tatum excused herself to go to the restroom and Becca had jumped up, hot on her heels like it had just occurred to her that she needed to pee because her sister suggested it.

As soon as they left the room, Finn rolled his eyes and apologized. "I forget sometimes that to a normal person my family appears certifiable. And maybe they are, and I've just been around them too long."

It made me smile, because of the three of them, Finn seemed the most like an outlier and his sisters reminded me of parts of myself. "They're great. It makes me realize how much I've missed having friends around."

"You mean, since you moved? Don't be so hard on yourself. It's rough trying to meet people in a new city. It can take a while."

It wasn't entirely what I meant but I didn't know if I wanted to correct Finn's assumption and let him know about the part of me that often pushed people—including friends—away for fear of getting burned. Janelle was a case in point. I hadn't fully let her in. It was so much easier to protect my heart and know I'd always be okay when things went south than to open myself up to getting hurt. Why would I do that?

"Yeah, I didn't think I'd mind not having a big friend group here but it turns out, I think I do," I said.

Finn didn't seem put off by my admission. He ruffled his hair and ruined it, as seemed to be his habit, and smiled at me. I liked it when he smiled. "Do you miss your friends in the Bay Area?"

"A lot." My friends were an odd assortment of people I'd sort of collected over the years. I didn't think he'd be all that interested in hearing about them. He surprised me, however, and asked.

"Tell me one story. Something you all did together that will give me a sense of the dynamic."

I had to think about it because I wanted it to be a better example than the four of us ambling into a bar in Oakland and ending up laughing all night long. I wanted to tell him about an adventure, and I was starting to fret because nothing came to mind.

"Annie..."

"Yes?"

"This isn't supposed to be stressful. I'm sorry I phrased it that way. Just tell me the last thing you did with your friends before you moved here."

I exhaled a breath I hadn't realized I was holding. "Okay, I can do that. We were all at my friend Kell's house. She bought a cool California craftsman-style place up in the hills above Oakland. And we had a cheese party." I didn't mean to leave it at that, but my phone buzzed, and I was expecting to hear from a judge, so I checked it.

"What's a cheese party? Is that a euphemism for something else?" he asked.

"God, I hope not. No, this was actually a party that revolved around eating cheese. We each brought different types of cheeses and we had a tasting."

"Was it a blind tasting? Like with wine, where you had to discuss its overtones and guess which one was the vintage one?"

"No, but it sounds like you've been to some interesting wine tasting events."

"I've been to exactly one, and I'll tell you about it after you tell me about the cheese party," he said.

"We ate a ton of cheese, we drank wine, and we laughed our heads off. Two of my friends are twin sisters. We all joined an amateur co-ed rowing league after college. It was ridiculous. Crazy hard workouts and most of the people in it were former college rowers. It was supposed to be amateur, but they took it super seriously. And we decided we were going to out-train them and show them up when it finally came time to get in the boats."

Finn leaned on the arm of the couch with his arms folded. "And did you?"

"I wouldn't say we showed them up. We lost most of our races, but they took us seriously after that. So that's Kell and Taylor. They both work in tech. And my other good friend, Sofia, is a police detective. She's legitimately badass."

"How'd you meet her? She arrest you?" he asked with a smirk.

"No, we were in a book club, which we hated. But we liked each other so she convinced me to take a ceramics class, which we sort of liked. Then we decided we didn't need a club or a class as a reason to hang out."

"Sounds like a good group," he said. Something about his expression seemed wistful, and it occurred to me he hadn't mentioned friends who weren't colleagues. Maybe his friendships were all mainly work relationships. Maybe he was just discerning.

Before I could ask him anything about his friends, Becca and Tatum came back holding hands, looking like they'd hatched a plan. "You two look evil. What's up?" Finn asked.

"We like her," Becca said, gesturing to me as though I wasn't standing in front of them.

Finn kept his arms folded and glared at him. "You two promised to behave."

"We're behaving," Tatum said. "But this is important." She took a step closer and focused as she spoke directly to me. I noticed her eyes were a pale shade of Finn's green, but they didn't lack for intensity. "Finn is a good guy, but he sometimes loses the big picture for the details. You may have noticed he only cares about research and data." Now she was talking about Finn like he wasn't there, and I wanted to disagree because I saw more in him than the portrait she was painting.

I suppressed a smile because I could tell she was serious. "I'm aware of his love for data," I said.

"Yes, well, you may have also noticed that he's damned stubborn, and he doesn't care if he does his work at an ivory tower academic institution or in a prison library," she continued.

"But we care. We care a lot," Becca said. "We need him to be exonerated."

"Not *need*, like we want him to do some sort of service for us. We need it because he doesn't belong in jail if he's innocent, even if he's too stubborn to understand that."

"It's not a question of being stubborn," Finn said. "There's an order to things, and I need to finish the work. It's an important economic theory and I don't want to risk potential abuse of the data."

Becca swatted him across the shoulder. "Seriously, Finn, if you say the word *data* again, I'm going to pirate it myself from you and put it on the internet."

"What we want to know…" Tatum said, her voice quiet and her eyes focused on mine. She reminded me a lot of Finn. "…is how you're going to defend him so he wins. No offense, but we wanted to make sure you were smart enough to do the job, and we think you're smart and nice. But what's the defense, specifically?"

Finn folded his arms across his chest and continued to glare at her, but he didn't speak.

I gestured for them to sit, and they both took seats on the couch. Finn moved to the arm of one of my chairs, and I stood. "This is the basic defense. I need to convince the judge that the information Finn relied on was publicly known. In other words, it was information any person could use to make the exact trades he made. It's tricky because he previously consulted for the companies, even if it had nothing to do with mergers, and he's the only one who timed his trades to make that kind of money. So it looks very suspicious. But the hope is that I get a motion to dismiss the case based on lack of evidence, as long as the whistleblower doesn't have something up his sleeve that he hasn't given us so far. Right now, all he seems to have is a belief that Finn traded on insider information, based on the timing, not proof."

"But there's no guarantee you'll win. It sounds like 'he said/she said,'" Tatum said, looking dissatisfied that my strategy wasn't foolproof.

"It kind of is," I admitted. "But that works to our advantage because the whistleblower hasn't provided evidence for his claim."

"Because he's a weasel?" Becca said. "I met that guy. He tried to hit on me when I came to visit you a couple years ago."

"He did?" Finn seemed surprised by the information.

"Sure did. I didn't tell you?"

Finn shook his head. "No, and that's especially troubling because he was married at the time."

Becca lit up. "Ooh, can we use that? I can be a character witness."

"This isn't one of your crime shows, Becs," Tatum said. "Him hitting on you has nothing to do with him ratting out Finn."

"It might. Maybe he felt jilted by me and is taking it out now on Finn. We can use that!" she said.

Finn stood in front of her as if to make her disappear and dug his fingers into his temples. "There's no *we* here. You two are not involved in this. I think it's time for you to go."

As much as I liked them personally, I could see that they were working Finn's last nerve. But they came with him because they had an agenda.

Tatum finally spoke. "Here's the deal. Finn's been a brother and a father to all of us, and we can never repay him for that. And maybe this sounds like we're asking for one more thing, but…"

"He can't go to jail. You have to keep him out of jail," Becca said.

"Pay the fines or give up the money or do whatever you need to do, Finn, but please…" She looked at me, and I noticed her eyes had the same sparkle as Finn's but in a hazel color. "I know he doesn't care if he goes to jail or not, but we care. He's too stubborn to ask you to do whatever you can to keep him out of jail, but I'm not. Please… do everything you can."

"You guys—" Finn started to speak, but Becca cut him off.

"No! Stop it. We know the money you've sent us over the years was money you made in the stock market, and we love you for that. But we're all good. Mom's good, thanks to you. We all have jobs. We're fine. So whatever you're doing—and I don't care if it was illegal or you trying to be smarter than everyone else— just stop it. Tell them what they want to know or pay the fines— whatever. And you—" She pointed at me, "please… keep him out of jail."

Finn himself didn't care where he worked, as long as he could keep compiling data. His sisters knew that. I pictured his brilliant mind sitting in a prison library, trying to cover new ground in economics, in between shifts sorting laundry. I didn't like the image of that either.

I nodded at her and looked at Finn. "You heard them."

# CHAPTER TWENTY

ANNIE

TWO GOOD THINGS and one bad thing happened at the end of the week. First, Jackson, unbidden, gave me a trove of research on whistleblower cases and the arguments that had been made in the past about the bias of whistleblowers when they stand to make money by turning someone in.

He'd been so fascinated by Finn's history lesson that he'd stayed late one night and compiled data on qui tam cases around the world and the arguments against allowing them. To say I was grateful was an understatement. "Jackson, I don't know what to say. I'm... I appreciate this so much."

"Don't get your award ribbons out. I did it partly for my own edification. I'll need to know this for future cases unless you plan to take all the qui tams from now on."

"I do not."

"Okay, then. You keep me posted, and I'll do the same."

"Absolutely. Thanks, Jackson. Now please go home so your kids can see you before they go to sleep."

He nodded. "Going now. See you tomorrow."

Then, because the universe doesn't dole out good without bad, I was called into Tom Chavez's office because apparently Janelle, my new work bestie, had ratted me out to Tom after I'd told her about Finn. It was the only explanation. "Annie, are you romantically involved with your client?" Tom asked, leaving no room to interpret the question for any possible alternate meaning.

I thought back to the frozen girl talk with Janelle and tried to remember the extent of what I'd confided.

Did it matter? It was a mistake.

Then she'd used it to her advantage. Given what she'd told me about her father and the pressure to make partner, I could only figure she thought a partner desk might open up if she told Tom I was involved with a client and he fired me. I was stupid to trust her, but it was too late to change it now. I readied myself for whatever Tom had to say.

"Attorney-client romantic relations… that's a firm line, legally, that you can't cross," he said, shrugging as though he didn't understand it himself.

But I understood. This was a warning, if not an edict.

"Tom, I know. And I haven't. I won't. It was the one evening before I knew he was my client. And I mentioned to you that we'd met. Nothing's happened since." Not exactly nothing, I reminded myself, but I was working hard at resisting him. That had to count for something.

"Yes you did. I recall," Tom said.

"But I've drawn a firm boundary line, and it's a purely professional relationship now. I'd never do anything to jeopardize my job or the client's case."

"Annie, relax. I'm just telling you what I think you already know. This is your first case at the firm and I'd hate for you to get off on the wrong foot. Clients make assumptions sometimes and you have to be firm."

"I know, and like I said, I'm one hundred percent professional."

"Okay, great. Keep me posted on how it goes with the deposition."

He then turned away from me and went back to a game of Solitaire on his computer, and I took that as my cue to leave, feeling like I'd been called into the principal's office for making out behind the bleachers. And I'd done everything in my power *not* to make out. What good was getting reprimanded without having any of the fun? I might as well have fucked Finn on the Ferris wheel if I was going to get detention for it.

I was busy shrugging off that disappointment when the second good thing happened: my cell phone rang, and according to the caller ID, it was Nikki.

"Hey!" I was dying to hear about the honeymoon. Two weeks on an island was unthinkable at the moment and I needed to live vicariously.

"Hi friend! How are you?" she said.

"I'm good. Wait, what day is it?" I looked at my calendar and realized it hadn't been yet two weeks since the wedding. "Did you come back early? Is everything okay?" I asked, concerned.

"Oh, it's amazing. I'm still in Anguilla. This place… I can't even do it justice by describing it."

"Try. Please."

"Oh, I just wish you could see it. I wanted to FaceTime you, but I barely have a Wi-Fi connection as it is and the call wouldn't go through."

"Nik, you're an artist. Use your artistic eye. Adjectives. Please. Now."

She laughed and the reception crackled. She sounded far away. "The sand is white, it's soft beneath my feet like powder, and the water is this color blue I've never seen before. It's a pale, clear aqua, and it goes on for miles and there's nothing else here. I'm taking so many pictures."

"It sounds incredible," I said, realizing how long it had been since I'd taken a beach vacation. "I'm so glad you called, but shouldn't you be naked in a cabana with your new husband? And please don't tell me you're naked in a cabana with him right now."

"I'm not. He's at the gym."

"The gym? You're supposed to be having so much sex you can't lift your limbs. Do I need to coach you on how to have a honeymoon?"

"No, we're good. Plenty of sex. In all kinds of gorgeous locations. But it's just a thing—Chris needs to get his gym time in."

"Well, I'm not complaining. I'm glad it gave you a minute to call—" I was considering asking her about Finn and thinking about how to broach the subject when Nikki yelped.

"Okay, we have to talk! I want to kill Chris even though I love him to death because somehow he thought it was okay to wait until a week after the wedding to mention that you hooked up with Finn! How did I not know this?!"

Despite the wonky reception, the fact that Nikki was shouting was abundantly clear. "Relax, of course I'll tell you everything."

"You'd better. Why didn't you tell me that night?"

"Are you kidding? It was your wedding. You had a billion other guests to spend time with, and the last thing I was going to do was bend your ear about some guy I'd never see again. I restrained myself."

"Never do that. Do you hear me? Never again."

"I hear you. Okay, where do I begin?" I recounted our time together at the wedding, his bizarre departure, and the fact that he was now my client. "Tell me how you know him? He said you went to grad school together, but he's an economist, so I don't understand that part," I said.

"What, didn't I mention I have a PhD in economics? I thought you were my friend. Were you not listening?" I loved that Nikki could dish out sarcasm as well as I could, and I had no trouble distinguishing it.

"Haha. How'd you meet? Give me the Cliff's Notes version."

"He was finishing his PhD, I was doing my communications degree, and we ended up both taking a cartooning class."

"What? What does that have to do with communications or economics?"

"Nothing at all. I was allowed to take one class outside of my department and so was he. We both happened to pick cartooning, and we were the only ones in the room who weren't graphic design majors and neither of us had any idea how to draw an oval. It was just a crazy serendipitous thing."

There was that word, *serendipitous*. Finn had said it in our first meeting with Tom Chavez and Jackson. I wondered if they'd both learned that word in their cartooning class.

"Okay, so you were bad artists. That was the big bond that's lasted eight years?" I asked.

"Um, yeah. You should have seen these design students. Super Type A, had to get the best grades, bugged the teacher if they didn't get one hundred percent on everything, and we were just there to goof around and draw comic strips about aliens." I tried to picture this side of Finn but couldn't. I couldn't imagine him doing anything that didn't have a mission attached to it. He seemed to have a firmly pointed compass at all times.

"And you've been friends ever since? How come you never mentioned him to me?" I asked.

She didn't answer right away, and for a moment, I wondered if we'd been disconnected. Then she sighed. "I dunno. You were in San Francisco and I was in LA. I'm sure I didn't mention lots of my friends."

"Okay, but they're not all hot economists. I have questions," I said. "Lots of questions. First of all, as someone who's known Finn a while, is there any part of you that could see him trying to get away with breaking the law?"

She didn't hesitate. "No. He's not like normal people who might get seduced by the idea of making a quick buck by trading on information that no one else has. His whole belief system is based on equality of information. He wants everyone to know what he knows. That's why he's always publishing stuff. It doesn't make sense that he'd go off and do something based on a trick or a cheat. That's not him, and I say this after knowing him for eight years. If he's telling you he didn't do it, he didn't do it."

"Well, he'd be the first. Every client I've ever had who was accused of insider trading was guilty of insider trading. This is my job; it's what I do. So when I hear hoofbeats, I don't think zebras."

"I know. You're used to scumbags who try to cheat the system. And I have endless admiration for you for giving them their legal due. But Finn isn't one of those guys. Can't you tell?"

That was the problem. I was so charmed by him that I'd stopped trusting my judgment. "I don't trust myself because I like him."

"You like him! Okay, let's talk about that."

"I like him a lot. And honestly, it's kind of freaking me out."

"Why? He's a badass genius. And he's sweet. And hot, if I do say so myself."

"Exactly. That's a few too many good qualities in one person. I'm not used to that."

Nikki laughed. It was a snort laugh which made her laugh even harder. I waited while she tried to control herself, doing my best not to be paranoid that she was laughing at me. "Oh, I'm sorry. That just sounded funny to me. You're right; you're not used to that, but you so deserve it."

I still didn't understand the humor. "Thank you, but why are you finding that so funny?"

"Because… it's you. You always go for guys who are so far beneath you."

"You're saying that like I do it intentionally. I just haven't met a lot of great guys of late."

I could hear her exasperated sigh. "Of late? Oh, come on. You've never dated guys who were worthy of you. You're always in control. Of *course* you do it intentionally."

"It's not like I only date people when I know the relationship will fail," I said.

*I don't do that. Do I?*

"I'm sure you're not doing it consciously. I just think you pick these guys who are kind of meh so you won't feel like it's any great loss if it doesn't work out."

I hoped she wasn't right about that. If she was, it meant I was unintentionally—and sort of intentionally—sabotaging every relationship I'd ever had. And guess what? They'd all ended.

"Oh crap, that's Chris. He's back. I think I need to run. Not because he's a demanding jerk who won't let his girlfriend talk on the phone—"

"You're his wife, if I'm not mistaken. And it's your honeymoon. I'll talk to you when you get back."

"Oh shit, you're right. I'm someone's wife. I've gotta go. Okay, love you. See you in a week."

And she was gone. I was left with a whole bucketful of thoughts, most of which I'd been ignoring my entire life.

# CHAPTER TWENTY-ONE

ANNIE

I RUSHED BACK to the office after a quick errand to pick up prescription computer glasses that had ended up taking almost two hours. Finn had been right, of course. I needed them, and the optometrist had said she was shocked I could see the screen at all, given how strained my eyes were.

With the pile of work waiting for me, it would have been easier to save my confrontation with Janelle for another day.

Would have, should have.

Janelle was eating a salad at her desk, and judging by the smell emanating from her office, it involved tuna. I didn't knock, so she didn't notice me standing there for a few seconds. In that time, I steeled myself for confrontation.

"Oh, hey," she said between bites. "How's it going?"

I shook my head at her. There would be no pleasantries. "No, we're not doing that." I stepped into her office and lingered in front of her desk, which gave me a height advantage over her seated position. I hope it would intimidate. "Just be honest. Were you working me from the beginning, playing the friendship game so you could find a weakness to exploit?"

"What's that supposed to mean?" she asked. Her forehead creased and she seemed confused.

"It means I can play dirty too, if that's what we're doing," I said.

"Friend, you're not making sense. Is everything okay?" She tried to play it off with a dismissive wave of her hand and another bite of salad.

"No, it's not okay. I thought we had an understanding. I would never have betrayed your confidence and told Tom about your dad helping you. I can't believe you told him about Finn."

I'd known women like Janelle in law school—women who sabotaged other women in order to get ahead. They pretended they were doing it out of moral obligation, but the truth was self-preservation. "Honey, I didn't."

"Tom just confronted me. He seemed to know an awful lot."

I hated her annoyingly-clean office. Where was the blood, sweat, and tears of doing her job without an assist from her dad? I so badly wanted to say something to Tom, but I couldn't stoop to her level.

"Annie, back up a minute. I swear I said nothing. I wouldn't do that to you, even though we're new at this." She gestured between us. "I don't have a lot of work friends either, which is why I'd never go low like that. I want to be your friend."

I wanted to believe her, but it didn't make sense. No one else knew about Finn except Finn and he'd never say anything to Tom. Right? But what if he did? I was losing it. I couldn't go around accusing everyone of betraying me.

"You promise? Really?" I asked, feeling suddenly drained. I loved arguing in court but I hated confrontations with people I liked.

"I do. I promise." She looked sympathetic. "So what happened? Tom figured out you're crushing on Finn?"

I flopped on her couch and grabbed at my temples. "I don't know what he figured out or how he did it."

"Could be the big bunch of flowers that showed up in Reception. Maybe he suspected," she said before taking another bite of salad.

I must have been looking at her blankly because she finished chewing and explained without me having to ask. "Have you not seen them?"

I shook my head. "I took the back stairs and Tom called me right in. Oh God, I'm such an asshole." I felt terrible for wrongly accusing her. "I'm sorry, Janelle. I'm all over the place. And Finn, he's got me feeling things—big things—and I'm not used to that and I don't want to lose my job."

"You won't. At least not over this. So… friends?" she asked.

"Of course. Yes, please. I'm really sorry, Janelle."

"Hey, now we're really friends. Now that you've gone irrational on me. And I've seen you in your underwear."

"I guess it's official," I said. It took some effort to drag my sorry self up from her couch, but I did it, giving her a little wave before slinking away.

I went back to Reception and found a giant arrangement of sunflowers on the credenza and a basket of bar snacks. There were tiny wrapped cheeses and olives. There was even a bunch of asparagus spears, limes, and the ingredients to make a martini. An edible memory of our night at the wedding.

And there was a card sitting open next to it. It read, "I find you as brilliant as you are beautiful. Thank you for riding the roller coaster with me. Love, Finn."

My heart fluttered at his words. It was adorable. Except that it was a career killer. The flowers and snacks could have passed as a nice thank you gift from a client. But the card left nothing to the imagination. What if Tom actually read it?

I didn't even have words for how annoyed I was at Finn and before I could call and explain attorney-client boundaries in a very loud voice, I needed to calm myself and choose the best words to get my point across.

I stayed at work, I risked verbally annihilating the next person to cross my path, so I packed up my laptop and headed for the beach. An hour staring at placid blue would calm the zoo in my brain and I needed a break. I'd never taken a personal day in eight years, but I could rationalize a personal two hours.

I didn't bother to say goodbye to anyone on my way out the door and I didn't obey the speed limit on my drive due west. But when I saw the rippling blue water from Pacific Coast Highway, I knew I'd made the right call. I needed to be alone and I needed to remind myself of my priorities. I was good at work and I couldn't let Finn get in the way of that.

I would deal with him first thing in the morning.

# CHAPTER TWENTY-TWO

FINN

"ANNIE, stop. Just... listen to me for a minute. I didn't send you flowers. Or bar snacks. I kind of wish I had because they got you to call me all hot and bothered and for once we're not talking about my case, but I'm afraid I'm as much in the dark as you are."

The bleating ring of my cell phone had pulled me away from reading a news article about the efficiency of bees and the honeycomb hexagons they build. I'd set the ring tone to alert me to calls from Annie but the second I heard her voice, I could tell she wasn't calling to ask me to breakfast.

"Finn. Seriously. Do you expect me to believe someone else sent me those things and signed your name on the card? Why would someone do that?"

It took me a minute to digest the information she was hurling at me and another minute to get her to slow down enough to tell me exactly what had shown up at her office and what the card had said.

Then I worked at calming her down and swearing on everything good and holy that someone did in fact send her those items and sign my name.

"That's crazy, Finn. Who would do that?"

Shaking my head, I noticed that my house was awfully quiet for nine in the morning with two meddling sisters. "I think I have an idea," I told her. "I'll call you in a minute, okay?"

I SHOULD HAVE KNOWN something was up when so far, both sisters had stayed out of my room. I'd heard the surge of shower water earlier and knew at least one of them was awake, but it was still odd that no one had barged in yet. Maybe they knew something I didn't.

Before I'd finished my coffee, both Becca and Tatum burst through the door.

"Morning, sunshine," Becca said.

"Do you have any boundaries at all?" I asked.

"Ew, why? Do you sleep naked or something?" Becca asked.

"No, because it's the normal thing to do when you enter a room, and the door's closed," I said.

Becca waved her hand like she thought I was ridiculous. "We're family. Family doesn't knock."

"I would've knocked," Tatum said quietly. She knew how to pick her battles with Becca. She always had. With five siblings, Tatum had to make herself heard but she also knew when to raise her voice and when to let her older sisters make the mistakes so she didn't have to.

"Oh my God, you have coffee in here? No wonder you haven't come out of your room yet," Tatum said, charging over to the machine and popping in a pod in to make herself a cup.

"You just made it in the kitchen," Becca said, shaking her head. "And you were tsk-tsking me for being rude."

"I want to know what it tastes like to live like royalty," Tatum said, holding her pinky out when she lifted the cup.

"I'd hardly say shoving a coffee machine on a table connotes living like royalty. Besides, aren't you here to fret over me and mother me? That seems more like a 'cook breakfast in the kitchen' situation, not a 'come in my room and bug me' situation," I told her, surveying my room and trying to see it through her eyes.

"Well, I live in a 'single person's expensive-ass apartment' situation, so I'm coming for the good coffee. That's what I came here to experience," Tatum said.

"Fair enough," I said.

It was a large bedroom by anyone's standards, but I'd seen Tatum's place and it was a crime how much she paid for what was basically a closet with a shower and a hotplate. By comparison, my room was a palace.

"Tate's right. That's why we're here. To experience new things. I am most definitely not here because I'm fretting about you or because I'm mothering you. In other words, no cooking," Becca said.

"If you're hungry, Finn, I made a fruit salad. It's in the kitchen," Tatum said.

Becca rolled her eyes. "Of course you did. Right after you ran fifteen miles or something before dawn, right?"

"I ran five. And damn, this neighborhood is hilly, Finn. Do you run these hills?"

"No. I use the treadmill. You're welcome to it."

"Oh please, you two health nuts are making me wanna drown myself in sausage fat," Becca said, swiping her filled coffee cup, dumping a load of nut milk into it from the mini fridge, and slouching in one of the leather chairs.

Becca was the wild child, and we all knew it, almost from the time she was born. She was also our father's favorite, and even though she was only fourteen when he died, it affected her in a way that changed her forever. She went overboard, testing boundaries, pushing limits, and generally driving our mom to the point of surrender.

She'd calmed a little bit as she'd grown older, but the wild streak that drove her had become so much a part of her personality that madness seemed to define her, despite her occasional attempts to temper it.

"Okay, as much as I love the wakeup joy you've brought to my room, I need to have a word with you both," I said, standing up from my chair so I could lecture them like the children they were.

Becca waved her hand at Tatum. "He's a bore. I say we discourage his words."

Tatum smiled, which was as close to laughing at her sister as was possible.

Undeterred, I leveled them with my wrath. "Flowers? Did you actually send flowers to my lawyer with a card saying I'm dying to get her undressed?"

"It didn't say that," Becca said.

"Aha! So you did," I said. Becca had the good sense to look contrite and Tatum just seemed embarrassed.

"Tater, seriously? You let her talk you into this?"

"It was her idea," Becca said, still slouching in the chair like she expected someone to come give her a pedicure.

Tatum shrugged. "We really like her and we think she's good for you."

I couldn't believe them. "I don't remember asking you to weigh in on my love life."

"We saved you the trouble," Becca said, sipping her coffee. "You're terrible at this." She waved her hand at me like the totality of me was a failure.

"What? What am I terrible at?" I asked. No one spent as much time telling me all the things wrong with me as my sisters. I should've been used to it, but I always thought they'd eventually concede that I was pretty good.

"Dating, relationships, wooing, courting, whatever you want to call it. You suck, Finn. You don't date. Ever. Why is that?" She didn't wait for me to finish. "It's because you're either lazy or you think you're too good for all the women out there, and I don't think you're that good, so you must be lazy. Focused on your work all the time. Just... stop it. Take Annie to dinner, romance her a little, get her to fall in love with you. We just gave you a little head start with the flowers."

"You shouldn't have done that. Her boss saw the card, apparently," I said.

Becca waved that off as inconsequential. "So what? You'd already kissed her before you were her client. You're in the clear. We did some research."

Oh, this was too much. "You did research? What kind of research?"

Tatum walked closer to me, and I could see a page with the diagrams from an econometric model I'd given my students as an assignment last semester. I'd put the recycled stack of pages in my printer to save a tree, and Tatum had used the printer with her laptop to churn out whatever was on the other side of the page. She held it up in front of me. I saw a lot of text, but what jumped out at me were the words: "client-lawyer relationship" and "lover."

Becca started talking before I could read the page and ascertain its meaning. "It turns out it's not against the law for a lawyer to sleep with a client if there was a consensual sexual relationship before they started working together."

"Wait, this is what you're doing when I'm not babysitting you?" I was processing multiple thoughts, and they were colliding in my brain, fighting for prominence. Was this a good thing? Did I have a consensual sexual relationship with Annie based on our time together at the wedding? Did I want that to mean we could have a consensual sexual relationship now? Did it matter if she wanted to have a strict attorney-client relationship? Why were my sisters involved?

It was a new feeling, this warring of thoughts. I was accustomed to sorting my thought agenda in order of importance of the topics for consideration. Suddenly, the idea of a consensual sexual relationship with Annie had all the synapses staging a mutiny and threatening to crash the system.

"We researched it because we wanted you to know you have options. You have relationship options," Tatum said.

"No, no, no. I hardly think having sex with my lawyer is a relationship option. She's very serious about professional boundaries. You two have gone round the bend and entered Crazyland. She's going to fight to get me the best outcome because she's a good lawyer, and that's what I've hired her to do." I had to make my sisters accept a world where reason ruled, not emotion.

I was surprised Tatum had gone along with this. The research had nutty Becca written all over it, but Tatum surely had to see my side. I needed her to agree with me. Two against one in my family never boded well for the one, especially when it was me.

Becca laughed. "You're the one who's in Crazyland if you think she won't be more invested if she loves you." I couldn't help flinching at the word.

"Stop saying that," I said.

"Stop what?" Becca asked.

"Stop saying that if she loves me she'll do a better job. That's not what it's about."

"Okay, forget about the case." Becca looked at me like I was as dumb as a rock. "Your life will be better if she loves you. How about that? Focus on that. You love her, she loves you—make that happen." Becca twirled out of the room in her usual style.

Tatum smiled at me, but she left the piece of paper on the coffee table in my room before she followed Becca out the door. "I'll bring you the fruit. You read that." Then she closed the door behind her, and I was left with the pleasant silence of my room. I was glad I didn't live with a house full of sisters anymore, much as I loved them.

Once they left, I glanced over the printout and saw that Tatum was right. Not that it mattered if Annie was set on maintaining a strictly professional relationship, but according to the rule of law, there was leeway.

It was a beautiful word, *leeway*.

True, I wanted Annie focused on winning my case, but I also wanted her in ways that went far beyond legal advice. If there was the tiniest chance that she wanted that too, I had to explore the leeway.

# CHAPTER TWENTY-THREE

ANNIE

FRIDAY HAD NOT BEEN GOING WELL. The problem was that I'd spilled my smoothie all over the counter in the morning before I left for work, which made me late. Everything else was a problem after that, and by the time Finn came to my office, I had a splitting headache and the mood of a cranky goat.

I'd skipped lunch so my blood sugar had plummeted and Finn was two hours late. He'd called, but still.

When he finally showed up, he seemed tentative, standing in the doorway of my office.

"Come in. It's not your fault I'm having a crappy day. Well, not entirely your fault," I muttered.

"My sisters are sorry. And I've sent them packing. They're both on their way home as we speak."

"It was a sweet gesture. You didn't have to send them home."

"Well, to be fair, they were planning on leaving today anyway. I just drove them to the airport. And I honestly didn't mind the yelling this morning. I like talking to you."

I couldn't believe him. "It's nice that you can categorize yelling as pleasant conversation."

"And because I'm an optimist, I'd say your day still has promise."

"Ugh, no. When it starts bad, it stays that way. It's like eating cookies for breakfast."

"How, exactly?"

"It sets your day off on the wrong foot and all day long you crave sugar." I felt strongly about this. I may not be an economist, but I was the progenitor of many theories. Most of them had only been proven by me and my experiences, which I knew was too small of a sample size to be significant. Nonetheless, I held fast to my ideas.

Finn was skeptical, as I expected he might be. "There are too many variables that you can't control for that idea to work," he said. He'd produced a tub of raw almonds from his bag and offered me some.

"No thanks," I said, automatically. I usually turned down food people offered me, not because I wasn't hungry, but because it was easier. It saved me from having to assess whether I liked the kind of food proffered, whether it might get stuck in my teeth or cause some other unforeseen situation. Easier to decline.

"Would there ever be a situation when you'd say yes to my snacks?" He was smirking and, once again, I had no way of knowing if he was truly talking about snacks or something else.

I tried to play it off. "I can't say for sure. I might say yes, but it would depend on whether your snack seemed appealing." I decided not to explain my general snacking policy. There was already too much to discuss relating to the theory of good days and bad days. "And I know, Finn. I know my whole thing about starting a day off wrong isn't steeped in the scientific method, but I still believe it."

"Okay."

"Okay? You're just going to let me off the hook? You don't want to argue with me about it?"

"No, I do. But based on your theory, your day hasn't been going so well, and I don't want to make it worse, so I'm choosing not to argue."

His expression betrayed nothing, but I was still suspicious. "You're messing with me, aren't you? You're trying to make my day better so you can claim that my theory holds no merit."

"How dare you accuse me of trying to make your day better simply to suit my scientific beliefs?"

Now he was smiling, and that was enough to make my day better, so my theory was going to hell. Somehow, he had the power to turn everything I thought I knew about myself upside down. I loved it, which made it harder to keep convincing myself I could avoid loving him.

*Boundaries…*

He offered his tub of almonds once more, as though now that he'd swayed me from one of my principles, I'd give them all up.

"No. Thank you. Let's get back to the case."

"I don't want to talk about the case, at least not in here," Finn said, gesturing to the walls of my office.

"What's wrong with in here?" I looked around the room to see what he might find objectionable. I'd added a couple of knick-knacks to my desk in an effort to make it feel a little homier. A stack of coasters from a San Francisco bar now sat on the corner of my desk next to a paperweight that the twins had given me as a gift after I ran the San Francisco marathon. I didn't have any papers in danger of blowing away, but the round glass half-orb brought back good memories.

Finn didn't seem to have issues with my desk. He started pacing the room like a caged animal. With his long legs, it only took a few strides before he was standing right in front of me, dangerously close.

I'd been carefully avoiding close proximity for days, partly because I felt heat creep up the back of my neck every time I got hear him. My stomach nearly exploded with a butterfly stampede when he accidentally grazed my skin. For my sanity and my professional ethic, I needed distance.

"I mean, I can't sit anymore. I'm starving, and I don't want almonds. Can I take you to dinner? I'd like to take you to dinner," Finn said. He sat back down on the couch and stretched his legs out in front of him, crossing his ankles. It baffled me how he could always look so at ease and comfortable even though every discussion we had included the possibility of him spending time in prison.

"I don't think so. That wouldn't be a good idea," I said, robotically.

"Why, do you not eat? Or are you still thinking you can't trust me around your bacon? I promise I won't fondle it unless invited to do so."

"Finn…"

"What?"

"We can't do this."

"Do what? Have dinner? I call bullshit. I know lawyers have big expense accounts for wining and dining clients. Why haven't we wined and dined?" he asked.

"Finn, you know why."

"I don't. What, because you turn into a gremlin if you eat after dark?"

"No, because of this." I gestured from him to me and back to him with my hands. He observed my movements and said nothing. Finally, I settled my arms back on the desk. "Why do you do that?" I asked.

"Do what?"

"Just… observe me like I'm an oddity."

"You're projecting. I'm observing you because I find you engaging and beautiful to watch. And I want to give you the respect you deserve and let you finish your thoughts—or gestures—before I interrupt."

*Gah… if he's going to keep saying things like that…*

I shook my head. "Seriously, Finn, you're making it really hard for me." I knew I sounded like a whiny five-year-old but I was exasperated with him. "You can't be this good and nice all the time and expect me to feel nothing and go about my normal business being your lawyer. Could you just be an asshole and stop being so perfect so I can do my job?"

He held up a finger. "Not perfect. Hardly perfect... But I'll accept nice. And I can be nice to you all the time because you're nice to me."

"You're paying me to be nice to you."

He stood up and shook his head. Then he walked around the desk to where I was sitting and faced me. I turned slightly away and busied myself extracting a red and white mint from the jar on my desk and unwrapping it. I offered him the jar.

"No thank you. And quit avoiding the conversation. I'm not paying you to be nice to me. I'm paying you to use your brain and mount the best possible defense. And in order to do that, I think we need to get out of this office and act like humans. I think that half the reason you have a headache is because you've got your hair up in that tight clip."

He pointed at the offending clip with one finger. He was probably right, so I reached up and loosened it a little.

"It might be part of it."

"Have dinner with me. You need to get to know me better. If you want to understand me, you need to know me. I'm not that complicated, but maybe I'm different from what you're used to."

"You're right. I don't understand you," I said.

"So let's fix it. Come to dinner, and we'll talk. Not about work. We can talk about anything you want, and you'll see that I'm exactly what I purport to be," he said, watching me wrestle with indecision. True, I needed to eat, but someone had to mind the attorney-client boundaries. Tom wasn't going to warn me twice.

"You promise this isn't some kind of ploy to get me to eat your snacks?" I asked. He raised an eyebrow, but before he could throw the innuendo back at me, I pointed a finger at him. "Don't say it."

"Look, I know this is hard for you. I'm asking you to break out of your comfort zone. I get that. But you're the one in control here, and if at any time you're not having an excellent time or you feel like you're compromising your boundaries, you can leave. I will put it in writing, and you can carry it in your purse."

I wanted to do the smart thing.

*I'd like to state that for the record, Your Honor. I wanted to resist him.*

But fuck, if he wasn't completely irresistible.

"I don't need you to put it in writing. But I... appreciate that you respect that this is... at the very least, unusual for me in a work setting. If we're going to have dinner, it will be an attorney-client dinner. You will have to behave," I said.

"Meaning?"

"Meaning, no saying funny or cute things, no suggesting things about my bacon or any other food groups, no looking hot—you must do your best to appear haggard and unkempt."

"Fine. I will wear a bag over my head if you'll agree to have dinner with me."

"You don't have to go that far." I tried to look anywhere in my office but directly at him. Those eyes would do me in and I'd agree to much more than dinner.

"So?" he asked, patiently.

"Fine." I gave in like a surly toddler who'd finally agreed to eat something green. He infuriated me with his niceness and his logic. I tried to focus on those facts so I wouldn't give in to feeling anything else.

We would go to dinner, and I would do my best not to enjoy it.

# CHAPTER TWENTY-FOUR

FINN

I'D BE LYING if I said I hadn't already made a reservation for dinner. I figured we both had to eat, and I was getting tired of our meetings in the office. It felt like we weren't getting anywhere. Let me clarify: we were making progress on how Annie would argue my case, but we were making zero progress personally. My sisters had a point. I didn't know if she could love me, but it would be nice if she at least *fancied* me.

To that end, I'd booked us at an Italian restaurant on Sunset Boulevard not far from my house. No, I wasn't mapping the shortest distance between a dinner table and my cloud sofa.

She'd probably never go for that.

I was, however, planning to show her a good time and let her live a little. I couldn't keep coming up with outdoor locations for meetings. We needed to go on a date.

The place was charming in a trendy restaurant kind of way. In other words, it had an outdoor patio set around olive trees with pea gravel on the ground, rustic wooden chairs, and beige linen on the tables. Our table had a small votive candle burning in the center and a tiny vase holding a few sprigs of lavender. There were string lights overhead. I wouldn't have been surprised if my landscaper had been involved.

Annie was wary when we walked in. "This looks like a date place, not a business place." She looked nervous. Then she looked away, but I could see the indecision in her eyes. She didn't want to step outside her ethical boundaries. Even if it wasn't against the law, it was against her principles.

"Do you want to go someplace else?"

"No, I like this place. It just seems awfully charming."

"And that's bad?"

"I'm not sure. But I think my morals are being compromised by the quaintness." Then she inhaled a deep breath, exhaled, and said, "Oh, well. Do you drink wine?"

Everything was damn near perfect from there.

The food was lovely. She was lovely. My heart was protesting my mistreatment of it the entire time that I sat there like an obedient lump and didn't wrap her in my arms and kiss her.

As a proponent of science and empirical facts, I knew the draw I felt toward Annie the night we met was an undeniable truth. Yet, talking and laughing with her outside the constraints of work proved that it was more than physical chemistry. We fell seamlessly in sync with each other each time we had a conversation and my brain had been courting her brain ever since.

All I wanted was to have dinners like this, with her, until the end of time. If I'm honest, I also wanted other things—many other things before, during, and after dinner—but for now I'd promised to behave, and I wanted to keep my promises to her.

"Come up with your best, most significant questions—write them down if you have to— and ask me those now, right away. Let's get right to it," I said. That way, she'd start to relax because she'd see that having dinner wasn't a ploy to evade her questions or prevent her from doing her job.

Also, by getting the business part out of the way first, I hoped we could spend the rest of the time talking about other things—

any other things. I was so fucking tired of talking about my legal case and explaining how I didn't do anything wrong that I was starting to doubt what I knew to be true.

But before we could talk about other things, I had one more information dump to make her understand the trading.

It was taking longer than I'd hoped, pushing us through the first glass of wine and into the salad course. I was determined to be finished before the entrees.

"How did you come up with the money in the first place? Did you save it from your salary? Did you borrow it? What?" she asked.

Annie had taken her hair out of the clip that had held it back while we were in her office, and now it hung past her shoulders in soft waves. It made her look more relaxed, but I'd been trained by my sisters never to give what seemed like constructive advice about a woman's appearance, so saying something like "Your hair looks so much prettier down" was an invitation to the doghouse.

"You have gorgeous hair," I said, admiring her hair and everything else I could see above the table. "If I'm honest, you have gorgeous everything."

"Thank you." She blushed, and I conceded that my sisters were geniuses. "But Finn…"

"I know. It's unprofessional to say that to my attorney. I apologize."

"Apology accepted. Just don't push it."

"It's hard."

"I know," she said quietly. I felt like I was wearing down her resolve to keep fighting me. "It's hard to get mad at you."

I poured us each a fresh glass of wine from the bottle that was chilling in a silver bucket next to our table. Then I finished my explanation of how I made my trades. I really wanted to get finished with this part of the discussion so we could get on with the relaxing and getting to know each other part.

"I bought my first shares using money I'd saved. It was about a ten-thousand-dollar investment and that was ten years ago," I said.

"You were still in grad school and you were making investments?" She seemed surprised. It wasn't that unusual. Some of my friends who'd gone to business school had investment competitions with their stock picks. They're the ones who mostly lost their money.

"Yes, who better? I had ideas about how the markets worked based on what I was learning, and I decided to put it into practice. In fact, I wrote my PhD dissertation on the early underpinnings of my theory of perfect market information."

"Okay, back up. I need to take notes." She started to take her legal pad out of her bag, but I put out my hand on hers to stop her. It was unconscious. I didn't mean to touch her, but even that tiny contact sent a thrill of electricity through my bones, ending at the bone in my pants. I needed to keep the horses in the barn if she wasn't going to think I was a horny asshole. Quickly, I pulled my hand away.

"You don't need to take notes. This is just background stuff. I promise I'll write it all down for you later if you need it. Right now, we're just talking."

She left the notepad in her bag and straightened up, looking a little wary. "You promise?"

"I promise. This isn't a trick. So backing up, I took my theory of perfect market information and tried it out with a few trades. This is something hedge funds have been exploiting for years, by the way. It's not new."

"If it's been going on for years, what's the big deal?" she asked.

"You mean, how did I get away with writing a dissertation about something that wasn't new? I made it new. I had an angle that was a little contrarian. Again, the details aren't important for this discussion."

"But you'll tell me later if I need to know?"

"Yes. Geez, woman, do you not trust me?"

"No, I do. I just feel a little insecure without my legal pad."

"Even at dinner?"

She shrugged and took a sip of her wine, which seemed to take the edge off. Slightly.

"Fine, if it makes you feel better, use the legal pad." She joyfully plucked it from her bag and scribbled on it with her pen to make sure the ink was flowing.

"Okay, go on."

"I made my trades, all of which were used to bolster my theory. And guess what? The theory held. It worked. I made money. But to be sure it wasn't a fluke, I needed data."

"Right you and your data." I noticed she wasn't writing. As soon as she had the security of her legal pad at the ready under her elbow, she'd taken to watching my face as I spoke. She took another sip of wine.

"Yes, me and my data. It's the key to understanding the universe, at least my universe, and I was starting to get some really good data. To be honest, I didn't care about the money. I was more interested in knowing whether my theories held water."

"It sounds like they did," she said, twirling her pen. I plucked a slice of bread out of the basket and dipped it in olive oil before taking a bite.

"They did. I was endlessly pleased, and my dissertation got published and won an award. You can enter it into evidence if you want. It's publicly accessible."

Her eyes lit up. "Can I read it?"

"Sure, if you want. It might help your case because it's the basis on which I made all the other trades for the next ten years."

"So you've been making decent money in the stock market since you were—what—twenty-five years old?"

"Twenty-six. And yes, I've done well, which brings me to the last piece, which is how I had enough cash to make the investment that led to the recent profit taking that's in question." I bit into another piece of bread and realized I hadn't eaten lunch.

Had I eaten breakfast? Who knew anymore?

Annie was shaking her head at me in disbelief. "Is that how you refer to it? Recent profit taking? We're talking about seven million dollars."

"Yes, that was what I made on the sale. But to be fair, that's not all strictly profit."

"Oh, whatever." She picked up the cork from the table and threw it at me. "It's still a shit ton of money, and you're talking about it like it's just more 'data'." Yes, she made air quotes. I tried not to get annoyed by her seemingly disparaging opinion of data.

"You're funny," I said.

"I'm funny? No, I'm normal. I come from a world where I was taught to buy a couple blue-chip stocks and keep them forever. Earn some dividends. That's it."

"That's one way to go."

"No! You don't believe that. You have data and theorems and your own way of looking at the markets. I have data I don't understand and I need to convince a judge you didn't trade on insider information. And there's no proof!"

I really wanted this part of the conversation wrapped up before the entrees arrived. "Annie... I do have proof. I have absolute proof. Pages and pages of it."

"Wait, what?" She looked at me in utter disbelief even though I was pretty certain I'd been saying the same thing from the time of our first meeting. Minus a few details.

"I have proof."

Having already thrown the cork at me, she was at a loss, looking around the tabletop and finding nothing. "I thought you had data. You're saying you've had proof you didn't make illegal trades all along? And you've withheld it from me?"

I nodded. "And I will continue to withhold it from you. But not for the reason you think."

"What? What do I think?"

"I don't know. That I'm playing you? Or toying with you because this is my twisted idea of fun?"

"Maybe I think that. Really, I just think you've been making me work on your case without all the information."

"No. I can't give you my proof because it's a work in progress. It's a model I created that isn't ready to be released into the public domain, which it will be if it's part of your case. I can't make it available until I'm ready to publish. You still have all the information, which is to say you have my word and you have all the data I used, which is all publicly available. I've given you all the inputs. They're available to all. I just did something with them that other people didn't and I made money. The one thing I can't give you is my theorem because it's not ready. Unfortunately, that's the one piece of iron-clad proof."

"Finn, you promised you'd be straight with me."

"And I have."

"You never mentioned that you had proof you made the trades without insider knowledge."

"I told you I had a theory I was proving with my trades. I brought my data to our first meeting, every piece of data I used to decide what to trade and when. I've told you I was innocent from the beginning, and I asked you to believe me."

She stopped talking and dug the heels of her hands into her eyes. "I know you did. And I mostly believed you." She removed her hands and looked at me.

"And now?"

"I do believe you."

Hearing those words made my heart surge with delight. "Excellent."

"But I can't defend you because I don't have all the information."

"You'll think of something."

She let out a frustrated groan. "How? I don't understand the subtext of what you're saying when you speak to me, and I know there's always subtext. And I hate that I don't understand the underlying economics because if I did, maybe I could explain exactly how you were able to make all that money when most normal mortals couldn't. I want to understand, Finn. I feel so dumb for not understanding. Please, even if it takes a year, help me understand."

Her rant was interrupted by the arrival of our entrees, and I thanked the gods of fine dining because I didn't want to talk about this anymore.

We waited while the server set down the linguini with clams in front of her and my pasta with eggplant in front of me. We sat silently, locked on each other's eyes while he offered freshly grated parmesan cheese and cracked pepper from a long brown pepper mill.

"Buon appetito," he said, leaving us alone at our table in the corner.

Annie's comment gave me a further clue into the way she thought, and it astounded me. She was not only brilliant, but she wanted to understand my world. Even my family, who loved me, looked at my field as unwieldy. They were happy I was happy, but in no way did they want to understand it.

And here was this woman—this stunning, complex, intelligent woman—who wanted to understand so badly that it was painful for her not to know what I knew.

"Annie…"

I reached for her hand, which she'd placed on the table near her wineglass. I'd promised to behave, but I needed her to know that what she'd just said mattered to me. She looked down at our fingers, and for a moment, I could see the conflict behind her eyes. She wanted to pull her hand away. But she didn't.

Instead, she turned her palm and intertwined her fingers with mine. Then she met my gaze, and I could see her fighting the urge to look away.

"Yes?"

"You're kidding, right? How many economics courses did you take? One? Two?"

"I took one."

"One. Well, I took more than thirty. I've thought about almost nothing else for half my life, do you realize that? And honestly, if you wanted to understand it all, I'd love nothing more than to teach you. But you don't need to know what I know to defend me in this case. You need your expertise in the law, you need the information I have, and you need to believe that I'm innocent."

"I do believe you're innocent. What next?" she asked.

"Next, we enjoy our dinner. Buon appetito." I lifted my glass and she raised hers as well, not letting go of my hand on the table.

# CHAPTER TWENTY-FIVE

ANNIE

I FOUND it hard to concentrate after Finn took my hand. The feel of his skin and the touch I'd been avoiding for weeks made me feel light-headed.

If this was how it felt to hold his hand, I couldn't imagine what white-hot version of euphoria I'd feel if he touched me anyplace else. But I wanted to know.

We talked less from that point of the evening onward, but it felt like we said more.

He was right. We'd spent enough time talking about the case. He was also right in thinking that if I got to know him, I'd believe that cheating the system was not something he would do.

It wasn't about deciding whether he was arrogant or confident. He could be both or neither. The point was that he didn't want to cheat the system. And he was smart enough that he didn't need to.

I finally saw him for him. "How's the vongole?" he asked, gesturing to my plate.

"Pretty delish. Yours?"

"Great. Do you like eggplant?"

I shrugged. "Depends how it's cooked. I love the color of eggplant, and sometimes I buy it and hope I'll turn into someone who knows how to cook it right. But I've had a few disasters."

"They tend to soak up oil like a little sponge. Sometimes it tastes great, but it can lead to an oily mess that's awful."

"I can attest to that," I said.

The small votive candle flickered, and we watched it burn to a liquid puddle of wax as we talked. And talked. And laughed.

"The last time I was in the Bay Area was for my mom's birthday in April," he told me while we mopped a second plate of olive oil with a second basket of bread.

"Was it a big birthday? Milestone?"

"She's reached the age where she says they're all milestones. But yes, she turned sixty."

"Wow, she had you young. When I was twenty-four, I was still in school and way too confused and irresponsible to be a parent."

He lowered his voice. "I might have been unplanned… my parents weren't married until after my second sister was born. I think they waited to get married because they were making a point, like they intended to have kids before they were married."

"So you think they had two more kids without getting married first just so you wouldn't feel bad later on and think you were an accident?"

"It's a decent theory." I loved the way he looked at everything as a theory to be proven.

It was just a matter of time before the conversation turned to my family and I had to reveal exactly how small my small-town upbringing had been. I prepared myself for questions about cow tipping and moonshine because most people I'd met who hailed from cities assumed I grew up in a barn in a field.

Not Finn. The first thing he asked was the population size of my town. When I told him it was in the tens of thousands, he immediately compared it with a couple of places southeast of the San Francisco Bay which were similar. He'd met people from those places. He'd even visited them. He made no jokes about cow tipping. He did, however, think it was hilarious when I said my mom wore slacks at her job as assistant principal at an elementary school.

"Slacks? I think my grandmother wore slacks in the fifties, but I'm pretty sure they've been replaced by trousers by now."

"Trousers are for men. And she definitely wears slacks. They're made of polyester, and they have a permanent crease in the front. She also wears turtlenecks, fringe vests, and go-go boots."

"How can you allow this to take place?" he asked, leaning back in his chair. He was smiling and seeing the crinkles around his eyes made me happy.

I shrugged. My mom's fashion sense had stopped progressing sometime in the seventies. "She's got style. Granted, it's from another era, but who am I to tell her to change?"

"Fair enough," he said, pouring a little more wine.

Our conversation for the rest of dinner was easy and familiar. The wine probably helped, and by the time I noticed we'd finished the bottle, we'd also finished our food. Finn insisted on dessert.

"I'm not a huge dessert fan. As I said, I tend to go for the cheese plate instead of chocolate or whatever," I told him.

"Okay, let's get both," he said, perusing the small card that listed desserts. Our server looked delighted when Finn ordered a panna cotta with raspberry coulis, a cheese plate, and two glasses of dessert wine, and he returned with all of it a few minutes later.

The cheese plate was a thing of beauty. One might think that after a salad, a plate of pasta, and a half bottle of wine, I might not be able to stomach another bite of food, let alone an ample cheese plate. That person would be wrong.

We shared the cheese and the panna cotta. "Oh my God, I'm so happy right now," I said, savoring the last bite of a creamy sheep's milk cheese.

"I feel the same way," Finn said, looking at me the way I'd

been looking at the delectable plate of cheese. Ordinarily, I'd warn him against innuendo, but my resistance to him was weakening.

I'd been forced to take my hand back in order to eat and drink my way through the decadent array in front of us, but now that we were mostly finished, I was craving the feel of Finn's touch while giving myself a stern lecture about remaining professional.

*Kissing a client is wrong. Imagining his hands on your body is wrong. Jumping his bones in a restaurant is wrong.*

With my glass of dessert wine empty, I knew I wasn't thinking entirely clearly and that was becoming a problem.

I excused myself and went to the restroom because I needed a minute away from the gravitational pull of Finn's face and body to turn my head back around and regain control.

In the restroom, I expected to find the face of reason looking back at me in the mirror. In fact, I'd counted on it. She was supposed to cast her wise seasoned eyes on me and remind me how hard I'd worked to make partner and have a successful career. She was supposed to crank down the blaze of heat I felt just looking at Finn, let alone touching him. She was supposed to restore order.

Instead, she looked flushed from what had ended up feeling like the best date she'd ever had. She looked like the kind of person who'd abandon her principles and her job security because the guy she'd spent the evening with made her feel things. Good, good things.

I spun around and headed back to the table because this woman couldn't be trusted. The best thing I could do would be to thank Finn for getting me out of the office and grab the nearest Uber home. I wouldn't sit back down at the table, and I'd keep my hands secured behind my back so I wouldn't be tempted to reach for his one last time.

When I got back to the table, Finn was paying the bill. "Finn, you're the client. This dinner was supposed to be on my expense account. I thought you wanted to be wined and dined." I stood adjacent to the table, a few feet away.

"It's my pleasure. You'll get it next time."

"There won't be a next time," I said, hating the truth of it. "All our future meetings need to be at my office."

"Why?" He looked up. Those eyes would be the end of me.

"Because this is dangerous." Again I was gesturing to him, to me, to the trouble between us, and in that moment, I forgot that I needed to keep my hands behind my back. Finn reached and stilled my hands. Then he used them to pull me a few steps closer.

As I stood in front of him, I started to come up with my next words of protest, but Finn was too quick. He wrapped an arm around my waist and pulled me toward him so I was sitting sideways on his lap, which was exactly where my body wanted to be. However, my brain still gave a last-ditch attempt at prevailing, but when I turned to tell Finn this was a bad idea, I had no words —only want.

Leaning toward my ear, Finn whispered so softly it gave me chills. "I may be going to prison, but not without doing every single thing I should have done the night we met. And more."

He encircled me with his arms and reached for my face, gingerly brushing my cheek with his fingers and tracing my cheekbone. I felt pulsing heat that started at my heart but didn't stop until it culminated in an ache between my legs.

He was going to kiss me. Not accidentally and not briefly. I wasn't going to resist. It was going to be impulsive, irresponsible, and possibly career-changing. And I was powerless to stop it.

# CHAPTER TWENTY-SIX

ANNIE

I'D NEVER BEEN SO glad to have a corner table. Not that it shielded us from the rest of the patrons—in any way—but it was marginally better than being in the middle of the room since we had no ability to censor what neither of us could resist any longer.

Finn's lips brushed against mine, lightly at first, hinting at possibilities. I immediately wanted all the possibilities and didn't see any point in waiting, but he was slow and luxurious when he pressed gently and savored every… languid… pass. It felt like he wanted to make sure I was on board with his mission before he insisted too firmly. I was done resisting. My internal protests went unheard and unheeded.

I was also done with gentleness. The gentle kiss was lovely, but it wasn't half what I wanted from him, which was why I felt fine moving us along. I wrapped my hands around his neck and dug in my nails to bring his mouth more firmly against mine.

Finn pulled me closer—as if closer was even possible—and took full control of the kiss, like a pirate intent on ravaging his enemy and claiming everything for his own. I hadn't seen this side of him, the fierce, possessive side, but I liked it.

It was not a restaurant-appropriate kiss.

Nor did it comply with dining etiquette when his tongue began to devour my mouth in strong sure strokes that left no question unanswered. We weren't going to stop at kissing. It wasn't even up to us anymore. There was a massive undertow in the current and we were pulled with it.

I had a momentary twinge of awareness that there were people around us, people who might be partners at my firm, past or future clients, but for once I didn't care about how every action could impact my career. I felt relieved of the burden of caring.

His kisses were intense, then soft and enticing, then demanding, all in a matter of seconds. I was swept away with the feeling of how much I needed this. He pulled back only so he could change the angle of the kiss, taking a moment to nip at my bottom lip before taking it into his mouth.

All I could think was that I was glad he couldn't read the thoughts in my head because they were of the "I'm yours," "you can have whatever you want," "I'm helpless against you" variety. I couldn't have him know—not yet—but that's what I was feeling.

We had to leave the restaurant before our heat burned the place down. Somehow, we had to mobilize ourselves as one because there was no longer any distinction between us. I don't remember how we managed to move.

All I know is that we were in motion. Finn had somehow pulled me to my feet without removing my arms from his neck or his from around my waist. He'd done it without depriving me of a single touch of his lips, and suddenly we were outside.

I only knew this because I was aware of a sudden shift and a chill in the air as he pushed me against the outside wall of the restaurant and kissed me again without restraint.

"I live five minutes away," he said, his voice low.

"Convenient," I said. His eyes locked on mine, maybe unsure if I was going to accuse him of planning it. "Let's go."

If he'd planned it, I applauded his genius.

We were quiet in the Uber, but that's only because we couldn't take leave of each other's lips. We'd already talked a lot. Plenty. There were no words superior to what he could do with his mouth on my hot skin. I was desperate for him, his lips, his tongue. I wanted them everywhere.

I think we thanked the driver. I think we closed the car door behind us. But I couldn't say for sure.

"I'm finally grateful to my landscaper for all these fairy lights," Finn said as we walked through his yard to the front door. "It's kind of romantic."

"Yes. Romantic. Enough talking." I was driven by need.

In our desperation to move down the path and past the threshold of Finn's house, shoes were discarded, lights were left off, and we tumbled through the entryway and onto the nearest flat surface, which happened to be the couch.

"Finn..." I said, barely willing or able to remove my lips from his for more than a second.

"Yes?"

"All those things you wished we'd done the night we met, let's do them now."

"Fuck, yes."

I was grateful to be lying down with Finn kneeling above me. I wanted his lips, but I needed his skin. My fingers desperately tugged at the hem of his shirt, freeing it from his pants and I felt the familiar contours of his muscles under hot skin that I'd been dreaming about for weeks.

"Take this off," I said, working on the buttons, but when I'd unbuttoned a few of them, Finn grabbed the hem and tore it over his head.

He was already freeing me from my thin sweater and lavishing his attention on my breasts, first with light teasing fingers, then with his tongue through the lacy fabric of my bra.

"Not red satin. Sorry," I said. It was beige lace.

"This is better. It's the best." He lifted me gently and

unclasped my bra behind me before laying me back on the couch. He slipped it over my arms and gave the lacy fabric a quick kiss goodbye before throwing it somewhere in the room.

I pulled him back down to kiss his neck, desperate to feel the heat of his skin. I couldn't get enough. I felt like I'd waited years, not weeks, to feel his skin flush against mine. But now that we were finally here, I didn't want to rush. Seemingly, neither did he.

He moved slowly above me, his hips circling over mine and his hard length grinding against me and giving me the friction I craved. "You're amazing. Don't you dare stop," I said. His mouth fell against mine, his lips insistent, his tongue circling and tasting.

We lingered in these kisses, making up for lost time. It felt like there had been so much lost time. My attraction had been building with each fascinating observation Finn made that caused me to want to know him more, in every way possible.

"Every time I saw you… it took all my self-control not to slam the door to your office and take you on the desk." He cupped my jaw in his hand and traced the line from my chin to my ear with one finger. I felt myself tremble and flush with heat. Then he followed with his tongue and I lost my mind.

"This is better. Desk is hard." Caveman English was all I had. I wasn't going to be coherent for much longer if he kept it up with that magical tongue, and he didn't stop. His breath came hot and fast against the spot where he'd just licked my neck. I felt chills down to my feet, and I think I moaned. Or maybe it was him. But I'm pretty sure it was me.

I traced the contour of his chest, appreciating every carved inch. Then I made my way lower, feeling the ripple of his abs beneath my fingers. But I wanted more. I wanted the taste of his skin, so I followed my fingertips with a long, slow graze with my tongue and his head dropped back with a low growl.

My hands were at his belt buckle, unbuttoning and unzipping his pants because I needed him urgently. But he backed away. "Finn, please," I practically whimpered because I desperately wanted to touch him. But he stayed just out of reach, moving down my body, kissing my throat and my breasts while his hands roamed lower.

"I can't get enough of you," he said, gently pressing my knees apart and settling between my thighs. He ran one finger along the elastic at the top of my panties, then kissed the skin just above it. He kissed me lower, over the fabric, and ran his hot tongue straight down my center. I felt a pulse of aching desire grow into an unstoppable rush. The heat from his mouth drove me crazy, but his tongue made me insane. His finger looped in the waistband and pulled the unnecessary fabric down over my legs.

This was the part I'd missed during his virtual sex tour in my office, so I was especially interested in the live version. He did not disappoint.

Watching my face as he planted a row of kisses up the inside of one leg, Finn's hands lightly massaged my hips. His kisses ended at the apex of my thighs and his exhale against my skin caused my toes to curl once more. He didn't ask me what I liked. He didn't need to ask. Everything he did could have come from an expert guidebook to making my body melt with sensation. Clearly, he was the author.

"Oh my God, Finn…" He met my eyes and smiled.

"I know…" he said, his voice low and sensual. "You good?"

I blinked heavily and nodded. Words were superfluous.

Finn flattened his tongue against the throbbing center of me, slowly licking until I writhed against his mouth. Then he worked me into a frenzy with quick strokes and long, languid passes with his tongue. I felt my orgasm building. It was beyond my control.

As Finn's tongue swirled against me, he drove a finger inside, curling it expertly to reach the perfect spot. When he added a second finger, my back arched and my hips rose up to meet his mouth. I couldn't stifle the new series of moans that escaped while I grabbed his hair and ran my fingers through it, messing it up the way he did himself.

"Finn… I want you badly."

"You've got me, baby. Any way you want me. But not just yet."

He wasn't done with his assault on my senses. Hitching one of my legs over his shoulder, he sucked and licked and drove me right up to the edge and over into sheer bliss as I pulsed against his tongue and fingers. There was no holding back. There was no thinking. I felt the mounting sensations push me closer to infinity until the heat shattered me to bits.

And in my hazy spiral back to earth, the one thing I knew was that I wanted him closer to me. I wanted him pressed against me. I wanted him in me. I wanted him to feel every sensation I was feeling.

"Finn... please." I reached for his face, cradling his cheeks as he moved up my body, planting kisses along the way. When he reached my breasts, he took one nipple in his mouth and cupped them both in his hands. I returned to his pants, pushing them down until he kicked them off his legs.

Ah, yes. I slipped a hand inside his boxers and wrapped it around his erection, reveling in how hard and good it felt. His breath hitched, and he looked up at me, his eyes fiery and gorgeous. I stroked him and watched his eyes watching me, and in that moment, I knew we were long past reenacting a casual hookup from the night of the wedding. This was real in a way I hadn't felt before, and I wanted it.

He kissed me deeply, ravaging my mouth with a desire equal to mine. I shoved his boxers down, tired of all the fabric that was holding us back.

Finn grabbed his wallet from his pants and extracted a foil packet, which he ripped open with his teeth. "You don't keep them in every room in your house?"

"I will now." He rolled the condom on, and my insides clenched in anticipation.

Then Finn took both my hands, pulled me up so he could slide underneath, and rolled me on top of him. He teased my entrance, but neither one of us had any willpower at that point, and he'd given me the advantage of being on top.

So I moved—slowly, gently against him—until finally I sunk down, inch by incredible inch until I felt him fill me completely. "Oh, that's so, so good," I said.

"You are. So good," he said, breathless. His eyes were dark and unfocused. His breathing hitched every time I moved above him, circling my hips and working us both toward another cliff. I was glad to see he could lose control. I intended to push that boundary as far as I could.

Finn reached for me and tucked a few loose strands of hair behind my ear and pulled my face toward his. He kissed me slowly, his tongue moving in rhythm with his hips. It was a languid dance, his hips rolling under me, my body moving against him until going slowly was too damned slow.

Finn drove harder, thrusting with each circle of his hips. Our mouths were fused, and our bodies found a rhythm as one. Then I felt a new wave building until it shattered my world again, bringing Finn with me over the edge into his own mad moaning climax.

It was the best thing I'd ever felt. If I was forever ruined for anyone else, it was so worth it. But I couldn't imagine ever wanting anybody else.

For a while, I couldn't speak. My mind was still seeing stars and I was only vaguely aware that Finn had kissed me and was smiling.

"Finn…"

"Yes?"

"Thank you for inviting me to dinner."

He laughed. "You're welcome, you crazy, incredible woman."

# CHAPTER TWENTY-SEVEN

ANNIE

IT WAS nice sharing a bed with Finn. So nice that I didn't intend to leave for the foreseeable future.

We'd decided that since it was the weekend, there was no need for me to put my metaphorical pencil skirt back on and push Finn away as professionalism dictated. I'd already punched a hole in professionalism, and if I was going to ruin my career, it could wait until Monday.

I also planned to have Finn explain as much as he could—in broad strokes—of how his theory allowed him to predict market behavior so I could explain it to the prosecutor.

But we could do that later.

He was lying on his side, gazing at me the way he did, with his impossible eyes seeming to see something deeper within me that I didn't want most people to know about. There were so many of those somethings, secrets I never felt comfortable sharing. But I liked him knowing. And I liked that he instinctively seemed to understand the sides of myself I usually kept hidden.

I left my leg looped over his while my hand traced over the hard muscles of his chest and abdomen. "You have a seriously ripped body," I said, not caring any more that words tumbled out of my mouth when I was around him, some of them the sort I'd normally keep to myself. Letting him know more of me no longer felt like a risk.

He laughed quietly. "Thank you. I think. That was a compliment, right?"

"Um, yeah. A big one. First of all, it's insanely hot, and I can't stop touching you."

He put his hand on mine and drew it to his lips. Then he placed it back on his upper abs so I could continue touching him. "I wouldn't want to stop you from doing something that makes you happy."

I smiled at that. "But also, I'm just... impressed that, with all you have going on with authoring theorems and being a master of the universe and all, you have time to spend six hours a day at the gym."

"One hour."

"Oh come on. I spend one hour working out and I don't look like that."

"I'd kind of hope not. Hard pecs aren't what I'm looking for in a woman." With that thought, he showed me how much he appreciated my very not-hard pecs by lavishing attention on my breasts with his hands. And then his tongue.

With that, most of the other thoughts left my brain, and I gave in to the idea that we'd probably spend the entire day in his bed. That would mean I'd miss my morning run and sideline the normal Saturday morning laundry list of errands and activities I'd had in place for the past umpteen years of my life. I had no problem giving it all up.

I ran my hand up Finn's chest again, marveling at the way I could feel the muscle fibers beneath his hot skin. He was like my own personal anatomy lesson. I worked my way from pectoral muscles to latissimus dorsi, appreciating every curve.

He moved his hands away from my breasts, looking longingly down at them and even more longingly at my lips, which he kissed gently. Then he ran the back of his hand along my jaw and up to my temple, kissing me there too.

Backing away slightly, Finn combed his fingers through my hair and watched my expression, which had to be somewhere between dreamy and total bliss.

"You've never told me why you left San Francisco."

He was right; I hadn't told him. It wasn't a secret, but it hadn't come up. "Yeah, I've always wanted to live in LA, so I decided to make the move, even though it meant changing firms." That was the party line, the words I'd been trained to say in every interview. I'd grown so accustomed to saying the words, I let them roll out of my mouth without thinking. Then I saw Finn's questioning look and realized what I'd said.

"You've always wanted to live in LA? Since when? You keep saying you hate it here."

"I haven't said I hate it."

"Maybe you've been too polite to use the word hate, but I can tell you don't like it."

It was challenging to be with someone who never let me get away with pretending something about me wasn't true. Sometimes, I wanted him to see a better side of myself. "Okay, fine. I don't love LA. And I'm sorry I gave you my bullshit line that I had drilled into my brain by the headhunter who was helping me look for jobs. That's not the reason I moved at all."

"Well, now, I'm dying to know the real reason. And I also want to know why the headhunter encouraged you to lie."

I sighed because as much as I could tell that Finn didn't mind the imperfect parts of me, I hated to be the one to point them out. I blinked for a long moment and psyched myself up. Maybe Finn could tell I wasn't ready to share, or maybe he wasn't so invested in the answer.

"Now, you've given me too much time to come up with my own scenario. Did you have to flee the city? Are you a fugitive from justice? Maybe the two of us can find some fake passports and blow this joint," he said.

He was still running one hand through my hair and using the other to rub my back. I couldn't tell him. I didn't want him to see me as a failure. "I am a fugitive from justice. I figured that working for a law firm was a good cover. Hiding in plain sight. Who'd think to look there?" I said.

"Well, lucky me. I'm glad you fled to LA to work for Bristol, Chavez, and Greeves and be my lawyer. Clearly, I came out on top." He rolled so he was, in fact, on top.

I smiled at him. "Is that why you're currently hovering over me? Is that a demonstration?"

"Yes. It's about to be a demonstration of exactly how good I can make you feel when I'm on top."

"I'm not going to argue with you," I said, wrapping my arms around his strong back. "I'm finding that you're very smart and persuasive when you want to be, and you're usually right. I'm not sure that fighting you is a good use of my energy."

"I'm so pleased you see it that way, though I might take exception to the word *usually*," he said. Then he kissed me madly, and I forgot what we were talking about.

A COUPLE HOURS LATER, we were in the same spot, contemplating a basic set of needs: food, coffee, and more sex. Not necessarily in that order.

Finn was sitting up, leaning against a stack of pillows, and I lay on my side, curled in a ball with my head on his chest. His hand was lazily rubbing my back, and I had to continually pinch myself to accept that I could feel this good outside of a dream state.

"We could order takeout, but one of us would still need to get out of bed to retrieve it from your front door," I said, feeling decadently lazy and unwilling to move. Even for food.

"I might be willing to make the sacrifice, but only if you give me a say in what we order."

I debated whether I was willing to make that concession for the sake of him opening the door. "Don't we like the same thing?" Maybe I could convince him to order food I liked and grab it from the delivery person so I could spend the entire day in bed. I'd never done it in my life. Since it was now two in the afternoon, I considered that I might have a decent chance of achieving it.

"Ha. Not at all," he said.

He was right, but I didn't want to acknowledge that it was because I didn't trust his taste in food. But my traitorous mouth jumped in. "That's because you eat vegan food where there's no hope for a normal person who likes meat."

"I don't eat all vegan food, but I eat some. You could try. Some of the dishes are so good you wouldn't even notice there's no meat involved."

"Fine."

He shifted so he could meet my eyes. "Really?"

"Sure."

"Why the sudden change of heart?"

I moved over a little so I could look up at him without wrenching my neck. It was then I noticed the ceiling fan lazily drifting in circles over our heads. I didn't recall Finn turning it on. "Where did that come from?" I asked, pointing at the fan. "When did you get up and turn it on?"

He reached over to the bedside table and picked up his phone, on which he showed me an app. "I did it from here. But you didn't answer my question about the food?"

"Right, that. I decided that I should give your vegan crap a chance. I've been eating like a runaway hamburger train since I moved here, and it has to stop. Now, I'm not guaranteeing I'll come out on the other side singing about plants, but I'll try it your way."

He nodded and scrolled through menus on his phone. "I applaud your open-mindedness. So I'll pick a place that isn't going to drive you away with cashew foam or jackfruit meat substitutes."

"Okay, that's completely disgusting, what you just said. I don't want to think about how it would taste, but I'm saying 'veto' to anything that's supposed to substitute for meat. If I want it to taste like meat, I'll order meat. Show me the glory of vegetables in their native environment, and I'll go from there."

He turned the phone screen toward me. "Want to have a look or should I choose?"

I shook my head and kissed my fingers. Then I reached for his cheek and patted the kiss there. "You choose."

But instead, he tossed his phone aside and flipped me onto my back and hovered over me. "I'll choose. But none of this lazy 'kissing your hand instead of kissing me.' That's not allowed." He leaned in and kissed me lightly. "Not." Then he kissed me harder and his body sunk into mine. "Allowed."

"Understood," I said, pulling him hard against me until there was no space between us. "Never again," I said against his lips before I felt his teeth sink into my bottom lip, lightly but hard enough to set off fireworks in my belly. His tongue soothed the temporary pain and sought mine with a new urgency.

"Just so we're clear," he said, his voice a low growl. He kissed me again, his hands in my hair, and his velvet lips so deeply satisfying. I again forgot about the need for food. He was enough. I'd sooner starve than let him move an inch from where he was.

But he moved. He rolled to the side and again picked up his phone. He scrolled for a moment and clicked a few boxes before returning his attention to my waiting gaze. "Okay, forty-five minutes, give or take, and you can experience the finest in plant-based cuisine."

I nodded, thinking it couldn't be as bad as I imagined it would be, but my expression must have given me away because Finn grinned at me. "It's going to be okay, trust me. And if you hate it, I'll make you a burger."

"Deal." Then I pulled him back to where I wanted him for forty-five minutes, give or take.

# CHAPTER TWENTY-EIGHT

ANNIE

NIKKI CAME BACK from her honeymoon and insisted on an urgent meet-up to talk about Finn. She didn't explicitly say that was why she wanted to meet, but I knew. She'd probably spent the remainder of her honeymoon planning the toasts she'd make at our wedding.

I invited Janelle to join us, figuring I'd buy her the first of many apologetic drinks to make up for wrongly accusing her of trying to sabotage me.

"Yes, but only if you really want to hang out. Not because you feel guilty about the thing," she said because she already knew me.

"I do feel guilty, but I also want you to meet my best friend and we need to get out of the office more," I said, realizing I was succumbing to Finn's way of thinking. I was also really starting to hate my big brown desk and the lack of warmth in the space. Changes would need to be made in there.

"Enough with the guilt, but I'm not above letting you buy me a drink—or four."

"Deal. I'll let you know where," I said.

Nikki was happy to make it a threesome and suggested we meet at the Waldorf Astoria Hotel rooftop. "I know you love it there," she said, remembering that when I'd visited in the past, I'd stayed at the hotel and loved the bar on the roof. She was right. One of the highlights of coming to LA had always been having drinks and looking at the view.

"Awesome, works for me," I said.

That was how I came to be sitting amid potted plants on a well-appointed rooftop, holding a cocktail with a large sprig of mint sticking out of the glass, and being badgered and berated by not one, but two unforgiving women.

It was pretty up on the roof, just as I remembered it from the last time I was there, which had to have been over a year ago. The clear views of the nearby hills made me feel like I was worlds away from my life on the ground. The life of a bird.

"Cheers," Nikki said before sipping the wine she'd ordered. "Now tell me about Finn. Please assure me you've done more than kiss him." Then she glanced at Janelle, as if she shouldn't have asked in front of her.

"It's okay, she knows there's... stuff," I said.

"I know she's fighting her feelings for the guy. I don't know what we're gonna do to get her to take the leap into his bed," Janelle said.

"*We?*" I asked. "When did this become a group effort?"

They shrugged concurrently and I knew I was doomed. I was never going to be able to shift the conversation to shoes and bar snacks, so I relented and told them everything about my weekend with Finn. "It was... I mean, you'll think I'm exaggerating if I say it was the best sex I've ever had with the best guy I've ever met, right?"

"No, because I know he's a great guy and I know you deserve that," Nikki said.

"Thank you. But I seem to have taken leave of my professional boundaries. I just got to the firm and the first big case I have, I tear my client's clothes off? Who am I?"

Nikki gulped her drink and shook her head. "Sounds like you've got it bad for him."

"I do, and it's a problem."

"Why?" Janelle asked. "Why is that bad? What am I missing?"

"Because I can't throw away everything I've worked for in my career for great sex. It's a slippery slope. First I'm spending a weekend with him; next I'm leaving work early to see him and asking for vacation time and losing sight of what's important to me."

Janelle and Nikki shared a look. I didn't like this dynamic.

"If it's just great sex, then I might agree, but I've never seen you like this. About anyone," Nikki said.

She was right, but I wasn't sure it mattered. "This is not good, Nik. All I can see is a downward spiral in my career because I don't care about anything as much as I care about being with Finn. I'm completely lost."

"You're saying that like it's a bad thing," Janelle said. "Man, if I felt that way for five minutes in a relationship, I'd take it and run."

"You're forgetting he's my client," I said. Tom implied any 'improprieties' could get me disbarred."

"Well, that's not true, you know that, right?" Janelle said. Did I know that? I'd always assumed attorney-client relationships were a clear violation. I looked at her quizzically. "It's in the Model Rules of Professional Responsibility. Article 1.8. 'A lawyer shall not have sexual relations with a client unless a consensual sexual relationship existed between them when the client-lawyer relationship commenced.'"

"You memorized the professional responsibility code?" I asked, surprised.

"Let's just say, it's come up." She winked.

Nikki looked positively gleeful. "I love Article 1.8. Well, there you go. It's allowed by law. Now you just have to get out of your own way."

"Plus, soon your case will be wrapped up and you can have at him without it being an issue," Janelle said. "Tom can't even slap you on the wrist."

"Unless it goes to trial—" I objected.

"Quit making excuses!" they said at the same time, then looked at each other and laughed. I couldn't help cracking a smile at that. Without intending to, I had found a second Nikki in Janelle. And they were right—I was great at making excuses.

I felt defeated. I hated when my emotions made decisions my brain didn't see coming. But they'd gone and done it without my consent. They wanted Finn. They wanted him completely, without boundaries.

Nikki edged my drink a little closer to my hand. When I felt the glass touch my fingers, I heeded her hint and took a sip. Then I gulped a deep breath.

"That's better. Now, just listen for a minute while I tell you what you're doing wrong with your life," she said, smiling. It was hard to imagine her taking a hard stance with me because she was normally so kind. But she didn't hold back. "You've been using your job and how much you love it as an excuse for years. You can't meet new people, you can't date, you can't find hobbies—all because the job you love requires so much of your time and energy."

"It does. It requires a lot. And I'm good with that. It's all good." I wanted to abort this conversation. I didn't really want to think about things I may have given up along the way in favor of my job because the sacrifices had brought me to where I wanted to be. I'd succeeded.

I glanced around, hoping my gaze would land on something that warranted urgent discussion. Instead, I saw nothing but a group of men in sport coats taking selfies by the railing.

Janelle sipped her drink silently but her sympathetic eyes were on me.

Nikki pulled her hair around over one shoulder and began braiding it while she spoke. "You know I respect you so much and I'm so impressed with how well you've done in your career. You're a freaking partner in a law firm, and you're barely over thirty. That's amazing. But I also know you've been pushing toward that goal since college, almost to the exclusion of everything else."

"It's what was required."

"I know that, honey, and you did it. You made it. All I'm saying is that there's nothing wrong with it if you look around from the top and decide it doesn't fulfill every part of you."

"But it does." I tried to protest, but my voice lacked fortitude.

"Okay, great. If it's what you want, then all good."

Janelle touched my arm. Her eyes were warm when she said, "It's a job. Or even a career. But it's not everything. You are aware of that, right?"

Was I? I'd spent most of my adult life telling myself that work was my sole purpose. I was good at work. That made it okay to be bad at relationships, even if it wasn't turning out to be true. "Fine. It's mostly good. It's mostly worth the sacrifices."

Janelle sipped her wine and looked at me as though her point was obvious.

"Fine. I get it. I should want more than mostly," I said.

"Do you?" Nikki asked.

"I never did before. But now…"

"Finn…"

"Yeah. I can't explain what he does to me. It's… complete madness."

"It's only madness if you keep making up excuses not to be with him," Nikki said. Janelle nodded in agreement.

I hated when Nikki was right, not because I'd begrudge her that, but because it often meant I was wrong. I really hated that. I looked at the view from the rooftop I'd always loved so much, and even that felt less convincing.

When I thought about Finn, my heart ached to be with him. It also ached a little bit for me because I would have liked nothing more than to wrap him in my arms and I couldn't.

*Why, exactly? Because of your stupid excuses?*

And suddenly, it hit me. I had a lot of stupid excuses.

Where had all of my insistence that I put professionalism above all else actually gotten me? I'd been passed up for promotions and reprimanded for having unprofessional relations with a client, when apparently the law was on my side.

And for what? So I could go home alone every night and deny myself the one man who I hadn't been able to get out of my head from the moment we met?

I needed a brain transplant, pure and simple. I needed to reexamine my priorities. And I needed to chill.

Everything I'd been fighting against for the past few weeks suddenly felt like the wrong battle.

# CHAPTER TWENTY-NINE

ANNIE

I WOKE up prepared to fight the right battle—a least when it came to work. It was deposition day and I wanted to nail it.

Nailing Finn was a secondary consideration. For the moment.

When I'd decided to move to LA, I'd been deliberate in choosing where to live and where to work. I made sure the commute was no more than a few miles because I hated traffic.

After being in LA for only a few weeks, I'd realized that my plan was irrelevant, and there was no way to avoid sitting in traffic for light years on end. For one thing, the couple of miles between my job and my home could translate into forty-five minutes of stop and go traffic, as I waited for ten minutes sometimes to make it through a single traffic light.

"This isn't normal," I told Finn, who was sitting in my passenger seat.

"They have traffic in the Bay Area. You're acting like you've never seen it before. Or is it just LA traffic you hate?" He was smirking at me. I could knew it from the sound of his voice, even though I had my eyes on the road.

"I'm an equal opportunity traffic hater. I guess I worked long enough hours in San Francisco that I didn't drive in much traffic. Plus, I used BART a lot."

Not that I minded time in the car with Finn. We always had a lot to talk about. But I'll admit I was a tad nervous about the deposition, partly because Finn had insisted on coming and the opposing counsel had okayed it. I hadn't expected that. In fact, I hadn't expected the lawyer to keep the appointment at all since he'd already canceled three times. But he surprised me and said that Finn could be in the room as long as he observed silently. I considered it a win to have him there. His colleague was less likely to tell lies he knew Finn could refute if he was in the room.

"Silently," I reminded him, knowing it would be a struggle for him to keep quiet if Dr. Warren Craft, the whistleblower and his colleague, said something he thought was false.

"I know. You've told me sixty-three times. I won't speak. I promise," he said. I could tell from his lack of joking that he was nervous too.

We pulled into the underground parking garage at Fifth and Grand and rode the elevator to the fifteenth floor.

"You're here to see…?" the receptionist asked.

"David Grape," I said, wondering how often people made comments about his last name and wondering what the best ones were.

"Concord or white grape? Do you plan to stomp on the opposition?" Finn asked as we took our seats in the waiting area.

I glared at him and pressed my lips together in a failed attempt not to smile. "Please stop. You're going to make me lose my train of thought."

"Should we ditch? There's still time to get out during the parking grace period. Let's go to the museum instead. Or The Last Bookstore."

Before I could tell Finn to behave, David Grape appeared, and all hopes of us having a bantering relationship that would lead to him telling me about the best jokes about tiny fruit disappeared.

David Grape stood about five feet, nine inches, and had salt and pepper hair, round glasses, and pale skin. He didn't smile, which conveyed that he saw me as his client's nemesis before I'd even asked a single question.

In my time practicing law, I'd found that lawyers tended to fall into two buckets: one group took their client's word as gospel and behaved like anyone who questioned them, sued them, or looked at them funny was the enemy. The other group behaved like we, as lawyers, more or less knew how everything was going to turn out and we, as lawyers, needed to work together to find an outcome that our clients could stomach.

As a litigator, I'd grown accustomed to the second group. We worked as opposing counsel, but our goal was one: a settlement.

I could tell within five minutes of meeting David Grape that he fell into the client-worshiping bucket. After introducing me to Dr. Warren Craft and getting us all seated in a drab conference room, he said, "Your client has committed a crime, and my client is here willingly at your request to answer questions." He said it as though Finn wasn't sitting right there under the ugly fluorescent lighting.

When I looked over at Finn to gauge his reaction, his face was impassive. Except when he looked at Craft. Then the expression turned to a glare.

David Grape was essentially a personal injury attorney, only he masqueraded as one who advocated for whistleblowers. In my mind, lawyers like Grape weren't judicious about which cases they took. The more lawsuits filed, the greater their opportunity of collecting on one of them, like playing the lottery. It was darts of the legal system variety.

We went through the niceties of sworn testimony, and then I started questioning Dr. Craft about his relationship with Finn.

"Norman Finley is the department chair of the Economics Department, and as such, he decides which courses I will teach, oversees my curriculum, and weighs in on my research," Craft said, robotically. He wouldn't look at Finn—Finn made him uncomfortable. Good.

"When did you become suspicious that Dr. Finley had broken the law?" I asked.

"When he made approximately seven million dollars betting against the mergers of two telecom companies," Craft said.

"How did you know he made those profits?"

"It was common knowledge in the Econ Department."

"He told people he made seven million dollars?"

"Objection. Asked and answered," Grape piped in. He didn't need to object, but I figured he wanted to feel useful.

"Why do you think he'd tell people if he made the money illegally?" I asked.

"Objection. Speculation." Grape smirked, then he signaled to Craft that he could answer.

"Because he's an arrogant SOB who wanted to lord it over me because I was consulting for those companies."

I felt Finn shift in his chair next to me, but he said nothing. I was impressed with his self-restraint. I glanced at Finn who sat motionless, his gaze boring into Craft's face.

"My client explains it differently. He said you came to him, said you heard he made 'big money' betting against the merger and asked how he knew it would fail. Do you agree with that account?"

"More or less, yes. I did ask him about it because it was contrarian. Everyone expected the merger to proceed."

"So you're recanting what you said earlier, correct?"

"Objection," Grape said. I wanted to lash out at him on the record for objecting relentlessly for silly reasons, but I decided it was better to let a judge make that determination later when the transcript was finished.

But when Craft excused himself to take a restroom break, I laid into Grape for his incessant objecting.

"Are you serious with this? Are you going to object to everything?"

"Not everything." He looked satisfied with himself, and my dislike for him grew.

It wasn't normal for a lawyer to object to every damn question. I felt like Grape was using it as a strategy to throw off my momentum. I couldn't let him succeed, and I felt my concentration waning the more he stopped me in my line of questioning.

"Do you really object to the content of all of my questions, or is there something about the way I'm phrasing them that's tripping you up?" I asked. I heard Finn stifle a laugh.

"I object to the questions. There's no nuance," he said.

"Yes, but the whole reason we're here today is so I can ask questions."

"That doesn't mean I have to let you ask whatever you want. If I find your questions objectionable, I'm going to object." Grape looked smug and I rolled my eyes. If this was his whole strategy, he was going to lose.

"I understand that, but when you object to everything, it dilutes the power of what you're doing. A judge isn't going to focus on any of your objections as actually meaningful." It was a gamble, but I thought there was a chance he might keep his mouth shut if he thought he was jeopardizing his credibility. Neither one of us had any way of knowing how a judge would view his questions, but most of the ones I'd met hated superfluous objections.

"Fine. I'll be more judicious."

Under the table, Finn put a hand on my leg and gave it a squeeze. The heat of his fingers sent a shock of pleasure directly to my heart, but I forced myself to stare at Grape's lopsided sideburns and my focus returned. I reached down and grasped his fingers in reassurance.

"You good?" I asked, casting him a side glance. He nodded. Ever silent, as promised. "Remind me to tell you all about Article 1.8."

He leaned in and whispered, "I'm familiar." His breath in my ear made my toes curl.

Craft returned looking a little calmer. For the moment. "Mr. Craft, are you aware that you stand to make fifteen to twenty percent of the money the government could potentially recover from going after Norman Finley?" I asked.

"Yes."

"Are you aware that on a seven million dollar profit plus interest and penalties, your portion could be over two million dollars?"

"I hadn't calculated it because I have no idea how much will be recovered," he said. Finn coughed loudly and I swallowed hard. I shot him a warning look and he put up both hands.

"Sorry, dry throat," he said, reaching into his bag for a bottle of water.

I turned back to Craft. "You didn't calculate it?"

"Objection. Asked and answered," Grape said, looking smug.

"I only ask to be sure that's your sworn testimony because if I were filing a suit against a colleague, I'd probably have a vague sense of the potential value to me."

"I had a vague idea," he said.

"Mr. Craft, how much does an associate professor at your level of experience make annually?"

"I make ninety thousand dollars, unless I consult."

"How much did you earn from the consulting job with Cellcom and Blink?"

"I'd prefer not to answer. That's proprietary information."

"It's not proprietary. Did you earn two hundred thousand dollars from the consulting job?"

He hesitated and looked at Grape, who shrugged. "Yes."

"So the amount you'd stand to gain through the qui tam suit is a better bet, isn't that correct?"

"Objection," Grape said. I glared at him.

"Can you please answer the question?" I asked Craft.

"Yes, it would be more money. But that's not why I filed the suit," Craft said. Grape cleared his throat in an overly-obvious way and both of us looked at him. He twisted his lips into a tiny sour smile but said nothing.

"Let's move on. Do you have any documentation to show that your colleague, Norman Finley, used insider information to make his trades? Do you have any proof he had insider information?" I asked. I felt Finn tense next to me. The answer to this question could change everything.

"I do not have documentation. But the timing speaks for itself."

"How does it speak for itself?" I asked Craft. So far, he hadn't even told me enough to know why he filed his lawsuit.

"He made his trades right before the companies announced that the merger fell through. He knew details only people at the companies could know," Craft said.

"And to be clear, you consulted with the companies. Did you share any of your research with Dr. Finley?" I was enjoying referring to him as Dr. Finley.

"No."

"Were you aware of anyone at the company who had a relationship with Dr. Finley such that he'd have access to company financials or your economic projections or anything else related to the merger?"

Craft hesitated, and I could tell he so badly wanted to lie. But he couldn't. "Obviously someone did because he knew when to sell shares of one company and short the shares of the other one."

"Is that why you filed the qui tam? Because you had a hunch?"

"Objection," Grape said.

"Just because I don't know where he got the information, doesn't make it illegal to be a whistleblower. I'm not the criminal here," Craft said.

"But it is illegal to file a fraudulent suit for your personal gain when you know there's no merit." I let my words hang and stared at Craft, waiting for a reaction. It took a couple seconds, but I saw a few tiny beads of sweat form on his brow.

There was something he wasn't saying. I hadn't gotten to the heart of it yet and I needed to. Why would he file a suit he couldn't definitively prove unless there was some reason other than a hunch. Revenge?

"Objection. He's not on trial," Grape said.

"Please stop objecting. I need to ask him questions and he needs to answer them. Mr. Craft, why did you file this suit?"

"I told you," he said.

I shook my head. "No. The real reason. Were you angry because Dr. Finley advised you not to consult for the companies? Did you think he was out to get you? Was this whole thing about petty revenge? Or were you just pissed because you weren't the one who made seven million dollars? So you made a guess and figured you could make some money betting against him."

Craft kept opening and closing his mouth even when words weren't coming out. He looked like a fish out of water. I wanted to yell at Grape to please get his client a glass of water. "Please answer the question. Was this a frivolous suit because you're a poor sport?"

I wasn't expecting Craft to jump up from his seat and point his finger at Finn like a dagger. "He thought I would fail! *He* bet against *me*!" Craft said. Grape looked surprised at his outburst and possibly surprised at the information he didn't know about. I was surprised too. I'd intended to wear him down until he admitted he'd filed the suit based on an unevidenced hunch, but this was interesting.

"Can you elaborate?" I asked. Finn shifted again in his seat but I kept my eyes fixed on Craft.

"When I got back from my consulting job, I heard some of my colleagues talking in the department. One of them said Finley had shorted the stock because he knew the merger deal would fall apart... and they said it was because I was the consultant. Finley was betting against me. He didn't think highly enough of me to believe my research would convince the government to bless the merger. And he used it to make money right before the news was announced that the deal fell apart."

Trying to keep my facial expression from revealing my feelings, I nodded at Craft. What he'd just said was irrelevant in a court of law.

Grape closed his eyes and nodded. He knew his client didn't have a case. His darts play had failed, and he'd move on to the next case. Even if Finn had thought Craft was a hack who'd fail at his job, it wasn't insider trading. As to the rest, the deposition made it clear Craft had an axe to grind with Finley, and he'd produced no preponderance of evidence of anything.

But I had a different problem. Finn had lied to me.

I felt the sickening leaden lump form in my throat and the taste of bile in my mouth. He'd dazzled me with sideshow antics about his fabulous theories but he was just a guy who didn't think another guy was smart enough to do his job.

He'd never said anything about Craft being one of his data points, or possibly his only data point. He'd never said that he sold his stock because he was betting against Craft's ability to produce research that would convince the government regulators to bless the merger. And the bottom line was if he was betting against Craft, he'd made a ton of money for very different reasons than he'd said. All his theorems and data were irrelevant to the case.

Even though a part of me wanted to curl up under the table and cry over my stupidity for falling for Finn's bullshit, I forced myself to focus.

I wrapped up the rest of the deposition, confident this part of the suit would go away. Now we just had to deal with the SEC. When Grape extended his slimy hand and said he hoped we'd work together again, it was all I could do to smile stiffly and leave before saying something I'd regret.

Finn followed closely behind. I couldn't even look at him.

# CHAPTER THIRTY

FINN

WE RODE the elevator down to the lobby in silence. I wasn't sure of Annie's process and I wanted to give her space if she needed to reflect.

She'd killed it in there. My respect and admiration for her had only grown over the past forty-five minutes. But she still wasn't talking. Shouldn't she be celebrating that Craft basically admitted he only filed the suit because he was annoyed?

When we exited to the lobby, I reached a hand out to bring her into an embrace. "Hey, stellar work in there, Counselor. I knew I made the right pick."

She shrugged me off. "Not now, Finn. No."

Wait, what? She was striding toward the other set of elevators that would take us down to the parking garage, but I didn't know what had just happened. Clearly, she was upset and I was confused.

"Annie, what's going on?" I asked, turning her to face me. The expression on her face was stern. I didn't like that face. She didn't look me in the eye and the warmth was gone from her demeanor.

That had me even more worried than I had been before the deposition. "Talk to me. Please."

Annie closed her eyes for a moment. When she opened them, I saw they were glassy. She looked defeated. She looked worn out. "The one thing I asked from the beginning, Finn, was for you to be honest with me," she said.

Those were not the words I was expecting. She looked so upset and I wanted to wrap her in my arms, but I had the sense that wouldn't go over well. "I was. I am."

"Craft?" Her voice broke when she said his name and I knew her well enough by then to know she hated appearing weak.

"What about him?"

She threw up her hands. "That was the key to your trades? Betting against Craft? Well, congratulations. You win. He looks spiteful and the SEC will probably take your word for it that you didn't cheat and you'll be just fine. That's how it works for you people who live above the law, isn't it? Everyone just falls at your feet?"

"Annie... what are you talking about?"

She took a deep breath and let loose on an exhale. "You. You happened. You came into my office and said you'd tell me everything. Then you got me all confused about your data and your theorems and your 'proof' and I believed you. But you never said the whole thing was just an expensive fuck you stock bet against Warren Craft. You thought he'd fail, you thought the merger would fall through? Well, news flash, it doesn't take a Nobel Laureate to make a bet against the underdog. Trust me, I know. We always lose. Doesn't take a genius economist to predict the future."

I'd never seen her like this and it killed me. I wanted to explain—needed to explain—but I couldn't get a word in. "Annie... it's not what you think."

She turned away from me, walking back toward the elevator. "You don't know what I think. Don't tell me what I think."

Not wanting to have her scream at me in the lobby of the

building, I guided us out the door and onto the sidewalk. She didn't seem to be paying attention but started striding down the sidewalk, so I followed. I needed to get her to understand. If we kept going a couple blocks to Maguire Gardens outside the LA Library, we could sit. It was nice. It had benches and a cool fountain.

I couldn't let her believe what Craft said, not without explaining. "Annie, please. Just… listen for one minute. Please."

"I don't want to hear it. I've heard enough. Too much." She was walking next to me, clearly not paying attention to where we were going. I steered us toward the garden.

"No, you haven't. Not if you think I lied to you. I didn't bet against Craft." Coaxing her to look at me wasn't easy, but after I put a hand on her shoulder, she turned, then looked back at the ground and avoided my eyes. I'd have to settle for that. The garden was empty and shaded by a row of trees on one side and the library building on another.

Much nicer surroundings than the office building, even if she was planning to yell at me. At least her words wouldn't echo as much as they did in the lobby. The marble floor in there made for hideous acoustics.

I stood in front of her and tried to explain. "Annie, I did not make my trades because I was betting against Warren Craft. I made my trades because of perfect market information theory, using the data I gave you."

She crossed her arms. "I'm not stupid, Finn. Do you even have a theory?"

That, for some reason, made me laugh. "Oh, yes. I have a theory. Ten years' worth. And the reason I cautioned Craft against taking the job in the first place was because of that theory. My data was already pointing to an inflection point and a sea change in the way the government would view mergers. Then I used my models to figure out the timing. That's why I dumped the stock. My theory was correct. And I based it on information everyone has. I didn't want Craft to ruin his reputation by consulting on a losing proposition, but I couldn't tell him why. He took my warning as a personal slight. And yes, I know about the rumors on campus that I was betting against him. All untrue."

Craft was an idiot but betting on him or against him never entered my imagination. And now, I couldn't believe I'd cared enough to warn him against taking the consulting job.

Her face softened as she heard my words. "Really? Swear to me, Finn. I'm not fucking around here."

"Annie, I swear." I looked her in the eye. When she locked on my gaze, I could see she believed me. She knew me.

"So you let him think you were out to sabotage him, watched him file a baseless lawsuit which then had the SEC all over your ass, all because you were trying to save him from taking a job that would hurt him?"

I nodded. "Well, I did make the trades. But... yeah."

She looked around, apparently realizing for the first time that I'd steered us to a park.

"Oh my God, Finn. Another park? How do you turn a fight into something that feels like a date?"

I shrugged. "I guess I just always really want to be on a date with you."

"I want to be mad at you..." she said.

"You do? Do you really?"

I watched as the fight seeped out of her, but she was still conflicted. "I don't know. I'm still trying to decide whether you obfuscated your feelings about Craft."

"If I did, it was unintentional obfuscation, I assure you." I leaned in tentatively. I wanted to kiss her so badly, but I wasn't sure if she needed more time to stew. Then I decided I wasn't capable of waiting and reached to cup her jaw in my hand and guided her face to mine.

Her lips tasted like berries and after a minute, I was fighting the urge to do more than kiss her. There was no doubt I was in love with this woman.

I'd been nervous about Craft, that little weasel. Even though I knew I hadn't cheated the system, he'd gotten me worried that he'd found something I'd unknowingly done wrong. Until the deposition, I'd been afraid he'd produce some piece of evidence that would blindside me and send me to jail.

But he hadn't produced a thing. Standing in the park was the first time I had hope of walking away from the lawsuits a free man. I kissed Annie again. "Thank you."

"You're welcome." Then she seemed to absorb the success of the day and she smiled.

I still felt like I'd let her down by not explaining my motives behind my advice to Craft. "I'm sorry I didn't tell you. I honestly didn't think it was relevant," I said, pulling her toward me.

"It's okay," she said, wrapping her arms around my neck. "You had no way of knowing."

I rested my cheek on the top of her head, endlessly happy to be with her. Still, I blamed myself for leaving out the one piece of information that almost cost me something I cared about more than my case—her.

# CHAPTER THIRTY-ONE

FINN

ANNIE SET up a meeting with the Senior Prosecutor for the SEC later that week in the hopes that she could get the case dropped based on Craft's seemingly vengeful motives. There was a chance we'd still have to go to court, and I steeled myself against that possibility. I could still go to prison. It wasn't over.

As we drove to the SEC's offices, she walked me through everything one more time. I had my data boxed up and organized. "There's a good chance the SEC will still pursue damages against you because of the timing of your trades. We will still need to prove you used publicly-available information."

"I get it. I know it's a lot of money. I look guilty, so they want proof I'm not."

Earlier in the day, she and I had talked over the case one final time to make sure I was prepared. She insisted I bring all the documents I had to show how much work I'd put into my theory of perfect market information. And she was ready with her broad strokes explanation of how I'd predicted events that allowed me to make money when other people didn't.

"You don't have to let them read your research. I understand why you don't want it to be put into evidence. But even showing the volume of work you've done will go far in showing how you could predict what the companies would do."

"I'm fine with that." I brought everything and I knew Annie understood why I insisted on holding onto my work.

The prep session continued as we drove into the parking structure and spiraled down to Level P4, where we finally found a space. "Here's how we're going to explain it. You wanted to make money on your trades, and you'd been doing that for years. There's a pattern of trading that never raised anyone's eyebrows before. But the trades you made two months ago were huge. Bigger than all the rest. And they were right before the merger was announced," she said.

"Correct."

"They will say that looks suspicious."

"Only if I was privy to the fact that the merger was happening, and I was not," I said. I felt like I'd been saying those words for months. Maybe because I had. But now it actually mattered.

"You hadn't consulted for any telecom company for over five years and all you know is what's publicly available. But from that information and your work in economics, you accurately predicted a tipping point—"

"Inflection point."

We pressed the elevator button and rode to the tenth floor. "An inflection point at which time antitrust laws would kick in and the merger efforts would fail, giving you a reason to short sell Cellcom and dump your shares in Blink."

"That's the crux of it."

"If you didn't have that information, how did you know to sell?" she asked.

"I anticipated a series of events. I compiled data and tested a working theory that had proven correct in the past. I knew it would happen. I just knew."

"Saying you just knew isn't enough, you know that right?"

"No one can prove that I used insider information. Who out there is saying they gave me information? No one."

"Correct. Just Craft. And he's been discredited."

The elevator doors opened and we were faced with a long hallway. Before we walked to the meeting room, I took Annie's hand and pulled her to me. "I just want to say thank you. For everything."

"Don't thank me yet. We're not quite done," she said. Then she smiled. "But I think we're good." We started walking.

"Good as in, you can win this case? That kind of good?"

"I'd say the odds are favorable."

"You know I don't care about odds. That's for statisticians. I care about data."

"I know you do. I'm starting to love your data."

"I'm starting to love you."

She stopped walking abruptly and looked at me, tilting her head as though trying to figure out if she'd heard me right. And maybe the timing was shitty, given that she was focused on my case, but oh well. There was no holding back how I felt about her anymore.

"Annie… if I do end up going to jail, I need you to know… I'm in love with you. For so many things. Your brilliant mind, your gorgeous body. But mostly for your giant heart. Thank you for taking a chance on me." It felt good to tell her. I'd never wanted to love anyone so much that it felt dangerous, but I couldn't help the way I felt about her.

"Finn…"

"Yes?"

"First of all, you're not going to jail. Okay? Think positively." She kissed me. "And second, I think I made it clear I only wanted to think of you as a client," she said. She swallowed and I worried there wasn't more to the conversation.

Then she continued. "I tried not to love you. I tried to put up boundaries and you tested every one. And now I don't have any left. I love you too... because you made it abundantly clear to me that I don't have any other choice."

More than the trades, the theorems, the legal arguments, that piece of data sealed my fate.

So I made a decision—there was no way I was going to jail. No matter how much of my research I had to give up, I'd do it to be with her.

THE SEC'S prosecutor had already read Craft's deposition and didn't think it was relevant. "There are all kinds of red flags there. Sounds like he had some issues with you personally as well as professionally," he said, adjusting his maroon tie under the grey jacket that matched his grey hair. He looked exactly how I expected an SEC prosecutor would look—serious and grey.

We sat in a small wood-paneled conference room without windows. Annie had brought bottled water for me, which was thoughtful, but after a few minutes, I realized that being nervous made me parched. She'd anticipated well.

"His credibility is questionable, and his proof is flimsy, mostly hearsay," Annie said, referring to Craft and his allegations.

"I agree. But as to the SEC's position, we see a pattern of trades pegged to the failed merger announcement. And it's a large sum of money, so the burden of proof is significant."

"In other words, you're going off of what looks like insider trading, but you have no proof that my client received any information from an inside source," she said.

"Correct, but because of the dollar amount involved, we can't just let it go. Your client did have relationships with both companies. It's not a great leap to think he had information from his consulting work or from relationships with company officials who knew about the merger," he said. He couldn't get past my prior work with the companies.

We went through the expected questions, and I answered

them. I held up the trove of documents as proof that I'd spent many years looking at industry behavior and trying to come up with viable models.

But the prosecutor had trouble taking that on faith.

"Are you saying you had no insider information? You made your trades at the time you did by happenstance? Seven million dollars is a lot of happenstance," he said.

I couldn't lie. The truth was I'd made predictions based on what I knew would happen. So I told him that. "I did know. I'm not denying that I knew. But not because anyone at the company told me. I knew because selling and shorting those companies was the most prudent course of action at the time I chose to sell. I suspected that the government regulators would act as they did and that once the companies figured out what I'd analyzed and believed to be true, they'd behave exactly as I predicted."

"The companies made their plans based on their proprietary data, having nothing to do with you," he said.

"Correct.

"You made your stock buys based on your own analysis."

"Correct."

"And this pile of documents, that's your analysis?"

"Yes," I said.

Annie began her explanation of market inflection points, industry saturation, government economics, and small bits of data which led me to my conclusions. She explained it beautifully.

The prosecutor nodded and looked at the pile of pages. "Then I'd like to enter these documents into evidence."

"Sir, that's not possible. These documents are proprietary research that my client has been working on for years. It's part of a body of work that will have major implications when it's published. I'm sorry."

"I don't know what you expect me to do. I can't just take seven million in perfectly timed profits on faith." The prosecutor was shaking his head.

Annie looked at me, sadness in her eyes because she believed I was willing to go to jail over this.

I grabbed her hand under the table and opened one of my files for the prosecutor to read. Yes, I let a stranger look at a potential Nobel Prize-winning material. "Hang on. Maybe there's a way we can make this work."

I outlined a proposal under which I would provide most of my research, enough that would allow someone who was paying attention to connect the dots from A to S or T. Enough to believe I was on my way to Z but protection enough for me that I could be sure no one could get very far with the data I entered into evidence.

"If you're willing to let me take these files and have one of our economists read through them, I'll consider dismissing the case, depending on his assessment," the prosecutor said.

Annie looked at me. "These are your babies. It's up to you," she said. "We can keep going, take it to a judge, and appeal it if it doesn't go your way. I'll stick with you on it as far as we need to go."

I squeezed her hand. "It's okay. Take them," I told the prosecutor.

He seemed satisfied and extended his hand. "Thank you for your time. There's some paperwork still to come, but if these pages check out, it looks like we'll dismiss the case for lack of evidence."

Maybe I was an idiot not to have figured out my A to S plan before or maybe I just never had a reason to care. Annie pressed her lips together, and I could tell she was trying hard not to smile. Just like I was trying hard not to kiss her in front of the prosecutor.

# CHAPTER THIRTY-TWO

ANNIE

FINN HAD ASKED me to lunch, and I'd taken a real lunch hour from work, something I hadn't done since... I have no idea.

There were lots of good restaurants in Century City, but we went to a place nearby that had a back patio and a menu of healthy-but-not-too-healthy food. We carried our trays out to the tables and I inspected his turkey sandwich. "That looks awfully normal. Very un-vegan and plant-based."

"I like variety."

I'd ordered a salad and was proud to note that I hadn't had a burger in a week. Progress was being made.

He looked at me like he had unfinished business to discuss. "What? You want to ask me something, I can tell." Maybe I was finally getting good at reading him.

"You never really answered my question—about why you moved to LA."

"I didn't?"

"No, you started to lie and tell me your great love for the City of Angels drew you here, but that's as far as we got. Care to amend?"

I thought back to when we'd had the discussion. "Right. That," I said, wondering if I should divert the conversation again.

But why?

Loving a person meant trusting him not to judge me. Or maybe it meant finally feeling free not to judge myself. I wanted him to know the whole truth, so I took a deep breath and spoke. "I was passed up for partner at my old firm. Twice." I waited for a reaction. He pressed his lips together and shook his head.

"That was a terrible mistake," he said, and he kissed me gently. "And I'm sorry. That must have been an awful feeling. And undeserved."

"Thank you." Hearing his words made me feel better about it. I'd worked hard not to care as much on my own, but having someone else validate my feelings was nice too.

"Anyway, they passed me up after saying I was next in line. Each time, they gave it to a man with fewer years at the firm, fewer billable hours. It was maddening."

"Did you consider calling them out on it? Sounds like blatant sexism."

"It's not the kind of thing you do if you want to make partner. Even coming to a new city and interviewing for jobs, I was told not to talk about my old job in anything but a favorable light. Even if people guessed that I was disgruntled after being passed up for partner, I was never to mention it."

"Well, that makes sense. New employers rarely love hearing people complain about their old employers."

"You have some experience in that area?"

"Absolutely. I've interviewed candidates for teaching positions who started disparaging their previous employers before we'd even finished making formal introductions. I generally don't hire them, but usually I lend them a piece of advice and tell them not to do that in the future."

"So you know. That's why I'm so accustomed to giving people

my rehearsed explanation about desperately wanting a change of pace that only a move to Los Angeles would provide. And at such a loss because I'd need to leave my beloved firm."

"You shovel the bullshit well."

"You didn't buy it."

"I have a finely-tuned bullshit meter. It comes with being a professor. Students are master bullshitters."

The sun was bouncing off the window of a brick building, hitting me in the eyes. Without a word, Finn swiveled the umbrella over our table to an angle so I could see again. "Thanks," I said. He nodded.

"Anyway, I understand why you'd be reluctant to call your old firm on sexism, and I applaud you for moving on to get the opportunity you earned."

"Thanks," I said, but I could tell there was more to his sentence. "You're thinking that by taking my toys and moving on, I let them get away with being sexist?"

"I'm not blaming you at all. I get why it doesn't behoove you to wave around your feminist flag. But you may be letting them get away with their behavior," he said, pulling the lettuce out of his sandwich before taking a bite.

"I know. The problem was I couldn't prove that's why I was passed over. It was never said explicitly. It's hard to prove. And I don't want to come off like a crazy person who's making blanket statements about men and their motivations."

"That's not how I see you."

"Thank you." I thought about that for a moment. He'd been passed from Jackson to me without a say in the matter. I didn't know if he'd researched my previous cases or my success rate in court. If he had, he'd have known I was just as capable as Jackson. But maybe he just went on faith because Tom told him I would be his lead counsel. Or maybe our time together at the wedding influenced him and caused him to make a business decision he might not have otherwise made. I had to know.

"How much of how you see me has to with the fact that you like me, wholly apart from my legal ability?" I asked.

He smiled and ran a finger up and down the length of my arm. "I do like you."

"I know you do. Did that influence your willingness to have me take your case? Instead of Jackson?"

"I told you. No, it didn't. I'd decided to work with Annie Prescott, kick-ass, white-collar litigator and partner at the firm based solely on her experience and bona fides. All things I'd researched before I met Annie, the gorgeous maid of honor at the wedding."

That made me happy. "Okay, good. I just wanted to be sure you didn't think you got the short end of the stick when Tom swapped me in for Jackson."

"Hardly. I was never supposed to work with Jackson. He was just filling in until the firm decided which female partner should take my case."

"Wait, what?" I put down my fork and stared at him.

"I was always going to have a female partner represent me."

I still couldn't make sense of his words. "What do you mean? I'm the only female partner at the firm."

"Oh. Yeah?"

"Um, yeah."

"So what do you mean, you were waiting for a female partner to take your case? Explain that part."

He shrugged like it was obvious. "When I interviewed firms, one of my stipulations for representing me was that I wanted a female partner on my case. It was my way of ensuring whatever firm I chose did, in fact, have women in partnership positions without having to put it that way."

I struggled against what he was saying because I suddenly felt like I was experiencing some sort of affirmative action I never knew was being enacted on my behalf. But Finn couldn't have made that request simply to get me to represent him. He didn't even know I lived in LA until he saw me at our first meeting. Was it too much of a coincidence?

"So wait, it was that important to you that your law firm had female partners that you'd have walked if there were none?"

"Yes."

"Why?"

He shrugged and reached for my hand, but it was dead weight when he grasped it. I couldn't deal with sexy Finn at the same time I was trying to sort through the motivations of client Finn. "Just the way I was raised. I told you that I have a headstrong mother and five empowered sisters. They drilled it into me that it wasn't enough to be a friend to women in the workplace. I had to be an advocate for them. I needed to set an example. It's the way I've always done things."

My brain was spinning, trying to figure out the chicken and egg timeline of Finn needing a lawyer who was a female partner and my fortuitous job offer at the firm. "When did you meet with Tom and ask for a female partner? When exactly."

His eyes traveled to the ceiling as he thought back. Then he looked at his phone because the tone of my voice told him I needed precision. "April twenty-third of this year."

I didn't need to look at my calendar to recognize the date as significant. But I couldn't believe it. "I was brought in for an interview on May fourth. The headhunter I was using told me there was a fortuitous opening at a firm for someone with my specialty, and partnership was on the table."

Finn's request had been the reason I'd been brought on as partner. It hadn't been my years of hard work. They needed a female body to land an important client whose case had the potential to gain attention for the firm.

I had to think hard about what that meant for me.

# CHAPTER THIRTY-THREE

ANNIE

IT ONLY TOOK the SEC economist two days with Finn's data and his partial theory to believe that he'd made his trades legally. The case was dropped, and Finn and I made plans for a celebratory dinner during which work would not be discussed.

"I promise," I told him. "Like the night we met. No talk about work."

"Deal. I'm making a reservation," he said, before rushing off the phone so he could call his mom and sisters.

Ordinarily, winning a case like that would have me over the moon, but learning the reason I'd gotten my partner position dampened my excitement.

I loitered in Tom's doorway without an appointment, which I knew was against policy. But I was mad. And sad. And even though Finn and I had spent a good hour talking about why he'd make the same request of any firm that represented him today, I still couldn't help thinking he'd somehow done it for me.

It was impossible. I knew that. Finn and I hadn't even met when I started my job search and I'd never heard about his case when Tom had presented vague details about an interesting insider trading case when we'd met for my first interview.

Of course, he wasn't going to come out and say that the only hope he had of landing a Nobel Prize runner-up client was having a female partner. But oh, how I wished he had.

Tom glanced up when he heard me speak, "Hey there, do you have a sec?"

He looked at his computer, and I knew he was checking to see if he had an imminent appointment. He then looked past me toward where his assistant sat, as if to ascertain how it came to pass that I was standing there without being vetted by her first.

Then he seemed to give in. "Sure, come on in. How's the case?"

"Done. All charges dropped."

"Fantastic. That's what we like to hear. Reason I put my faith in you."

So he was going to continue with the bullshit party line. "Yeah, about that. It's come to my attention that my client requested a female partner on the case as a contingency of signing with the firm."

Tom looked shocked. "He told you that? Why would he tell you that?"

"Was it supposed to be a secret?" I asked, leaning against his end table.

Tom waved his hand as if to dismiss the errant thought. "No, not a secret. Not anything. Clients make requests like that all the time. They want certain attributes in an attorney, and we do our best to accommodate."

"Right. It's just that... was that why I was hired as a partner? Because he insisted on a female partner and you didn't have one?"

Tom looked at me like I was a child who'd come to him demanding to know why no one had ever explained that the tooth fairy wasn't real. "Does it matter? You got what you wanted and so did he."

"It matters to me." As I said the words, I heard the echo of Finn's first request, when he'd said it was important that I believed he was innocent. I'd brushed him off, just like Tom was doing right now. It made me hate the lawyer I'd always thought I wanted to become.

"Fine. Yes, you were in the right place at the right time. But you're a white-collar litigator with an excellent reputation, so it was hardly a pity hire. And again, you got what you wanted, so I don't know why you're hung up on how or why it happened. Just be grateful and do the job you were hired to do."

I didn't know how to respond. I didn't like it.

"Okay, good to know. Just one more thing. I think it's important that we represent the cultural norms, which means at least one more woman in a partner position along with one more person of color. I know it cuts into the bottom line, but I'll be proposing it at the next board meeting. I hope I'll have your support." Maybe it was time to wave around my feminist flag.

Tom looked like he was going to be ill. He didn't say a word, but I had a feeling he understood that was the smartest move.

For the time being, I'd keep my partner chair and do the best work I could and use my voice at the table for something good. Maybe we could do more pro bono work. Maybe we could even help out some single parents who'd lost a spouse. There had to be some way I could still make a difference. I was going to find it.

As I walked back to my office, I felt the shiny glow of my fancy job start to dim into the wan beige of the conference room walls. I'd been so excited to embrace them. Now all I could think of was getting the hulking brown desk out of my office and ordering some furniture I liked. Maybe I'd ask Janelle too help. I liked her style.

Fall was coming and the days would be getting shorter, which meant I needed to leave work earlier if I wanted to make it home in time to see the sunset. A girl couldn't possibly be expected to spend all her time at work. There was more to life. Much more.

# CHAPTER THIRTY-FOUR

ANNIE

IT TURNED out I was right. Professors do compare office size, and Finn's was much larger than McCutcheon's. Still, his friend was happy to have him back, even if it meant that he'd notice the discrepancy on a daily basis.

Finn insisted I come to campus to meet his colleagues, and I couldn't help but notice the nameplate on Craft's door.

I tapped on it. "Still makes me mad that you tried to help him, but he believed a rumor and tried to ruin your life," I said.

"If I got mad at everyone who tried to throw me under the bus for something, I'd be mad all the time," Finn said.

I kissed him. "You are the calmest person I've ever met."

According to Finn, Craft's nameplate would be removed as soon as his position was filled with a new professor. Craft had been sent packing, and no one had felt especially sad to see him go.

After everyone had finished welcoming Finn back and telling him they knew he was innocent, Finn looked through all his files. He was like a mother hen checking on her baby chicks, counting to make sure the brood was happy and healthy. I stifled the urge to make a comment about his data. It turned out that his research and his data had saved him.

We walked through the main campus quad toward a bench that was out of the way of students walking to class. The air was warm but there was a late summer breeze that almost felt like fall. The leaves on the liquid amber trees were bright and green, but in another month, they'd turn all shades of orange and red before falling to the ground. "Hey, are you hungry? I have a faculty discount at the student union," Finn said, guiding me in that direction.

"You should donate your discount back to the school. Or someplace else."

"I've been doing a version of that, actually," he said, taking my hand and leading me up the stairs toward a coffee kiosk. He knew I'd rather have an iced coffee than a meal.

"What do you mean? Where do you donate it?"

He ordered two iced coffees and left a dollar in the tip jar. When the coffee was ready, he carried them to the bench we'd walked past earlier so we could sit in the shade. The late summer heat was fierce. "Did you ever wonder why I made all those stock trades? Why I wanted to make all that money?"

"You told me. Your theorem. I thought it was part of your research and your 'data'." I couldn't help the air quotes.

"It is part of my 'data,' but I don't need millions of dollars to prove my perfect market information theory."

"So why, then?" I asked.

"I started a non-profit up where my sisters live to provide financial and mental health support for parents who've lost a spouse. That was why I needed seed money five years ago, why I took the consulting gig. Then I continued to fund it with money from stock trades."

A surge of love welled in my chest for this man. His mom— he'd been worried about her and his sisters for so long. My heart ached for him. "Finn, that's amazing. When did you start it?"

"It's been a work in progress. One of my sisters oversees it and my mom runs support groups there. She's fine now, but she went through some really bad times right after my dad died and I always thought that if there was a place where she could have gone to connect with other single parents in her position, maybe it would have lightened her load," he said.

"You have guilt about not being there when he died?" I asked.

"I tried to take a leave from college to come home but she swore she'd disown me if I did. I heeded her wishes but I promised I'd make it up to her and my sisters as soon as I could earn a living."

"I hope I can meet her soon. Has she talked about visiting?"

Finn seemed to decide that we'd spent enough time on the bench because he pulled me up and along with him as he walked down another path on campus. This one led toward a wide-open quad where students were lounging on the grass.

"She's funny. She hates to fly and drive long distances. But she'll get in the water and swim like Becca or ride her bike twenty miles, no problem," he said.

"I can respect that. Guess we'll have to go visit her. In San Francisco. Twist my arm," I said.

When we'd reached an empty spot on the grass, Finn dropped to the ground, pulling me toward him. He lay on his back and I curled up on my side with my head on his chest. It was better than the bench. He always had good ideas.

"It's a date. Now we just need to see when we're both free. With my classes starting up and your new job, that should be sometime in the next four years, I'd imagine."

"I'm free," I told him. Because I finally was.

# EPILOGUE

FINN

Six months later

I COULD TELL the first night I met Annie that she was a Northern California girl at heart. Sure, she'd grown up in a small Central California town and given it a go in Los Angeles, but she was true to the song about leaving her heart in San Francisco.

So I didn't hesitate in booking a trip there when we both scraped together a few vacation days. I'd recently published my research and was starting to hear rumblings about a nomination for the Nobel Prize in Economics. Annie been working long hours at her law firm, doubling her load with pro bono cases in addition to her regular work. We both needed a break.

"What have you been missing the most about being here?" I asked Annie while we walked through the Ferry Building on our first day in the city. We were picking up provisions for a picnic, and there was a cheese shop Annie loved, so we went there first.

"Everything," she said, leaning her head on my shoulder. Over the past six months since my legal case had wrapped up, it had been such a relief to be with Annie without talking about how to keep me out of jail. There were so many better things to talk about.

We were staring at a case of goat and sheep's milk cheeses, some with washed rinds, others dusted with ash. I'd never been a cheese connoisseur, but I liked every type we sampled. Finally, Annie settled on a few varieties and had them wrapped up.

"There's a good bakery down the way, and we can get everything else at the market," she said, taking my hand. I could smell the bread long before we reached the stall where it was sold.

"Just promise me you won't tell my sister we cheated on her and ate other bread," I said.

"I promise, but does she really think you eat no other bread other than hers? If she doesn't send you a loaf, you're breadless?" she asked.

"Yes, that's what she thinks. So when you meet her, please toe the party line."

"Will do." Isla was the only one of my sisters who hadn't made it down for a visit since we'd started dating, but Annie would meet her on this trip. "I'm curious about her sourdough starters. She talks about them like they're her children."

"They kind of are. She's a nut. You'll love her." We picked out the bread and grabbed a few other things from the market before heading to Golden Gate Park. My mom had promised to drive over and meet us. I just hoped she'd remember what we'd talked about earlier. Sometimes, she could still be a little scattered.

We rented bikes and rode along the waterfront until we got closer to the park, and then we cut inland toward the giant green space. I thought we should go to Bunny Meadow, even though it got crowded with picnickers. It was a great spot and Annie had said she liked it there.

The rented bikes came equipped with baskets on the handlebars, so we had no trouble transporting our food and a blanket over to the park. I chained up the bikes while Annie found a shady spot and laid out the blanket.

"Come," she said. She was sprawled on her stomach on the

blanket with her feet in the air like a little kid, a giant grin on her face. I joined her and she rolled over onto her back and lay next to me.

"This is your place, huh?" I said.

"What do you mean?"

"Your happy place."

"Yeah, I guess it is. I do love it here."

I'd been listening to her as she talked about her law firm over the past few months, trying to gauge whether it was a love match or not. She liked being recognized for doing good work, but that would happen anywhere she worked. And the shiny perfection of the job had been replaced with a more sordid reality. She wasn't thrilled about the politics, though she knew they existed everywhere.

I had an idea I wanted to run by her, and it seemed like this was the place to broach the subject.

She pointed up at a cluster of leaves on a tree overhead. "Is that a nebula?"

"Funny. It may be a pooping pigeon."

"Is that visible only in the summer sky, Professor, or all the time?"

"You love my astronomy lessons, admit it." In the time we'd been together, we'd had quite a few nights under the stars in my backyard, and each time we'd one-upped the fantasy retelling of our dashed hookup hopes on the night of the wedding. To be clear, the sex wasn't virtual, and we didn't break up afterward. It had been a great six months.

"I love you. I tolerate the astronomy lessons," she said.

My phone buzzed with a text and I searched the surrounding grass for signs of my mom. She was easy to spot—a sixty-year-old woman in a pink dress and a straw hat, jumping and waving.

"Oh my God, I love her already," Annie said.

"I think the feeling's mutual." My mom had spotted us and was running toward Annie.

"I love that she's wearing running shoes with that dress. Does she run for fun or just on days when she can't wait to see you?" she asked.

"She jogs. Slowly. And she seems to think it's fun."

"Now I love her more," she said, waving back.

I knew they'd get along in the same way Annie had bonded with each of my sisters over seemingly-innocuous traits they shared. She and Becs realized they shared a love of old-school board games and she and Tatum discovered they'd read every book by a British author I'd never heard of. My sisters Cherry and Sara had visited a couple months ago and the three of them talked nonstop, all at the same time, and I had no idea how they heard what the others were saying, but somehow they did. My family loved Annie almost as much as I did.

Annie stood up, and my mom scooped her into a hug.

"I'm so pleased to meet you." She held both of Annie's hands and was looking her over from head to toe like she was deciding which part of her to eat first.

"And I'm here too, your favorite—and only—son," I said, arms crossed, waiting for her to hug me.

"Oh, I know, I brought bunches of love for you too. You are my favorite son." She hugged me around my waist and stood on her toes to kiss my cheek. Her dark brown hair only had a sprinkling of grey and she wore it in the same shoulder-length style she had for as long as I could remember.

My mom plunked down on the blanket, and we unwrapped all the food. The cheese was smelly and somewhat acceptable to me, but Annie raved about it. We layered the bread with different kinds of cheese and charcuterie, pickles, tomatoes, and Dijon mustard. My mom tore into a bag of kettle cooked potato chips, and Annie opened a bottle of wine she must have bought when I wasn't looking. It was a perfect picnic.

Annie barely had a chance to eat because my mom was peppering her with questions. "How long did you live in San Francisco?" "Did you ever run Twin Peaks? I used to do that back when my lungs were young." "And your parents still live in the house where you grew up?" Annie patiently answered every one until I finally intervened.

"Mom, let her eat, for crying out loud." She shushed me and they went right on talking, but my mom made an effort to push various food items toward Annie in between answers.

After a lazy hour of talking and laughing and eating everything we'd bought, my mom took a book out of her purse and encouraged us to go for a walk while she read. Before I got up, she slipped a small box into my pocket, as I'd requested.

We walked lazily hand in hand, just as we'd done every time we walked anywhere together. It was beautiful and clear, but there was a chill in the air. Annie buttoned up her jacket. "You cold?" I asked.

"Nah, I'm good. I like this weather."

"I know you do. After living in LA for so long, I forget that when the sun's out here, it doesn't mean it's warm."

"Not unless it's summer."

"I remember." It had been many years since I'd lived in the Bay Area but it always felt like home. I was counting on Annie feeling the same way, so much so that she'd consider moving back.

Annie had told me she loved the Dahlia Garden in the fall when the flowers were in bloom. It was the middle of winter, but we walked in that direction anyway. And if she agreed to my plan, she'd be able to walk over to see the dahlias every day from the house I'd bought in Cole Valley.

My intention was to wait until we got to the Dahlia Garden to propose, but I suddenly didn't have the patience to walk any further. So I stopped and turned her to face me.

"Hi," I said.

She smiled. "Hi." A light breeze blew a few strands of hair into her face. I slid them away with my finger and used the excuse to trace the line of her jaw.

"I love you. I could not love you more."

Annie stood on her toes and kissed me. "I know. That's how I love you. Boundlessly."

I felt a sheen of sweat on my forehead and I knew it wasn't because of the sun. I'd stood and lectured in front of hundreds of students, but nothing made me nervous like the idea of asking a question when I wasn't absolutely certain of the answer. I was almost certain, but the standard deviation from the mean could kill me if I'd miscalculated my odds.

So I stalled. I took Annie's hand and pulled her down to sit facing me on the grass. No one was around and it felt like our own island amid the verdant green. "I'm not sure if I've said this to you, but I really admire you for starting your life over in a new city. That's a big life change."

She nodded, but her eyes were questioning my non sequitur. "It was. I think about it sometimes and wonder… if I hadn't moved to LA before Nikki's wedding, would we have ever met?"

"We'd both have still been at the wedding, even if you flew in," I said.

"Yes, but… change the inputs, you get a different output. Econ 101. If I'd been in town for the weekend, would I have been in a different kind of mood or acted differently?"

"You mean, would you still have been looking for a hookup? I'd say the chances are high."

"I don't mean that. I mean, would I have been in a different place, mentally—unhappy in my job semi-happy in my life? I don't know. Maybe you'd have found me dull."

"I doubt that could ever be possible, but I understand what you mean." I still felt nervous even though I'd steered the conversation in a different direction. Now I had to find my way back. "Here's the thing—since I've known you, I've felt like you were trying to make things work in LA, I don't know, maybe to prove that you could. Even if maybe you'd rather be here? I guess what I want to know is, would you consider moving? Here, with me?"

She looked stunned. "You're moving?"

"No, not necessarily. But I was offered tenure at Berkeley, so moving is an option, is all I'm saying."

A dawning of understanding passed behind her eyes. "You put yourself up for a job at Berkeley because you know I love it here?" she asked.

"Yes."

"Finn…"

"Yes."

Annie reached for my cheek and caressed it. "That's amazing and sweet, but you don't have to move to the Bay Area to make me happy. I'm happy wherever you are. Including LA."

She wasn't understanding. I wanted to show her the house, which had great details and character, but we'd have time for that later. And if she didn't want to move, I'd keep it as a rental property. The point was the proposal, and I'd gotten off track.

I decided I was making it too hard. "What I'm trying to say is that I *want* to move here because I want to make you happy. You know, you saved my life."

"Finn, come on. The guy had no case. Any lawyer could've kept you out of jail by the time it all came out." She couldn't hide her glee. "But I did an awesome job."

"I'm not talking about the lawsuit. You saved *me*. I wasn't looking for you. Or anyone. I was fine. I had my house with my wall and my job and my theory. That's more than most people. I never presumed to deserve more than that."

As the words sunk in, she smiled. "I know. I was fine too. But I really wasn't."

"Annie…"

"Yes?"

I meant to get down on one knee, but we were already on the ground and I was too caught up in watching her reaction to my words. "Will you spend your life with me? Every day, starting now?"

Her eyes grew dewy and she answered. "Yes, please."

"To be clear, that was me asking you to marry me. I had a

whole proposal planned and you just... you make me so goddamned happy and nervous at the same time, I forgot every-thing. But... I love everything about you. And I can't fathom going another day without promising to love you forever. You'll marry me?"

She nodded, the dew now replaced by tears. I blotted them away with my thumbs and cupped her face in my hands. The only thing that made me happier than the idea of kissing her now was the idea that I could kiss her for life. Her lips were soft and warm and our sweet kiss quickly moved into territory unfit for a public park. "To be continued..." I said, nipping at her bottom lip and kissing her once more.

"I love you, Finn. Whether we're in LA or here or somewhere we haven't thought of yet, I will love you with all my heart," she said.

I was the luckiest man on the planet and there was no theory or formula to explain how I'd been graced with such good fortune, so I took it as one of the inexplicable beauties of the universe and felt grateful.

Oh, and I'd been so swept along with my feelings that I'd forgotten to take the ring out of my pocket.

"Oh. Shit." I pulled out the box and presented it to Annie. "This is for you. It was my grandmother's, and I was her favorite grandson."

Her smile spread across her face, but she wasn't looking at the ring. "Weren't you her only grandson?"

"Favorite. Favorite grandson." I slipped the ring on her finger.

"It's beautiful."

"You're beautiful," I told her.

Annie laughed and I looked over at where my mom was standing a respectful distance away in her pink dress with her hands balled into celebratory fists. "I take it she was aware of your plan today?"

"Yes, and it was all I could do to keep her from being a part of the plan. She wanted a role. Don't ask." I could see my mom's smile from a hundred yards away before she turned and walked back to the blanket.

"She's got her book. Want to take a walk?" I asked, looping my arm through hers and pulling her up.

"Can we see if there are any late-blooming dahlias? I know it's winter, but there's always hope."

"Of course." With her, there was always hope, of so many things.

We walked across the grass and I grabbed her hand. There was zero probability I'd ever let go.

THE END

BONUS EPILOGUE... Read an exclusive bonus conclusion to Finn and Annie's story!
https://dl.bookfunnel.com/oyjz3nzann :)

COMING SOON... The Finley Sisters Series — a spinoff series of standalone romances about Finn's five sisters. Make sure you're on my mailing list to get the first peek. https://mailchi.mp/bf6eeef2206e/newsletter-signup-travis

# A NOTE FROM THE AUTHOR

I hope you loved reading Finn and Annie's story as much as I loved writing it. If you did, please consider leaving a review on Goodreads, Bookbub or your favorite retailer. It takes an endless train of support to launch a book, and reviews help get the word out. But of course, no pressure. We're all busy. I get it!

This is a fictional story, but it's based on fact.

Whistleblowers are an important part of maintaining ethical standards at companies, and they're afforded legal protections from retaliation so they can speak up without fear.

I focused on the Securities and Exchange Commission's whistleblower program—informants who blew the whistle have enabled the SEC to collect over $1 billion in ill-gotten gains and return half of that to investors who were harmed. I thought it was interesting that whistleblowers could receive a bounty as a result of these lawsuits. In 2019, the SEC paid $37 million to a single whistleblower who provided evidence in a case. That followed awards of $50 million and $39 million to other whistleblowers in recent years. That immediately made me wonder whether there was the occasional bounty hunter who filed a whistleblower suit —a qui tam—as a financial play. There had to be at least a few people who were in it only for the money. Thus an idea for a story was born.

It is also true that economists are frequently hired as highly-paid consultants to companies that are pursuing mergers with other companies. They're responsible for creating the models which make these mergers look good to consumers and the larger industry. Are they good?

The antitrust argument is that American industry has never been more concentrated into an ever-dwindling number of companies. That means consumers have fewer choices and there's less competition among the companies who want our business. Their power gives them the ability to set prices and earn greater profits in the face of fewer competitors.

Check out recent headlines about Google, Apple, Amazon, and Facebook and you'll see that the questions about how big is too big don't have clear answers. The implications for Big Tech—and for consumers—are still undecided. Is bigger always better? Who loses out when there's less competition and fewer choices? Something to think about.

Thank you again for reading.

Lots of love,

Stacy

# ACKNOWLEDGMENTS

I must again default to the words of Hillary Clinton: "It takes a village." I work ridiculous hours—many of them during the traditional sleeping hours—to get these books out, but I couldn't even find my morning coffee without the village.

Readers, thank you. I'm grateful for every word you read, every kind review, every thoughtful click and like and comment. Love you all.

Jay, Jesse and Oliver: I've multitasked during movie night, I've crawled into bed when the sun was coming up and I've forced a few too many Trader Joe's lasagnas on you. Thank you for forgiving it all and loving me anyway. My deepest love goes to you three giant men.

To my beta readers, editors, proofers, givers of feedback, and supporters—Amy V., Betty S., Amy D., Samantha at Blazing Butterfly Edits. Thank you Dana K. and Jodi K. for the primer on legal issues and criminal procedure.

And enormous thanks to the people who I refer to as my SOS crew - no matter when I send a desperate text or email, you respond and talk me off the ledge: Christine D.R., Dylan A., and Melanie H. I'd be a pile of unpublished words without you.

Alyssa, your design genius amazes me and I'm grateful for your skill and patience.

Thank you Jenn and the Social Butterfly team for expert advice, brilliant execution, and other superpowers. Hilary, you went above and beyond the call of duty and this book is better for it - thank you.

Bloggers and bookstagrammers—thank you for embracing my books and exposing my writing to readers. Glad to have you in my village.

And to my fellow authors: as always, I am honored to type among you.

# ABOUT THE AUTHOR

Stacy Travis writes smart, steamy contemporary romance novels with feisty female characters and hot heroes who love them for their badassery. When not writing, she is probably dashing about in running shoes and complaining that all roads seem to go uphill. Or she's on the couch with a margarita and a large plate of cheese. Or fangirling at a soccer game. Stacy lives in Los Angeles with her husband, two sons and a poorly-trained rescue dog who hoards socks.

I love to hear from readers, so please connect with me!

Super fun newsletter: https://bit.ly/35pj0khnewsletter

Website: https://www.www.stacytravis.com

Awesomest Facebook reader group: https://bit.ly/2B1psS4fbgroup

Goodreads: https://www.goodreads.com/stacytravis

Email: stacytraviswrites@gmail.com - tell me everything!

Want more Stacy Travis wordsmithing? Read on for a Sneak Peak of Bad News, a standalone enemies to lovers romance

# SNEAK PEEK

## BAD NEWS - AN ENEMIES-TO-LOVERS ROMANCE

LINDEN

I can already tell today is going to be one for the books.

Specifically, the horror-novel type.

I've been awake for fifteen minutes and I've already stubbed my toe on the corner of my couch and knocked over a potted fern, leaving a trail of dry dirt because I haven't watered it in over a week. I guess wet dirt would be worse, so I have a glass half-full moment of contemplation before telling that sentiment to step off and shove it. Oh, and my hairband breaks and flies across the room like a slingshot.

It's the sort of Monday where I leave my apartment while it's still dark out and I already know it will be dark when I come home. That means I will only see winter's daylight through the windows of the newsroom if I have a moment to look up from my computer at some point during the work day. If news is breaking and I'm scrambling toward a deadline, I may not even see the daytime sky through the plate glass windows of our eighteenth-floor office.

It's almost just as well. Seeing the sun while not being able to get outside is its own form of torture.

But that's a problem for later.

For now, the soft shag rug feels nice on my feet, especially in the dark when I can't see the fern dirt amid its hideous mottled brown and beige swirls of synthetic fibers. I knew it was ugly when I bought it, but it was on sale and I appreciated that it was super soft and would hide dirt, so I wouldn't have to vacuum as often.

I wish I had the luxury of hiring a cleaning service occasionally to do it for me, but that's a fantasy for a day when I'm not gaming the system by loading up on mushrooms, sprouts, and other lightweight items at the Whole Foods salad bar to keep from spending my entire paycheck on one meal. I would never splurge on a fat cucumber slice or a weighty cube of tofu.

Someday...

For now, there's still a lot of ramen for dinner and protein bars instead of lunch. Reporters don't really make the big bucks, at least not entry-level reporters who still have years to work their way up to plum assignments and decent paychecks. Journalism is one of those jobs people choose for reasons of passion over paycheck, generally because they feel like it's a noble calling or a necessary check on government.

In my case, it's because I love finding a story no one else has and writing about it first. So yeah, I'm just a little bit competitive. I guess it's a labor of love, and I hope that if I hang in long enough I'll work my way up to a salary that allows for a decent robot vacuum and cherry tomatoes on my salads. Goals.

Truth be told, I do have enough money to shop for sensible dinners and modest-priced work clothes. But where's the fun in that? I'd much rather skimp on lunch all week and buy an awesome pair of stiletto boots that are as impractical as they are fabulous. I'd rather socialize with a barista for five minutes at Starbucks over an expensive vanilla latte, extra-shot, extra-hot, than watch my hand-me-down Melita drip machine churn out another depressing cup of coffee. I know I don't always make sound financial decisions. I'm twenty-eight. When I flout wisdom, I go big.

I hear my mother's voice in the back of my head, telling me I could be saving money if I made better choices. Then I actually hear it when I talk to her on the phone. "You have to have a plan. A savings goal. You need to commit to putting twenty percent of every paycheck away," she says.

"I know, Mom. I have a plan," I tell her.

I hate lying to my mother. There's no plan.

"Good girl. I didn't raise a dummy."

The economic term for my situation is cost-burdened. Anyone who spends more than half their income on housing gets to lug around that hyphenate until either they find a cheaper place to live or they get a raise.

And I'm not about to move.

I love my apartment. It's the top floor of a duplex, with blonde hardwood floors, cantilevered windows, and old dark beams across the ceilings. Even with my yard sale decor and bookshelves sitting atop milk crates, it has enough style to look amazing.

I moved in two weeks after I got promoted from news assistant to my reporting job at the Examiner, even though I knew I'd be financially stretched every month. The windows face east and west, and even though there's a tall orange tree outside one window, it's always really bright and perfect for houseplants. There are trailing ivy plants, hanging baskets, and a few fiddle leaf ferns in urns on the floor on opposite sides of my Ikea couch. I may have gone a little overboard with the greenery, but at this point in my life, plants make the best roommates.

Today, I haul myself up before the dawn to hit the gym because I know it's the only time I'll be able to fit in a workout. The lights are on dimmer switches and only turned on to the lowest light, not because I have a roommate or boyfriend I'm afraid of waking, but because I'm still half asleep and I intend to stay that way for as long as possible, toe stub notwithstanding.

If I keep the lights low and stumble around in a kind of fugue state, I can convince myself that I've actually gotten an extra half hour of sleep. That will come in handy later when I start feeling a little tired and need to fool myself into believing I slept a full eight hours. Well… seven. And really only six and a half. Or whatever.

Really, does it matter?

The regulars greet me at the gym, we adjust our bike seats and handlebars to the heights we like, and I take my usual spot in the back row. I like the vantage point from there. It helps me absorb the energy of everyone else in the class when I can see them all, and at this hour of the morning, I need that extra push.

"Hey Linden." I hear the voice before my eyes can adjust to the dim lighting in the room. But I know who said the words.

"So early," I whine to Cassie, a brunette with narrow hips and the kind of giant boobs that seem uncomfortable to manage in a spandex tank with shelf bra. She always takes the bike on the end and always gets there before me. "If it's still dark out, isn't it technically the middle of the night?" I ask.

Leaning down, I try to balance on one foot while putting the hard-soled spin shoe on the other. I tell myself that it's the early hour that makes me especially clumsy, but I know I could easily fall over at just about any hour of the day.

"I'm a naturally early riser. I did Pilates before this at five-thirty," Cassie says, spinning her legs quickly with light tension, making her bounce up and down on the saddle like she's riding a pony. She's kind of adorable.

"You're a beast," I tell her, repeating verbatim a conversation we've had at least six times this month. I'm not much for new thoughts before seven in the morning.

"I'm just lucky. I only need five hours of sleep," she says, and I mentally curse her and her curvy body. I swing a leg over the saddle and clip in. Then, I give my legs a mental directive to start pedaling.

*Come on, you can keep sleeping, just make circles.*

Feeling like leaden tree trunks, my legs obey, and I wait for the instructor to turn on the first song so I can lose myself in Lizzo and get my sweat on.

"Did you see *Bachelor Bay* last night?" Cassie asks, unable to keep the squeal out of her voice.

Discussing this reality show is half the reason I'm here. "Yes, and what *was* that thing with Diego?"

"Girl, there aren't enough hours in the day to crawl into his wacky brain."

The show is my guilty pleasure, pure dumb fun watching a bunch of guys get filmed doing stunts as they try to win over unsuspecting women on a yacht docked near a resort town.

Somehow the scenarios that unfold on those ships are beyond scandalous, beyond controversial: champagne-fueled sexcapades, lies, and justifications for infidelity; husbands pretending to be single to compete on the show, all while believing their wives won't find out—and of course they do.

People just seem to combust when they get in front of the cameras. The show has been on for a decade and it's ratings gold. Cassie and I figured out that we were both suckers for it a year ago and we dissect every episode.

"Dean, OMG. Could you believe Jake ended up making out with Sally while that other guy was lying naked next to her in the bed. And she was totally fine with it?"

"It was pretty awesome," I agree. Just thinking about *Bachelor Bay* makes me smile. It's so far-removed from reality that it relaxes me to contemplate it. I'm almost bummed when the instructor gets on the mike and starts coaching us. But not really. I need a good sweat-drenching if I'm going to counteract the day's bad juju so far. We cycle in time with the music, we stand and run on the pedals, and we raise the temperature in the room by at least ten degrees.

Cassie hoots and hollers from the saddle next to me and I sing Pink's "What About Love" out loud. No one can hear me and that's the point. What started out as a slog uphill has turned into a full-throttle, joyous race to the finish. Drenched in sweat and three degrees away from a heart attack, I am transformed.

By seven-fifteen, I am fully awake and feeling almost invincible. I have forty-five minutes to shower, drive to work and pick up my latte from the coffee place in my building before going upstairs.

I love my job, even on the days when I get nasty letters from people who think I've missed the point of a story or even threats of lawsuits from people accusing me of slander. I was taught early on that hate mail is the sign of good reporting. I've wanted to be a journalist since I was a kid, long before I became a reporter for the ThesBEE, a publication for theater news that no one read at my tiny high school.

I worked my way up over the next ten years, through a college major in journalism, internships, terrible beats in tiny towns and semi-successful attempts to freelance in bigger towns. Since I had only ever wanted to be a journalist, landing a job at the Examiner was my dream. The paper has its main headquarters in New York, but there are news bureaus all over the country in all major cities. I was lucky to get hired in the LA bureau, so I didn't have to relocate.

There is, unfortunately, one thing I hate about my job. And it sits in the cubicle next to mine in the fine form of Jack Galloway. He's a star reporter who's treated like he walks on water, which feeds his already-giant ego. Before I'd been at my job for a week, I learned that Jack consistently writes more stories and gets more exclusives—meaning he's beating every other media outlet to report on breaking news—than almost anyone else at the paper.

He also lays claim to the only Pulitzer Prize won by anyone in the Los Angeles bureau for a series of stories he wrote a couple of years ago about a pattern of sexual harassment at several major film studios that led to major reform in the industry. He broke a story each day for weeks and was responsible for billions of dollars paid to compensate victims. When I started my job, Jack's journalistic reputation preceded him. I was ready to kneel at the altar of his skill and experience, grateful to be able to learn what I could from a master.

But he was nowhere to be found.

For the first couple weeks after I was hired, Jack was working at the paper's New York headquarters, so I didn't meet him until I rushed in one day—a half-hour late—and found a broad-shouldered man in a navy sport coat hunched over the news desk. When he heard me and turned around, my first thought was *I'm done for*. As in, there's no chance I can work around this guy every day and not want to have sex with him on the daily, starting right at that very moment.

Yes, please and thank you.

His deep blue eyes did me in at first glance and his perfectly straight, white teeth and dimpled cheeks unleashed a flutter in my belly when he smiled at me. I'm sure he expected me to melt into a puddle when I looked at him.

I almost did.

The only thing saving me was the need to take in the rest of his face: the strong jaw, the cheekbones that could cut glass, and the plush lips that mesmerized me even when he wasn't talking.

He tipped his head up in acknowledgment, "Jack Galloway." Then he looked back at whatever had his attention on the news desk. It was fortunate that he didn't seem interested in conversation because I was having trouble stuttering out my own name. When I did manage to enunciate it, he looked up at me with a smirk, like he was all too familiar with the effect he has on women.

Oh shit, this guy's trouble, I thought.

And I'm a magnet for trouble. Or at least, I used to be. If there was an egotistical, emotionally stunted, magnificent-looking guy within a ten-mile radius, I would find him like a heat-seeking missile. Then I'd let him wreck my capacity to make good decisions until he decided to move on, and I was left like sad roadkill, wondering what just ran me over.

Guys like him were the reason I never got promoted beyond reporting on brush fires and "dog bites man" stories at tiny papers—because I overslept one too many times after making bad decisions. Like going out instead of working late and coming to work unfocused after blindingly good sex.

It's been years since I've made those mistakes because I finally realized that for me, ambition and dating don't mix. So here I am, with no blindingly good sex in my life, no boyfriend, but one hell of an opportunity to do good work for one of the biggest papers in the country.

I'm done with distractions. I'm leaning into the job and ditching all relationships. It's for the best.

But man, if I have to look at Jack every day, it's just going to be painful.

He's the kind of guy who uses his hair for emphasis, running his fingers through it when he's thinking, shaking it forward and back again to settle the loose strands in place whenever he needs to get someone's attention. He comes into work with it wet and slicked back, as if communicating he's just come from the gym. Then he goes ahead and communicates it himself, in case any of us happened to miss the swell of his biceps and the broad span of his shoulders from whatever he does there.

"I caught that on CNN at the gym," he'll say, jumping in on a conversation about how a company's stock took a turn after a bad earnings report. Or, "On my way to the gym, I saw a three-car pileup. We should do a piece about airbag technology." When he rolls up his sleeves, he has to stop midway up his forearms because his muscles prevent the fabric from going higher.

Some reporters wear jeans and T-shirts unless they have a meeting with an executive or a business lunch. Jack wears a dress shirt and tie most days, even if he's wearing jeans. He keeps a sport coat on the back of his chair for the off chance he has to run out and meet with someone important. He never gets rattled by anything at work. At least nothing that can't be solved by running a hand through his hair.

And while he's nice to look at, that's only when he's not talking. When he opens his mouth, it's usually to tell me something I'm doing wrong. "You shouldn't let a source dictate the terms of an interview" or "never agree to tell a person what quotes you're using in a story. If they say it on the record, you can quote it," he's told me. More than once.

While I appreciate the advice and know I can learn from the more senior reporters, it's the way he says things that annoy me. Like I'm a neophyte idiot who couldn't possibly get it right without his help.

Jack isn't my boss or even a person who has the power to fire me. But that's irrelevant. He's a highly respected reporter and people listen to what he has to say. Most of the time. Fortunately for me, the people who hired me didn't listen to him when he apparently objected, and they hired me anyway.

That didn't stop him from voicing his objection to the deputy bureau chief one morning when he thought I wasn't there. I overheard him say, flat out, "I think it was a mistake, putting her in that job. She's too green. It's going to blow up in her face."

I turned around and walked the other way so they wouldn't know I'd overheard the conversation. I felt a rolling wave of nausea in my gut and the urge to quit right then. There was no mistaking that the conversation had been about me. I'm the least experienced reporter in the bureau, by a long shot. I'm the only reporter who could be described as green. But instead of giving him the satisfaction of thinking I quit because of him, I went to the bathroom, cried for five minutes, and talked myself off the ledge.

Most of the other reporters treat me like they assume I'm capable unless I show them otherwise. From the attitude Jack gives me daily, I can tell he thinks the exact opposite. Which is why I need him to understand that he can level that blue-eyed stare at me all day long if he wants to, and I'll feel nothing.

Bad News is available at all retailers